THE NIGHT WHEN NO ONE HAD SEX

THE NIGHT WHEN NO ONE HAD SEX

Kalena Miller

Albert Whitman & Company
Chicago, Illinois

Library of Congress Cataloging-in-Publication data
is on file with the publisher.

Text copyright © 2021 by Kalena Miller
First published in the United States of America
in 2021 by Albert Whitman & Company
ISBN 978-0-8075-5627-6 (hardcover)
ISBN 978-0-8075-5632-0 (ebook)

Printed in the United States of America
10 9 8 7 6 5 4 3 2 1 LB 26 25 24 23 22 21

Jacket art copyright © 2021 by Albert Whitman & Company
Jacket art by Suzanne Dias
Design by Valerie Hernández

For more information about Albert Whitman & Company,
visit our website at www.albertwhitman.com.

For my mom, who's read every word I've ever written.

THE BEST GROUP CHAT EVER

Group Chat

11:58 PM

Julia: WHO'S READY TO DO THIS?!?!?!?

Zoe: Are you seriously texting during the last dance?

Julia: It's called multitasking. And so are you.

Zoe: Morgan and I bailed. We're waiting in the parking lot.

Today 12:00 AM: Julia named the conversation "LET'S DO THIS!!!"

Morgan: Julia, you need to chill.

Julia: I can't chill. Do you know why?

Kevin: Nobody answer her.

Madison: Why lol?

Madison: Sorry Kev

Julia: BECAUSE IT'S TIME FOR OUR FREAKING SEX PACT!!!!!

Morgan: Please don't call it that.

Julia: Fine. It's time for our intercourse agreement.

Morgan: Worse. So much worse.

Alex: Can we not talk about this around Leah? I don't want her to think I'm a creep.

Julia: Leah doesn't think you're a creep. She thinks you're very nice and somewhat quiet.

Alex: How do you know that????

Julia: We were talking in the bathroom. OBVIOUSLY.

Alex: Fantastic. Just fantastic.

Zoe: Where are you guys? There are too many people.

Julia: Coming!

Alex: Same.

Julia: YAYAYAYAY!!!

Morgan: Madison? You and Jake coming?

Zoe

"Do you see them?"

I survey the crowd of teenagers in formal wear spilling into the parking lot. The guys are impossible to distinguish because they all rented the same half-price suit from Men's Warehouse. The girls aren't much better. I thought I was being original when I chose this charcoal, two-piece ensemble, but apparently dark colors are popular this year. Ninety percent of the laughing girls running across the asphalt are wearing navy or black.

"Should I have gone with the red dress?" Morgan asks.

"You look gorgeous in this one." I finger the blue chiffon skirt that falls just above her knees. The bodice is a fun geometric print, but she did manage to choose the same color palette as every other girl in the senior class. "Predicting trends is a complicated science," I explain. "And when you consider all the variables—region, socio-economic status, access to consumer goods—I imagine it's nearly impossible to accurately predict fashion trends like prom dresses."

"Interesting," Morgan says in a tone conveying no interest whatsoever. "Do you think Madison will ride with us? Or with Jake?"

"I don't know."

That's a lie. In fact, I am very certain Madison will ride with Jake because (1) He's her boyfriend, (2) They drove here together, and (3) There aren't enough seats in Kevin's minivan for all of us. If Morgan were to assess the situation logically, this would be obvious to her, but my girlfriend is rarely logical when it comes to her twin sister.

"Are we sure this is Kevin's car?" I ask. Distraction is often the best course of action when Morgan starts obsessing. And there were a substantial number of students driving minivans to prom this year. Minivans belonging to their parents, but minivans nonetheless.

"YUP!"

"Holy shit—" I shriek as a sweaty human latches herself on to my back. I shrug my shoulders free and turn around to find a grinning Julia. She's pulled her blond hair into a ponytail and her cheeks are flushed with excitement. Standing behind her with one arm around her waist is her boyfriend, Kevin.

"Are you guys ready for tonight?" Julia bounces on her toes and tugs on Kevin's arm like a puppy. "Sex pact! Sex pact! Sex pact!"

Kevin tries to shush his girlfriend, but her energy is contagious and soon they're jumping around together. Morgan sighs pointedly. She's never been one for public displays of affection. Or public displays of giddiness in this case.

As we wait for the others to arrive, I consider the sex pact's probability of success.

Julia and Kevin are a slam dunk. They've been best friends since they were three, and they've been boyfriend-girlfriend since they were fifteen. I'm surprised they've made it this far without going all the way, especially when you consider how much time they spend in this very minivan instead of going to lunch. I'd give them a ninety percent chance. Maybe ninety-five percent. Julia rarely gives up on something once she's made up her mind. And the sex pact was her idea.

"Hey, guys." Alex and Leah join us outside the car. To her credit, Julia shuts up. Alex and Leah met for the first time five hours ago, when we all gathered in Alex's backyard to take cheesy prom photos. He was the only one of us without a date, so Julia worked her magic and set him up with her lab partner.

Alex and Leah are decidedly not part of the sex pact. I wouldn't judge anyone who wanted to have sex on a first date, but that's not Alex's style. I had to reassure him twenty times my uncle had two cabinets full of DVDs and every streaming service imaginable before he agreed to join us for the sleepover.

"Are we ready to go?" Kevin asks. "It's going to be a zoo getting out of here."

"We have to wait for Madison," Morgan says, her eyes darting around the parking lot.

"I thought she was riding with Jake," Kevin says.

"Yeah, I saw her getting into his car," Julia says. "We don't have room anyway."

Kevin unlocks the van, and Julia crawls into the farthest-back seat, her purple dress snagging on an armrest. She motions for Leah to follow her. Kevin is the only person allowed to operate his mom's vehicle, so he circles around to the driver's seat.

"You want shotgun?" Alex asks me. "It's your uncle's cabin."

"No, you navigate." While I possess above-average intelligence in a variety of arenas, spatial awareness has never been my strength. "I'll text you the address, and you can map it."

"Sounds good." Alex slides into the front seat, leaving me and Morgan standing alone outside the minivan.

"Come on." I take Morgan's hand. "Madison will be fine."

"She's the opposite of fine. She's participating in Julia's

stupid sex pact with her stupid boyfriend. How could that possibly be fine?"

I don't have an easy answer for her. I know from personal experience Morgan's not against having sex, but she's very much against Madison having sex with Jake. I sympathize with her point of view. Jake is nice in a goofy, clueless sort of way, but he's also a varsity baseball player who's headed to college next fall on an athletic scholarship. He and Madison have zero long-term potential. With the way Morgan and Madison have been arguing lately, though, Madison might have sex just to piss off her sister.

"You have to trust her." It's a weak argument, but it's all I've got. We need to get moving if we want to avoid spending the next hour in traffic.

Morgan nods almost imperceptibly. I squeeze her hand and we climb into the middle row of seats. "Thanks," Morgan says, though I can barely hear her with Julia and Leah accompanying the radio at an earsplitting volume.

"I can't even hear what song this is," I say.

"Nothing I know," Morgan says. "Do you think it's possible for them to sing any more off-key?"

"There's no way this counts as singing. Screaming, maybe."

"You can scream off-key."

I'm not sure that statement is technically accurate, but I decide to let Morgan win the argument. This is clearly a something-else-is-going-on kind of situation, but a carful of people singing—or screaming—at the top of their lungs isn't the right environment to engage in meaningful conversation.

As the duet in the back of the vehicle reaches new levels of awful, Alex turns around to face me. "Can you make them be quiet?" he shouts. "Kevin can barely hear me."

I repeat Alex's request to Leah and Julia. No response. Julia is now belting out the national anthem to the beat of whatever pop song is playing. It's an unfortunate mash-up.

I try again. "We need to be quieter," I say in my loudest, most commanding voice. It still doesn't work. It may be after midnight, but Julia and Leah are high on prom-night adrenaline. That's a good thing when you consider our plans for the evening. But when it gets in the way of safe navigation, it's not optimal.

Thankfully, Morgan is sitting beside me. "Hey! Everybody! Shut up!" she yells. The back seat falls silent.

This is why Morgan and I are a good pair. We're like the moms of the group. Morgan is the overbearing control freak who thinks she knows what's best for everyone. Granted, she usually does. And I'm the level-headed, logical one who kills the vibe by saying things like "Maybe you shouldn't take off your bra right now, Madison," or "Julia, how would your parents feel about you adopting a miniature pig?"

"Thanks, everyone," Kevin says. "The roads are super-dark."

"And my GPS keeps recalibrating," Alex says. "Zo, are you sure the address is right? We're in the middle of nowhere."

"His place is in the middle of nowhere, trust me."

I stare out the window into the dark night. Back in Eugene, there were streetlights for illumination. Outside of town, though, we're seriously lacking in visibility. Without GPS, I would have no chance of finding Uncle Ross's place in the middle of the night. But having sex in the woods requires driving through said woods.

Of the twenty-something members of my extended family, Uncle Ross is definitely the worst. He's arrogant and condescending and will lecture me for hours about the difference between a cabernet and a merlot despite the fact that I won't be able to drink legally for another three years. But even with his many flaws, I wasn't about to turn down the opportunity to use his second home for our prom-night extravaganza. He only offered us the place after two different renters canceled and my dad promised to stain his back porch, but still. It's better than renting crappy motel rooms like most of the senior class.

"It's easy to get lost out here," Morgan says. She's leaning between the front bucket seats to stare out the windshield.

"We'll be fine," Alex says. "I paid ninety-nine cents for an app with fancy directions. It's never let me down."

"I'm worried about Madison," Morgan whispers to me.

"She's fine." I squeeze my girlfriend's hand. Even in the

shadowy dark of the car, I can see her eyebrows scrunched together and forehead wrinkled. She's starting to panic. And when Morgan is panicking, it's usually about Madison. Madison's mood. Madison's health. Madison's douchey boyfriend. In this case, Madison in another car with her douchey boyfriend. Morgan takes her role as an older sister very seriously. She acts like she's five years older, not five minutes.

"It's really dark," Morgan whispers. "What if they get lost and something happens? I only agreed to the sex pact because I thought we would all be in the same house."

"We will be," I say. "I sent her and Jake the address. They're probably a few minutes behind us. Or maybe they'll be waiting when we arrive."

"Do you think I should text her, just to be sure?"

"Absolutely not." I take the cell phone out of Morgan's hands and slide it back into her purse. I have gathered enough anecdotal evidence over the years to state with certainty that Morgan checking on Madison is not a wise decision.

"Do you know what I realized?" Julia doesn't wait for a response. "This is exactly like the beginning of a horror movie. A bunch of teenagers going into the woods to have a good time, except the cabin is haunted or there's a serial killer on the loose or something."

"Can we not talk about that right now?" Morgan asks. She's treating my hand like it's a stress ball. I shoot her a sympathetic smile, but there's nothing I can do to make her feel better about Madison and Jake. If only the problem were a deranged serial killer. That would be more frightening, but at least there would be tangible solutions.

"Am I getting close to the turn?" Kevin asks.

Alex doesn't respond. He's too busy staring at the bright screen of his cell phone.

"Am I getting close?" Kevin asks again. "Alex, come on, man. I need directions."

Alex shakes his head. Kevin takes one look at him, then pulls over and slows to a stop. I glance back and forth between the two guys. If I had to rate the strongest relationship in the group, it might be Alex and Kevin. It's hard to top a bromance like theirs. Whatever Kevin is seeing on Alex's face must be serious.

"What's going on?" Kevin shakes Alex's shoulder. The entire van is silent as we wait for him to answer. "Come on, you're scaring me."

Alex looks up. He's blinking back tears and his voice breaks. "It's my grandmother," he says. "She had a heart attack."

Alex

I glance over my shoulder, then merge into the left lane, speeding up to pass the silver sports car driving a mere three miles per hour over the speed limit. I thought people who drove fancy cars were supposed to be reckless. Speed demons, my father calls them. But the balding man leaning back in his seat with one hand draped lazily across the steering wheel is the opposite of a speed demon. Does he not realize some people on the highway have elderly relatives in the hospital? Okay, maybe it's unreasonable to expect random cars on the highway to know my business, but even if he did know about Halmoni, I can tell by the man's casual slump that he wouldn't care.

I zip past with ease, then merge back into the middle lane. I check my own speedometer. Nine above the speed limit is pushing it, but at least I'm not in double digits. I read online the police won't pull you over if you drive five over the speed limit, but any faster and you're in trouble. When I told Halmoni this, she said I better not risk driving even a mile over the speed limit. I generally heed her advice, even if I'm late for school or hungry for Chipotle. Tonight is different though. Halmoni would understand.

I push my foot down and watch the speedometer tick past seventy-five, then seventy-six. I turn on my blinker and pull back into the left lane, this time flying past a dusty pickup truck with beams of wood jutting from the cargo bed.

"You should slow down." Leah places a hand on my shoulder as I get ready to pass a black SUV. "We'll get there when we get there. The last thing your parents need is you getting into an accident or being pulled over."

It's sound advice, but all I want to do right now is close the gap between me and my grandmother. Still, I force myself to slow down until I'm just five over the speed limit.

"You don't need to come with me," I say for the third time.

"We already spent fifteen minutes getting your car, and my house is on the other side of town. Of course I'm coming with you."

"We could be there a long time," I say.

"Don't worry about me," Leah says. "I can always Uber home."

"What about the after-prom party you were talking about? You're going to miss it."

Leah bites her lip at my mention of the party. She was okay skipping it for a night in the woods. A hospital waiting room with the family of a guy you barely know is a totally different thing. But then she swallows and smiles at me reassuringly. "Alex, listen to me. All that matters is getting you to the hospital, preferably in one piece." Leah nods at my dashboard, where the speedometer is creeping up again.

I feel guilty about hijacking our evening, but Leah makes a compelling argument. I don't need to stress about a pointless after-prom party. I have enough on my mind.

My first worry is Halmoni, who's about to be cut open by a team of doctors. She's younger than most of my friends' grandparents, but she's not *young* young. Then I worry about my mom stressing about her mother and my dad stressing about his wife and both of them stressing about my little sister. Mom and Dad like to brag Jenny is mature for her age, but no ten-year-old is mature enough to deal with our neurotic parents while Halmoni goes through surgery. And I worry that if something horrible happens, I'll forever feel guilty about my last moment with my grandmother.

It was earlier tonight when we were posing for silly

pictures in the backyard. Mom offered to take one of just me and Halmoni, but I said no. I wasn't trying to be rude or anything, but we were already running late for our reservation at Los Dos Amigos. Halmoni's smile didn't waver, but I knew she was disappointed. And now I'm filled with self-loathing.

My hands tighten on the steering wheel. I can't let my brain go there. I will see Halmoni again. And then I'll put this suit back on and take a million selfies with her.

Finally, there's the worry that's right in front of me. My parents are about to meet Leah.

Mom and Dad are middle-aged, church-going Korean Americans. They're not supposed to think about me as a sexual being. Especially my mother. I would rather burn my entire rare stamp collection than tell Mom about the sex pact my friends agreed to. It's not like she's overly strict, but she's definitely under the assumption I won't be having sex until marriage, which, in her mind, won't happen until I'm thirty. Dad is less likely to be judgmental, but a thousand times more likely to be embarrassing. Which is worse. Way worse. I managed to run interference while we were taking pictures this afternoon, but being stranded in a hospital with Leah provides my dad with ample opportunity to be, well, dad-like.

"Hey, so you know how Julia was talking about a sex pact?" I work to keep my voice casual.

Leah looks surprised by the sudden subject change but

goes along without question. "Yeah. She was joking, right?"

I keep my expression neutral. They may be lab partners, but Leah doesn't know Julia like I do. There is
nothing humorous about her commitment to losing her
virginity tonight.

"Yeah, totally joking," I say. "But maybe don't mention
that to my parents? Even though it was a joke, obviously."

"Alex." Leah places one hand on my thigh. It's a sweet
gesture, though surprisingly intimate for someone I met
five hours ago. "You don't need to worry about me. I've
interacted with adults before."

"Right, okay. Sorry. I have a lot going on inside my
head."

"I know you do," Leah says. Her voice is filled with
sadness, and I know she's acting out of genuine sympathy,
not token politeness.

Until two days ago, I had every intention of skipping
prom. I was the only one of my friends without a date,
and I didn't want to tag along like a third wheel. Or seventh wheel, technically. Besides, I'm not the prom type. I'm
the guy who floats through high school without making
much of an impression and then shows up at the twentieth
reunion with a million-dollar tech start-up. At least that's
what I tell myself when I decide to stay home instead of
going to football games or chili cook-offs.

Julia would have none of that. It was my senior prom,
she said, and I would regret it forever if I didn't go. When

I used my singleness as an excuse, she promised to find me the perfect date. All Julia told me was that my date was a white girl with brown hair. Which was extremely unhelpful because all of Julia's friends are white (excluding me and Kevin, obviously) and most of them have brown hair.

Still, I was pleasantly surprised by Julia's matchmaking abilities. Leah is sweet and pretty and isn't one of those people who takes prom seriously, which I appreciate. We spent most of the night mocking the tacky Hollywood-themed decor and brainstorming better causes the student council could have spent money on—like eradicating world hunger or better snacks in the vending machines. But the date wasn't supposed to extend beyond the confines of the high school gym or Zoe's uncle's cabin. Potentially grieving the death of my grandmother was not part of the plan.

My knuckles turn white as I exit the highway. I'm repulsed by my own brain. Dad said in his text Halmoni's odds were good. People have heart attacks all the time, he said, and they got her to the hospital immediately. I shouldn't be acting like Halmoni is on the brink of death.

"What's your grandmother's name?" Leah asks.

"Her name? Uh, I don't know."

"How do you not know her name?"

"I call her *Halmoni*. That's how you say *grandma* in Korean. Well, technically it's *weh-halmoni*, but she's always just been *Halmoni* to me."

"Okay, well, what do your parents call her?"

"My mom calls her *Umma*, or *mother*. And my dad calls her *Jangmo neem*, which means *mother-in-law*."

"So I should just find out the Korean word for *the grandmother of my prom date*?"

"Exactly." We've finally arrived at Johnson Memorial Hospital. I turn into the parking lot and follow the light-up signs for the emergency room.

"I'm being serious, Alex."

"Okay, okay." I turn into an empty parking space, between a police van and a shiny pickup truck. "She goes by Alice."

Actually, most people call her "Alice the Agitator" these days. Halmoni spent the past two years fighting a wealthy businessman who bulldozed her favorite park. She and her elderly friends made picket signs, marched in protest, and went door-to-door advocating for public spaces. The millionaire and his dozens of lawyers may have won, but Halmoni is still the local hero who tried to save Elmwood Park.

I don't tell Leah any of this though. The whole "my grandmother nearly got arrested for protesting capitalist greed" story isn't really first-date material.

I also don't tell Leah I have zero plans for her to be around when the surgery finishes. Unlike my mom, Halmoni has no qualms about me dating. In fact, one of her favorite topics of conversation—other than the evil man who destroyed her favorite park—is why I don't have a girlfriend. If she sees me and Leah together, she'll have our entire wedding planned before she gets off bed rest. If she gets off bed rest.

No. I'm not thinking like that. "I need to think positive thoughts. I can't let the scary stuff into my head."

I don't realize I'm speaking aloud until Leah touches my leg again. "Focus on the positive stuff if you can. But it's hard to avoid negative thoughts. There's not a right way to feel."

"Oh. Uh, thanks." I hadn't meant to tell Leah how I was feeling—I'm not usually a "share your feelings" kind of guy—but she's surprisingly decent with advice.

"Alex?"

"Hm?"

"Are you going to go inside?"

"Right. Yeah." I take the keys out of the ignition and adjust my cowlick in the mirror. I wish I had normal clothes to change into, but I'm stuck in my jacket and tie for the time being. Maybe I can find some sweatpants in the gift shop.

"Do you want me to come in right now?" Leah asks. "Or should I stay in the car for a while?"

"Um…" I hadn't even considered Leah staying in the car. If I left my keys, she could have air-conditioning, listen to the radio, and eat the bag of Starburst in my glove compartment. It would be like an after-prom party for one.

But then Halmoni's face pops into my head. She would be horrified if I left Leah in the car like a dog. She would probably disown me—if that's even a thing grandparents can do.

"No, you should come inside," I say, even though I'm less than confident about my decision. I push ahead with a blatant lie. "I'm sure my parents would love to meet you."

Leah's cheeks stretch into a massive smile and her dangly earrings jangle as she bounces in her seat. I'm not sure why, but she is genuinely excited about meeting my parents. Which only makes me dread it more. I try once more to head off the inevitable awkwardness.

"Listen, Leah. I'm sure my little sister is going to love you and my dad will be fine, but maybe take it easy with my mom. I'm not saying my parents are traditional in a stereotypical way or something, but we don't talk about girls. Or dating."

"Alex, I wasn't lying when I told you I had interacted with adults before. Can you trust me to be normal?"

I want to tell Leah interacting with adults is not the same thing as interacting with my mother, but I don't. I also want to tell Leah I made a mistake and ask her to wait in the car until further notice, but I don't do that either.

"I know, I know. You're right."

The glass doors slide open, and we're met with a gust of cold air that smells exactly how hospital air always smells—mashed potatoes from a box, latex gloves, and too many cleaning products. I know there's a silly cliché about hospitals smelling like death, but I've always found the scent of medical institutions oddly comforting. I like knowing there are people way smarter than me working hard to fix problems I don't understand. My mom might find solace in God or religion or her bible study group, but my brain doesn't work that way. I need to believe in something tangible. Like the medical professionals who have spent their entire lives developing the particular set of skills that might save Halmoni.

"There's the directory," Leah says, walking toward a sign mounted on frosted glass. I follow her lead. Johnson Memorial is a big hospital, and Dad didn't specify where they were waiting. "Do you think we should go upstairs? Or into—"

"Alex! Oh, Alex." Mom appears in the doorway of a waiting room and rushes toward me, a jumble of emotions pouring out of her in mixed Korean and English. Her short black hair is pulled into a ponytail, and she's wearing the thick-rimmed glasses she wears in bed. "I'm so glad you're finally here. How was prom? Your father said you were doing okay. What took you so long? Don't you worry about your grandma, now." She wraps me in a hug and kisses me on the forehead.

After a few minutes of hugging and kissing and asking me questions she doesn't give me time to answer, Mom extracts herself. She turns to Leah, and I cringe, expecting some kind of inquisition or judgmental comment. But Mom doesn't hesitate. She throws her arms around Leah and launches into the same confusing monologue.

"Alex's girlfriend! Oh, Alex's girlfriend. How was prom? I'm so glad you're finally here..."

Leah shoots me a look over my mother's shoulder. "See?" she whispers. "I told you I would be normal."

I shake my head and wander into the waiting room to find my dad and sister. Nothing about this is normal.

LET'S DO THIS!!!

Group Chat
12:43 AM

Zoe: Hey Mad, Alex's grandma had a heart attack so he's going to the hospital.

Madison: Shit is she going to be okay?

Zoe: Not sure. We just dropped him off at his house. He said he'd text when he gets there.

Madison: Alex I'm so sorry let me know if there's anything I can do <3

Zoe: So we're going to be late getting to my uncle's house.

Madison: Got it. Jake says he's really sorry to hear about

your grandma

Zoe: If you get there before us, just wait outside. But Kevin is driving fast.

Julia: KEVIN IS DRIVING TOO FAST.

Madison: It's okay I think we're stopping for snacks so you'll still beat us there

Morgan: Where are you stopping?

Madison: Idk somewhere with food

Julia: Oooh can you get me something sweet? Like twizzlers or gummy worms.

Julia: Actually, get me something sour.

Morgan: Is anywhere open this late at night?

Zoe: Kevin says he wants Doritos.

Julia: IF KEVIN WANTS DORITOS, HE NEEDS TO SLOW DOWN!!!

Julia: Don't go to that gas station off exit 9. There was a robbery there last month.

Morgan: Seriously Julia?

Julia: Although, if you were a criminal, would you really hit the same gas station twice?

Morgan: Julia!!!

Julia: I'm just saying that could be the SAFEST gas station because it's been hit recently. You never know.

Morgan: That's not how anything works.

Julia: Kevin slowed down, so you can get him Doritos. He wants the ones in the purple bag. And I want sour gummy worms.

Julia: I don't have any cash on me, but I know my mom's PayPal login.

Julia: Madison, are you still there?

Morgan: We have enough space for you and Jake in the van now if you want to carpool.

Morgan: Mad?

Alex: Hey guys. Leah and I got to the hospital and I found my parents. My grandmother was taken back to get prepped for surgery. I don't fully know what's going on, but my dad said it's not too serious and the doctor is going to come talk to us in a little while. I think she's going to be okay, but we won't know for sure until she's out of surgery and I don't know how long that's going to take. Thanks for driving us back to my house and I'm sorry I can't be with you guys tonight. But please get your sexy on without me ;)

Alex: God I can't believe I said that. Please ignore me. It's late.

Julia: HAHAHAHA OMG ALEX

Zoe: Thanks for updating us! We're all thinking about you!

Morgan: Madison, are you still there?

Madison

"Mad? What's going on, babe?" With zero thought given to his own safety or the other drivers on the road, Jake leans across the armrest and places a sticky smooch on my cheek. I wipe it away.

"Aww, babe. My lips taste bad?"

"You smell like brisket."

"Fuck, that brisket was good. I would have been more hyped if I knew there was gonna be food."

Thanks to an influx of donations to the senior class, the PTA decided to feature a catered buffet at prom. They thought food would decrease the amount of inappropriate touching, but it didn't work out that way. The barbecue brisket and fruit salad distracted everyone for a while, but once the buffet had been ravaged, it was back to grinding on the dance floor. With the unpleasant addition of meat breath.

"Aww, babe. You mad I didn't pay enough attention to you?"

I shake my head. I did spend a good portion of prom sitting with my back against the cinderblock walls of the gym while Jake wolfed down sliders and discussed a senior prank involving an alpaca, peach schnapps, and the fire escape, but I didn't mind. I was happy to hang out with Zoe and Morgan all night. Ever since I quit ballet, dancing hasn't really been my thing. I get overwhelmed by the conflicting desires to correct people's posture and sob hysterically. I've been told it isn't a fun vibe.

"Then what's wrong? You can tell me." Jake leans across the armrest again, causing his car to swerve into the bike lane.

"Jake, watch it." I push him back into his seat. There are many, many qualities I love about my boyfriend. His total disregard for basic traffic laws is not one of them.

"Only if you tell me what's wrong," Jake says while defiantly keeping his eyes off the road.

"Dude, okay. Just watch where you're going," I say as another text lights up my phone. "There were a bunch of messages in the group chat with my friends. Alex's grandma is in the hospital. She had a heart attack."

"Which one is Alex? The skinny dude or the not-skinny dude?"

"Come on, Jake. Don't be that guy."

As one of the heaviest guys in our class, Kevin receives plenty of snide remarks about his weight. He usually brushes off the ignorant comments, but Julia is like an attack dog when it comes to defending her boyfriend. She gets enraged at any mention of Kevin's size, even when it's not negative.

"I'm being serious, Mad. You know I'm bad with names."

"I'm just saying you should think about the words before they leave your mouth." I sigh. "Fine. Kevin is the bigger Chinese American guy who's permanently attached to Julia. She's the blond girl," I add when Jake still looks confused. "Alex is the tall, skinny Korean American one who was sitting with Leah. You guys talked about League of Legends?"

"Ohh, Alex!" Jake high-fives me like he accomplished something big. "He's my bro. We're gonna stream together."

"Well, your bro's grandma is in the hospital."

"Damn, that sucks. Tell him I hope she doesn't die."

I type a more pleasant version of Jake's sentiments into the group chat. Alex will appreciate the thought, even if the girls don't. Morgan used to be the only one who had a problem with Jake, but I think she's convinced Julia and Zoe of his faults by now. I'm sick of their negativity. I'm just trying to enjoy my senior year, to take advantage of the supposed pinnacle of high school. And Jake's a good dude. Unlike Julia and Morgan and Zoe, I'm not deluded enough to think I'm going to spend the rest of my life with my high school sweetheart. This isn't 1980.

But Morgan thinks everything I do is a threat to my very survival. When I was diagnosed with lupus at thirteen, Morgan appointed herself as my guardian angel. It was nice for about two weeks. Then it got annoying. She would sit next to my bed, even when I wanted to be alone. She would tag along at appointments and scream at the doctors when they couldn't make my pain go away. She ditched school on more than one occasion when I was too exhausted to attend.

Even when the treatment started working and I was able to resume a semi-normal life, Morgan's annoying protectiveness didn't stop. The doctors told her with a few small modifications, I would be perfectly healthy. My mom told Morgan I was lucky to have such a moderate case. I told her I was totally fine and she needed to leave me the fuck alone. Okay, I screamed the last bit. But she still didn't listen. She may have stopped sneaking into my bedroom in the middle of the night, randomly bringing me vegetables, and forcing sunscreen on me whenever there was a break in the Oregon clouds. But the concerned glances and the subtle questions and the tiptoeing around my emotions like I'm some porcelain doll that's about to crack? Those things never stopped.

Jake is the anti-Morgan in every conceivable way. He wasn't there in seventh grade when I collapsed. He isn't with me every morning when I take my regimen of pills. He knows about my diagnosis, but it doesn't faze him.

When we first started dating, I told Jake during lunch I had a disease that caused my body to attack its own immune system. First, he asked if it was deadly. I said sometimes, but not in my case. Then, he asked if I was going to finish my tater tots. I said yes, and he should buy his own tater tots. He hasn't mentioned it since.

"You want snacks? I want snacks." Jake pulls into the parking lot of a 7-Eleven.

"How are you hungry?" I ask. "You've eaten twice in the past six hours."

"I need to eat five thousand calories a day, babe. Coach's orders."

I roll my eyes and follow Jake into the convenience store. It's not the first time he's shared that little tidbit with me. I will never understand why athletes are so proud of how much food they consume.

"Let's be quick," I say.

I would love to get to the cabin, claim a bedroom, and be making out with Jake before Morgan has a chance to drag me back home in handcuffs. Unfortunately, Jake's version of being quick entails roaming every aisle of the brightly lit store and selecting a variety of neon-colored snacks. Sour Skittles. Pringles. Zebra cakes. Flavor-blasted Goldfish.

Really, he'll go for any food with enough preservatives to withstand nuclear attack. And yet, with his daily workout regimen, Jake's horrifying diet doesn't affect his physique. The dude has the biceps of a Greek god and the abs of a Hollister model—another thing about Jake my sister doesn't appreciate.

"You want anything?" Jake asks.

"Uh..." As I search the aisles for something, anything, I can eat, a symphony of concerned voices sneaks into my brain.

Eat less trans fats and processed foods.

Don't touch anything fried.

Do you know how much sodium is in that?

I try to force the voices out of my head. It's like having a hyperactive lupus conscience that keeps me from functioning like a normal human being. Even when I'm not with Morgan and my mom, their voices are there, worrying about me constantly, dictating my every move. It's fucking annoying.

"Here." I grab the first thing I see—a jumbo bag of Hot Cheetos—and add them to Jake's pile. Sodium, trans fats, and processed foods all in one go. Take that, stupid voices.

"Dope. Hot Cheetos are lit."

Jake and I circle through the store one more time. His arms are overflowing with junk food, and I can't imagine what else he needs. But he stops in the medicine aisle, in front of the condoms and lube. He picks a box of Trojans. "Yeah?" he asks me.

The sex pact was Julia's vision, but Kevin, Zoe, and I quickly latched on to the idea. Morgan was the only one who protested. It's not like my sister is a prude—I know for a fact she and Zoe have done it before. I've had the pleasure of being in the next room *while* they were doing it. But she's a prude when it comes to me. She thinks poor, sick Madison is too fragile to have sex.

The concerned voices again crash into my head. This time, it's just Morgan, berating me for behaving irresponsibly:

You'll get too tired and have a flare.

You deserve a better guy than Jake.

You should wait. You should really, really, really wait.

Sex is overrated. You should spend the night sleeping and recharging your body.

"Mad?" Jake asks, holding the condoms.

No, I tell the voices. *You're not going to control me. I agreed to the sex pact, and I'm going to follow through. Having sex with Jake will be nice. And, like Julia, I want to do it before starting college.*

"Yeah. For sure."

But it's not just about following through.

I *need* to have sex tonight. Not to please Jake, not to piss off Morgan, not to support Julia.

No, I need to do it for me. I want to prove I can.

Julia

"Zoe, this place is freaking amazing! This is your uncle's house?"

"Yeah, how have we never been here before?" Morgan asks.

"He rents it when he's not living here, but there was a cancellation this week. Somebody's sister-in-law went into labor early." Zoe wanders around the living room, turning on lamps and fans. "No AC, unfortunately. But it's still nice."

"Nice?! This house is spectacular!"

I'm not exaggerating. When Zoe said her uncle owned a house in the woods, I was expecting something primitive.

Bare floors, wooden cots, animal carcasses turned into rugs. That sort of thing.

But this place is the type of rustic mansion you see on Pinterest. Oversize wooden beams hanging from the ceiling, granite countertops in the kitchen, an elegant stone fireplace Zoe activates with the flip of a switch. And so many throw blankets. I feel like I'm standing in the middle of a Pottery Barn.

"Are there house rules or anything?" I hate to be that person, but I find it's easiest to have fun when I understand the exact parameters of the fun.

"What do you mean?" Zoe asks.

"Are there areas we shouldn't go? Stuff we shouldn't touch?"

"Probably." Zoe shrugs. "But I really don't give a fuck. My uncle is a total asshole. I'd be fine if we destroyed this place."

"So should we, like, start some fires?" Morgan asks. "That sounds fun."

"No, nothing quite so dramatic," Zoe says. "I don't want him getting all the insurance money. I'm thinking smaller acts of defiance. Like not replacing an empty toilet paper roll. Or tilting the picture frames so they're slightly crooked."

"Ooh, what a rebel," Morgan says.

"Shut up." Zoe smacks Morgan with a tasseled pillow. "Come on. I'll give you the tour."

Zoe leads us around the mansion, pointing out bedrooms, bathrooms, and a platinum record signed by Garth Brooks.

"Is that for real?" Kevin asks.

"Yep. My uncle bid a fortune at some charity auction. Talks about it nonstop too. It's so obnoxious."

Zoe takes us inside a small office she calls the "drawing room" and a third bedroom, this one featuring a four-poster bed and an attached bathroom with marble sink and claw-foot tub. Then, we head down a narrow set of carpet-covered stairs to the coolest part of the house, according to Zoe.

The basement living area looks pretty mundane (if you consider a leather sectional and full-service bar mundane, which I certainly do not), but Zoe ignores all of this. Instead, she strides across the room and flings open a set of wooden double doors.

"Ta-da!" she announces, stepping back for us to enter.

"Oh my god…"

I walk through the doorway, and it's like entering another dimension. Inside is a massive movie theater that looks at least two stories tall, which doesn't seem architecturally possible. There are rows of leather recliners, an old-school popcorn machine and candy station, and a gigantic screen that rivals the Cinemark downtown.

"This is so cool!" Morgan grabs some Milk Duds from the candy station and pops a few in her mouth. "If I were your uncle, I would live here full-time."

"You should see his real house," Zoe says. "It's even fancier."

"Kev, wouldn't this place be cool for gaming? It's like a giant monitor. Kevin?"

I look around, but Kevin is nowhere to be found. I should have noticed his absence when he didn't freak out about the theater. Luxury electronics are one of his favorite topics of conversation.

"Did you see where Kevin went?" I ask Zoe and Morgan. They both shake their heads. "He must have stayed upstairs. I'll go find him." I grab a box of Sno-Caps and head back through the double doors.

"Yell if you get lost," Zoe says.

"Yeah, we'll find you in a couple days!"

I find the living room without making any wrong turns, but then things get trickier. This might make me a terrible girlfriend, but I don't remember the last time Kevin was with us. I was too overwhelmed by the magnificence of the house. That's what a taste of opulence does to a person. I know Kevin commented on the Garth Brooks record, but I don't remember him saying much else. I obviously should have been more attentive. His best friend's grandmother is in the hospital, and I'm fawning over a vintage popcorn machine.

"Kev?!"

I run down the hallway, opening and closing doors as I go. Each door is ornately carved and has a shiny knob, so there's no way of telling bedrooms and linen closets apart. I come face-to-face with buckets of cleaning supplies more than once. Finally, at the end of the hall, I find Kevin. He's in the room with the four-poster bed and the marble bathroom. I always knew my boyfriend had good taste.

"Hey, what's going on?" I ask.

Kevin's sitting in an overstuffed armchair, his head resting in his hands. His shaggy black hair is flying in a million directions, and he's loosened the purple tie we picked out to match my prom dress. I perch on the edge of the ottoman.

"Sorry, I wasn't feeling great, so I let you guys go ahead."

"And you strategically claimed the best bedroom for us. I see what you did there."

Kevin cracks a smile but doesn't move.

"Are you worried about Alex?" I ask.

"Yeah, I guess. I wish I knew what was going on."

"He said he would text when he knew anything. But it might be a while."

"I know, I know." Kevin exhales through his nose and leans back in the armchair. "People survive heart attacks all the time. I just hate feeling so useless. I wish I could help, but I don't want to bother him by texting constantly."

"Do you want to head over to the hospital? I'm sure his family would love to see you." I try to hide my disappointment. I know it's selfish, but I had envisioned a perfect night for us (a perfect night for all of us, really) and none of it is happening as I expected. But clearly, if Kevin wants to be with Alex and his family, he should be there.

"I would be fine here by myself," I say, this time with more certainty.

"That's sweet of you, Jules."

"I'm serious. You know I'm more than capable of occupying myself with quality entertainment."

Kevin smiles and pulls me onto the armchair with him. I'm straddling his legs and our noses are practically touching.

"Hey now. I thought I was part of this sex pact. Are you telling me you'd prefer to watch porn and get yourself going?"

"Ew, Kevin! Why does your mind go there? I obviously meant I would watch Netflix."

It's not that I haven't been tempted to search for porn on the occasional Saturday evening when I was home alone, but I'm too paranoid about my risqué Google searches showing up on our internet bill. That is so not a conversation I want to have with my parents in this lifetime.

"Hey, I'm sure with your knowledge of the Netflix catalog, you could find something sexy to watch in my absence." We both start laughing, but then my lips brush against his and we're kissing amid the laughter. Kevin's tongue roams my mouth, but a new burst of giggles overtakes me and our teeth collide.

"Ow." Kevin pulls away slightly. He makes a big show of massaging his front tooth. "I don't know, Jules. Going solo might be a safer option. I was hoping to have all my teeth at the end of the night."

"Oh, stop whining. It was a tiny bump." I lean in to resume our romantic activities but pause when I remember Alex's grandma. "Are you sure you want to do this? I'm totally fine waiting if you want to go to the hospital instead."

"I'm sure." Kevin brushes my bangs out of my face. "Alex will send updates whenever he can, and in the meantime, I could use a pleasant distraction."

"Excellent. Let the pleasant distraction begin." I lean forward again, but something in Kevin's face makes me stop. "What's wrong with you? Are you worried about having sex?"

While the sex pact was my idea, Kevin had certainly seemed excited about the plan. But there's no denying he's always been a bit more hesitant than me with the physical stuff. Maybe he's changed his mind and decided it's too soon. I would obviously respect his wishes, but it would mega suck if we were the only couple who didn't follow through with the pact.

"Kevin, talk to me." I poke him in the chest.

"It's not the sex I'm worried about." There's a confused look on Kevin's face, and he's staring over my shoulder. "But I am slightly concerned about how you're going to react when you see the cat on the bed."

"What?" I turn around to see what Kevin's talking

about and then shriek at the top of my lungs. Sure enough, there's a cat sitting in the middle of the freaking bed. A mangy, orange, well-fed cat that looks capable of smothering me in my sleep.

"Oh my god. It's a demon cat!" I scramble off Kevin's lap and stand as close to the door as I can without letting the cat out of my line of vision. Something tells me that would be a bad move.

"Aww, I think he's kinda cute!"

"How is that thing cute? Do you see how his eyes are squinting at me? That's a demon cat right there."

"I always forget how weird you are about cats." Kevin tentatively approaches the bed, then scoops the lump into his arms like it's a puppy, not an evil being with murder in its heart.

"Aren't you a little cutie? We're gonna find out who you belong to." Kevin's talking in a baby voice that might be endearing if it weren't for the thing in his arms. "Until then, you can hang out with Uncle Kevin. Your Auntie Julia gets a little skittish around cats, but she loves you too, I promise."

"Don't tell that thing I love it." I back all the way into the hallway. "And I'm the appropriate level of skittish."

Kevin doesn't hear me. He's too busy scratching Demon Cat's head.

This night is really not going my way.

Zoe

Morgan keeps her thoughts to herself for a full ten seconds. That might be some kind of record for her. But the moment we hear Julia's footsteps going up the stairs, she explodes with pent-up worry.

"I don't trust Jake. Not one bit. Why the hell are they going somewhere for food at, like, one in the morning? There was food at prom, which I saw Jake eating all night. While he was neglecting my sister, by the way."

Morgan's eyes are wild and her frantic gesturing is causing Milk Duds to fly across the room. "This is not a safe time of night to be at a random gas station. Especially when Julia said there was a robbery there. And why hasn't

Madison texted me back? Do you think I should call my mom? We could still cancel this whole thing, you know. God dammit. I'm so stupid."

"Shhh, Morgan." I place one finger over her lips and remove the half-empty box of Milk Duds from her hands. "Getting worked up isn't going to fix anything. You have to calm down."

I realize what I've said before I even finish speaking. Over the past eighteen months, I've learned telling Morgan to calm down is almost always a mistake. She thinks I'm not validating her emotions. What I'm really doing is trying to keep her from hyperventilating. It's a fine line.

"How can you tell me to calm down?!" Morgan responds, right on cue.

"Sorry, sorry." I give her a quick hug. "I didn't mean to say that. I get you're worried about Madison, but there isn't any reason to panic. She's at a convenience store with Jake. Which means she's probably bored out of her mind listening to him talk about his pecs, but she's not in danger."

Morgan nods and takes a calming breath.

It's all about knowing your audience. With Julia, that means showing an interest in her latest passion, whether it's competitive Hula-Hooping, excessively long fantasy novels, or the European singer she's unironically obsessed with. Madison loves talking about the future—what kind of apartment she wants, where she's going to study abroad, what car she'll buy once she has enough money. And with Morgan, I can always score easy points by mocking Jake. I don't actually mind the guy. I wouldn't want to have a one-on-one conversation with him for longer than thirty seconds, but I think he's sweet. Morgan, however, sees everything in Madison's life as a potential threat. Especially Jake.

"If she's okay, why didn't she text me back?"

"Well…" I consider how to phrase the truth. "You were asking a lot of questions. In what could be perceived as a controlling manner." Morgan opens her mouth to protest, but I hear footsteps above us followed by laughter.

"You hear that? They must be here." I try unsuccessfully to keep the smug smile off my face.

"I hate it when you're right," Morgan mutters.

"You should be used to it by now, don't you think?" Morgan glares at me and snatches her Milk Duds back. We head up the stairs, but I stop before we reach the top.

"How about you let me show them around?" I ask. "So you can give Madison some space?"

"Why?" Morgan honestly looks bewildered.

I spend enough time with Morgan to know her compulsive need to protect her twin comes from a place of love. But I also spend a lot of time with Madison. Who frequently fantasizes about living in a different country than her sister.

"Remember what I said about you being perceived as controlling? Just let me show them around."

"Fine. But your uncle's candy stash may be gone by the end of the night." Morgan squeezes my hand and runs back downstairs.

I wait until I hear the sound of the cinema door closing before I round the corner and find myself face-to-face with Madison. Well, more like face-to-butt. Madison's legs are wrapped around Jake's waist, and they're oblivious to my presence. That's one benefit of dating a soon-to-be college athlete. An intense exercise regimen opens up an astounding range of sex positions.

From the back, Madison is the mirror image of her sister. Slim legs and arms, a long torso, and thick, chestnut-colored hair both she and Morgan decided to curl tonight. I distinguish the twins by their faces. Madison's lips are thinner, her eyebrows arched in a more dramatic fashion, though I'm not sure if that's a natural occurrence or the result of careful tweezing. Morgan's eyes are wider, her cheeks rounder, and her face tanner thanks to field hockey. The twins have never gotten tested to see if they're technically identical or just remarkably similar-looking fraternal twins. Most people say identical, but I've always leaned fraternal. Maybe I'm just used to telling them apart.

Thanks to the display in front of me, I can also attest that their make-out styles are entirely different. Morgan would never jump on top of me, even if I were strong enough to hold her. Which I'm definitely not. As a proud midsize girl, I may have the same body mass as Jake, but I definitely don't have the core strength.

I clear my throat. Madison and Jake look like they would have sex right here in the living room if I gave them another few minutes. Which I don't intend to do.

"Oh, hey." Madison twists her head around to greet me. Jake, still oblivious to my presence, begins sucking on her ear. "Jake, stop." Madison hops down from her perch on his waist and hugs me hello. I can smell Jake's brisket-y breath on her neck. It's not pleasant.

"Sorry to interrupt," I say. "But I wanted to show you around the house."

"No, we're sorry." Madison pulls a tube of ChapStick out of her bra and spreads it across her lips. "Aren't we, Jake?"

Jake whistles in response. "Damn, this house is sick! You live here?"

"No, it's my uncle's place. He mostly rents it out."

"The uncle you hate? The one who—"

I nod curtly, cutting Madison off mid-thought. I may be stuck in my uncle's house all night, but I'd like to avoid talking about him. Especially now.

"Come on, let me show you around." I take Madison's hand and lead her down the main hallway. Jake trails behind us, swearing appreciatively and running his hands across the wainscoting on the walls. I hope he's getting grease on everything.

"This is the drawing room, whatever that means. And there's one bedroom, but I believe Julia and Kevin already claimed it. Here's another." I push open the door to the smallest bedroom and the one that has always been my least favorite.

"Holy fucking shit." Jake runs into the room like a kid let loose in a toy store. "This is so dope. Madison, we've gotta claim this room. Man, I've always wanted to try hunting."

Madison scrunches her nose, her face perfectly replicating the disgust I feel whenever I'm in this room. In fact, I deliberately avoid this corner of the house during family get-togethers. Every single wall is adorned with multiple animal heads—deer and bison and three varieties of bear, a rhinoceros head my uncle imported illegally. All mounted on wooden plaques with their mouths open in threatening positions. All incredibly revolting.

"This is some sick loot," Jake says, admiring an elk head. "Does your uncle hunt?"

"No, he's very anti-gun. He buys these from online collectors." The man is the human embodiment of hypocrisy. He must experience serious cognitive dissonance.

"So cool." Jake turns back to Madison. "Babe, let's do it under the antelope. That's gotta be some good luck." Then, noting the look of horror on Madison's face, he adds, "Only if you want to."

Madison bites her bottom lip. I know she's weighing her desire to be agreeable with a very legitimate concern about having sex for the first time in a room full of animal heads. I'm about to show them the other bedroom option when my phone starts buzzing.

"Hang on, you guys." I fish my phone out of my back pocket, my hand clenching when I see the who's calling. "Sorry, I've got to take this."

I step into the hallway before answering the phone. "Hey, Uncle Ross," I say in my brightest voice. "What's going on?"

"Zoe, I just heard!" My uncle's voice booms through the phone. I wander into the kitchen, so nobody will overhear us. "What exciting news!" I place my cell phone on the granite countertop and rest my head in my hands. I don't even need to put it on speaker. That's how loud my uncle Ross is.

"Your parents tell me we've got another Ivy Leaguer in the family," he continues. "But not just any Ivy League school, Zoe. The best! The crème de la crème of educational institutions! Yale University. My alma mater, your father's alma mater, your grandfather's alma mater, your great-grandfather's—"

"Look, Uncle Ross..." I wish I could feel a fraction of the excitement my uncle is exuding. But ever since I opened that email—the email every waitlister dreams of receiving—I haven't been able to shake this feeling of unease. I don't know why thinking about Yale makes me nauseous. I don't know why I haven't told Morgan. I don't seem to know anything right now.

"Sure, it was a blow to be waitlisted the first time around," Uncle Ross says. "Especially when the rest of the family got in right away." I pound my fists against the countertop. I hate him so much. I guess that's one thing I know. "But it's where you end up that matters. And nobody at Yale will know you got rejected at first. We'll keep that embarrassing tidbit in the family."

"UNCLE ROSS!" I swear I'm going to torch this house. I am going to burn my asshole uncle's house to the ground.

"What, dear? Were you saying something?"

There's so much I wish I could say to my uncle. I want to explain that (1) Just because he thinks Yale is the best school on the planet doesn't mean everyone wants to go there, (2) Being waitlisted is nothing to be ashamed of, and (3) It's a billion times harder to get into college now than it was fifty years ago.

The thought of letting loose is tempting. But then I take a shaky breath and remind myself how awkward family events would be if I made any of those points aloud. I need to stay calm, be polite, and at most, make a few passive-aggressive comments. Sometime later, my mom and I can discuss our hatred for him over diet lemonade and banana bread.

"I was wondering why you called so late at night," I say. "If there was another reason, I mean. Other than to congratulate me, which is so very appreciated." I let a hint of sarcasm slip into my voice. Enough to make me feel better, but not enough to cause any drama. Probably not enough for him to notice.

"Well, actually, there was something else. I forgot to mention my cat is there. I'm afraid your aunt has been having some allergy problems, so we're trying a bit of separation. Can you make sure Bulldog has food and water?"

"Wait, I'm confused. There's a cat here? And a dog?"

"No, just a cat. The cat's name is Bulldog. I named him after Yale's mascot, the mighty bulldog."

"Of course you did, Uncle Ross." I sigh. "Of course you did."

Madison

I understand the appeal of hunting for survival. People who hunt their own meat in the woods instead of buying hamburger from the supermarket are pretty badass. Unfortunately, when your family is very anti-gun, it's difficult to justify hunting, even if that is the most environmentally conscious way to consume meat. All this to say, I understand the appeal.

What I don't get, however, is taking the dead body of some animal you killed, cutting off its head, and then paying a taxidermist lots of money so you can hang a trophy above your bed. Or, perhaps worse, buying that trophy on the internet. What kind of bloodthirsty weirdo would want a dead thing mounted on their wall? Well, clearly Zoe's uncle does. From her accounts, the dude sounds a bit outrageous, but I never would have pegged him for the corpse-on-the-wall type.

I close my eyes and try to focus on Jake, not the lifeless antelope staring down at me. Jake's lips are soft and tender, but the intensity with which he's kissing me is the complete opposite. A soft squeak of pleasure escapes my lips. It's so nice to be treated like a normal person, not some helpless doll. I press my tongue into Jake's mouth, but at the same moment, he pulls back.

"You okay? You made a noise."

I squeeze my eyes shut as annoyance surges through my body. I'm sick of everyone being so damn careful around me. But then I open my eyes, see the genuine concern on my boyfriend's face, and realize this is Jake being a good guy. And, of course, that also annoys me because why can't my sister and friends see how gentle and considerate Jake can be? Why do they have to judge every single thing I do?

"Mad?"

"I'm fine," I say. "Actually, I'm more than fine. That was…uh…really nice."

"Good. I was worried the animal heads would freak you out and…" Jake pauses. "Aw shit."

"What?" I roll over to one side. Maybe Jake finally realized it's creepy to have sex with dead animals staring at you.

"I left the snacks in the car."

I roll my eyes. Only Jake would be thinking about Cheetos while making out with me.

"It's just…the condoms are in the bag. Those are kind of necessary. Unless you're okay without?"

"Um, no. Very necessary." Morgan went on the pill last year to help with cramps, but my specialist advised against it. Plus, Jake and I don't talk much about past relationships. There's a good chance he's been around the block, as my mother would say, and the last thing I need is another disease.

"I'll grab the bags," Jake says. "You stay here with Melvin."

"Is Melvin the antelope?" I ask.

"Nope." Jake grins. "I named the antelope Theodore. Melvin is the arctic fox."

I lie back on the bed, pulling a pillow over my face to avoid Theodore's lifeless gaze. Jake closes the bedroom door behind him, and within seconds, the energy drains from my body. Moments ago, I had been making out with Jake and now I'm exhausted. I tell myself it's all psychological and I'll feel reenergized when Jake gets back. Lupus flares don't happen instantaneously. But then I start to feel a familiar, dull ache in my wrists and fingers. I shove my hands under my butt. Suddenly, all I can think of is my mom's stupid list of symptoms.

After a lupus flare hit me a few years ago and we spent

hours at the urgent care clinic, my mom tacked a laminated list of symptoms to my bulletin board. It was utterly humiliating. I felt like a six-year-old who couldn't remember how to tie her shoes, not a highly intelligent fifteen-year-old with a chronic illness. But now, anytime I start to feel achy or sick, that list of symptoms in twelve-point Helvetica pops into my brain.

1. *Unusual aching or swelling of the joints.*

2. *Prolonged or extreme fatigue.*

3. *Unexplained fever of more than one hundred degrees.*

4. *Development of a butterfly-shaped rash.*

5. *Mouth or nose ulcers.*

6. *Dizziness or difficulty focusing.*

7. *Digestive problems or abdominal pain.*

Right now, I have two of the seven. And since I never get the butterfly rash or the ulcers or the abdominal pain, I'm basically halfway there.

"No, no, no!" I throw the pillow across the room and force myself into an upright position. It's hard to move but not unbearably so. I get the vibe Jake likes being on top anyway.

"You listen to me, Theodore." I shake my finger at the antelope head. "I am not letting anything ruin this night. Not my dumbass body, not my mom and her list of symptoms, not Morgan and her constant worrying. You hear me?"

Theodore gazes back at me with solemn understanding.

If anyone gets my pain, it's Theodore. Actually, my issues probably sound mundane to him. Theodore had his head chopped off and turned into tacky home decor. He's an antelope with real problems.

There's a knock on the door, and I run my fingers through my hair, trying to get my part to fall like it did earlier in the evening. It may be two in the morning, but I still want to look nice.

"Jake? Dude, there's really no need to knock."

The door opens a crack, and Zoe sticks her head in. Behind her, my sister huffs. She hates it when I talk like Jake, but it's out of my control at this point. I was sprinkling "dude" and "bro" into my vocabulary ironically at first, but you can't spend an entire year with someone without adopting some of their quirks.

"Oh. It's you." The words come out ruder than I intended, so I hurry to explain. "I didn't mean you, Zoe. I was talking about…" Behind Zoe, a hurt look flashes across Morgan's face, and I realize I made the situation worse.

"We really didn't mean to interrupt," Zoe says. "I just got off the phone with my uncle, and his cat is living here. You'd think he would have shared that crucial bit of information with guests, but he decided to inform me of our feline co-inhabitant in the middle of the night. Among other things."

Zoe purses her lips, and I wonder what else her jerk of an uncle said to her. He's been making snide comments and subtly insulting Zoe ever since she got waitlisted at Yale earlier this year. As if not getting into her family's alma mater wasn't painful enough.

"So have you seen a cat anywhere?" Zoe asks.

I'm about to tell them a cat would likely avoid a room with animal heads mounted on the wall when I hear a high-pitched shriek.

"Is that Julia?" I jump off the bed, ignoring the pain in my knees chastising me for moving so quickly.

"Sounds like Julia," Morgan says.

"THAT'S A DEMON CAT RIGHT THERE!" Julia's voice echoes down the hallway.

"Shall we go rescue the cat from Julia's wrath?" Zoe asks Morgan.

My sister, who apparently has no intention of interacting with me further, is already halfway down the hall. Zoe turns back to me. "Have a good night with Jake, okay? And seriously, if this room is too freaky, you should move next door."

"Thanks. And I'm sorry about snapping at you earlier."

"No problem. I honestly don't even remember," Zoe says with a sigh.

She sweeps her perfectly straightened hair into a ponytail, then lets the dark strands fall back to her shoulders. I look closer at my friend, noticing the shadows under her eyes for the first time. The combination of the purple-tinged semicircles and her pale skin makes her entire face look gaunt. Zoe's the type of person who pushes herself too hard and never gets enough sleep because she's working on extra credit for AP Physics. But she doesn't usually look this exhausted.

"Hey, Zoe?" I say as she turns to leave the room. "Are you okay?"

"Just a lot going on in my head." Zoe shrugs and forces a smile. "Don't worry about me."

Alex

The second waiting room is identical to the first. Same stained carpet, same months-old magazines, same scratchy sofas. But this waiting room is on the third floor. It's closer to where the surgeon is operating on Halmoni and away from the distraught families and sick children streaming through the sliding glass doors. We were directed here by a kind receptionist who promised a peaceful waiting area, but the quiet of this room feels worse than the chaos on the first floor. The unspoken words are louder than the cacophony of crying babies and ringing telephones.

Leah and Jenny sit together on a sofa, doing one of those "spot the difference" puzzles in an old *Highlights* magazine. Jenny normally insists fourth graders are too old for kiddie games, but she agreed immediately when Leah suggested they play together. Since then, Jenny has been staring obsessively at Leah's manicured nails and sequined dress. Jenny always gets attached to my female friends, and Leah is no different. Hopefully she won't ask Leah about childbirth (like she did with Julia) or start fondling her hair (a constant occurrence with Madison and Morgan).

Mom is pacing in a tight circle next to the coffee maker, typing furiously on her cell phone. My mom has two older brothers, both living in Korea, so I assume she's sending updates about Halmoni. There was talk of my uncles getting on a plane and flying to Oregon, but Dad kept saying, "It's not serious enough yet." I don't know what "yet" means, but I know I don't want to find out. For a brief moment, Mom pauses and makes an impatient clucking noise with her tongue, but then she tucks a few loose strands of hair behind her ear and resumes pacing.

Dad and I are sitting on our own couch across the room from Leah and Jenny. He's been glancing back and forth between me and Leah, a smile tugging at his lips. Finally, he leans in closer and lets out with the question he's been wanting to ask for the past twenty minutes.

"So is this Leah your girlfriend?"

I kick at a lump in the carpet. I want to tell Dad his mother-in-law is in surgery and now isn't the time for gossip, but I know that wouldn't be well received. Instead, I answer honestly. "No. I met her tonight."

"She could still become your girlfriend." Dad waggles his eyebrows suggestively. And frankly, it's embarrassing for a middle-aged man to do anything suggestive with his eyebrows. "If you're anything like me and your mother…"

"Dad. I know how this goes."

It's my dad's favorite story to tell at dinner parties. And during dentist's visits. And at parent-teacher conferences when your teacher makes the mistake of mentioning biochemistry.

My parents were the only two Korean students in their sixty-person chemistry lab. Their professor, whose not-so-subtle racism got him suspended two years later, paired them together, assuming the two Asians would be able to talk to each other. My mom, an international student from Daejeon, spoke almost no English, and my dad, a Boy Scout from Park City, Utah, spoke even less Korean. But it was an instant connection, Dad always claims. Mom just smiles and nods, silently endorsing his revisionist history.

The language barrier wasn't a problem for them, Dad brags. Then he finishes the story with the one-liner that elicits giggles from my friends, awkward silences from my teachers, and probably a request to open wide at the dentist's office: *because there was very little talking involved, if you know what I mean*, Dad says with a wink and the eyebrow waggle. Always the eyebrow waggle.

"All I'm saying is love at first sight can happen."

"Okay, fine," I concede. "But that's not happening here. Leah is a friend of Julia's. It was a random setup when I didn't have a prom date."

"So now you and Leah can double date with Julia and Kevin." Dad has missed my point entirely. "Double dates are good for young people. It keeps things casual."

"Can we talk about something else?" I ask. We're getting dangerously close to discussing my sexual activity, a parental conversation I was hoping to avoid for the rest of my life.

"Your mother likes her. That's good. It's important for the women in your life to get along." He nods sagely, pleased with his analysis.

"Mom is in a state of shock," I say. "That's the only reason she doesn't hate Leah."

"Your mother is a very open-minded woman."

I fake a cough to avoid laughing. My mother is open-minded about everything in the world *except* the dating habits of her firstborn. I swear she'll let Jenny get engaged before she even entertains the thought of me with a girl. One time, she walked in on me and Kevin watching *Grey's Anatomy* and nearly had a heart attack because she thought it was porn.

I frown as those words flit through my brain. When did having a heart attack become a figure of speech? Heart attacks are serious business, not something to joke about.

I make a mental vow to permanently remove the phrase from my vocabulary.

"Alex…" Dad leans in close and covers his mouth with one hand like he's about to reveal a secret. "You and Leah know how to be safe, right? Because—"

"Bathroom!" I announce too loudly as I spring out of my seat. Everyone in the waiting room turns to stare at me. I lower my voice. "I mean, I need to go to the bathroom. I'll be right back." I hurry out of the room before my dad says something I can never unhear.

I pause outside, scanning the hallway for a restroom, but all I see are other waiting rooms, an empty nurse's stand, and doors marked *Hospital Personnel Only*. I turn left and head back toward the elevator. I announced to the entire world I was going to the bathroom, so I may as well follow through.

I stare at the directory posted next to the elevator, trying to orient myself within this maze of a hospital. I've almost gotten my bearings when I hear footsteps behind me.

"Alex, wait." I turn around and see Leah jogging to catch up with me.

"I'm going to the bathroom," I say.

"Yeah, the whole waiting room knows that," she says. I wince in embarrassment, but Leah smiles and tugs on my hand to let me know she's joking. "I was thinking about leaving to—"

"You're leaving!?" Again, my words are louder than I

mean them to be, but the thought of Leah abandoning me fills me with a surprising amount of dread. Less than an hour ago, I was seriously considering deserting her in the car. Now, I feel like the precarious peace in the waiting room will fall apart if she's not here. I clear my throat and attempt to look calm.

"Sorry, just surprised. It's totally fine if you want to leave. You have that after-prom party, right? You should definitely go. In fact, why don't you take my car? I mean, not permanently because it's technically my mom's car, but for tonight." I'm babbling, but I hold up my car keys to emphasize my point.

"Alex, chill," Leah says. "I'm skipping the party. I told Jenny we would do the word search next, and I take my puzzle commitments seriously."

I exhale loudly, not even trying to hide my relief. "What about the party?"

"Eh, Jason Womack was throwing it, and he kind of sucks." Leah shrugs, but I can see the disappointment on her face.

If I were a better person, I would tell Leah I was totally fine and force her to attend the party, which is clearly what she wants to do. But being in this hospital, listening to my mom panic, placating my father with pointless conversation while Halmoni fights for her life…it's like I'm drowning and Leah's my life jacket. There's no way I can swim on my own yet.

"Are you sure?" I ask. "I'd be fine if you wanted to go…" I trail off.

"No, really, I don't care about the party," Leah says, and she actually sounds like she means it this time. "But I was thinking about leaving for a few minutes to get some food for your family. It's been hours since any of you ate, and I heard your sister's stomach rumbling."

"Oh. You don't have to do that." I look at my feet, so Leah doesn't see the heat on my cheeks. It's a nice offer, maybe too nice. "I mean, that would be cool, but if it's too much trouble…"

"It's no trouble at all," Leah says. "I looked on my phone, and there's an IHOP across the street. Just tell me what you want."

"Uh, I don't know. A salad?"

"Nobody eats salad at IHOP." Leah suppresses a smile. "Forget it. I'm getting you chocolate chip pancakes."

At the mention of chocolate chip pancakes, my mouth fills with saliva. The food at prom looked too disgusting to touch, and all I had for lunch was a peanut butter sandwich.

"Here, at least let me give you money." I grab my wallet from my other pocket.

"No way." Leah pushes away my wallet but takes the keys still dangling from my finger. "My dad gave me two hundred dollars before I left the house. I've got it covered."

"Why did your dad think you needed two hundred dollars for prom?"

"No idea." Leah grins. "But it's not like I was going to say no." She punches the down button on the elevator. "You relax, and I'll be back in no time with food."

"Okay, thank you so much."

"No problem."

"No, seriously." I take her hands and look her straight in the eyes. "Thank you."

As I walk back to the waiting room, Leah calls after me. "The duck is green in one picture and brown in the other."

"Huh?" I turn around.

"Your sister can't find the last difference between the pictures. Tell her it's the duck."

"Oh, right."

"And, Alex?"

I turn around again.

"There's a bathroom literally right behind you."

LET'S DO THIS!!!

Group Chat
1:27 AM

Zoe: Update on the cat situation. My uncle's cat is living here because my aunt is allergic. I don't really know how that's working, but it means we're supposed to take care of the cat tonight.

Julia: IT'S A FREAKING DEMON CAT

Zoe: The cat is strictly an indoor cat so don't open windows and watch the doors!

Julia: What if I accidentally slam its head in a door?

Morgan: Wtf Julia?!? It's an innocent cat.

Julia: JULIA HAS A VERY RATIONAL AND JUSTIFIED FEAR OF CATS

Morgan: Why are you talking about yourself in third person?

Julia: BECAUSE JULIA IS STRESSED

Morgan: Kev, is Julia okay?

Kevin: Yeah, she's fine. What's the status of my Doritos?

Today 1:33 AM: Julia named the conversation "ALL CATS ARE EVIL"

Madison: Sorry forgot to tell you the Doritos and gummy worms are in the kitchen

Kevin: You're my hero.

Morgan: Seriously Julia??

Madison: I know I am

Zoe: As I was saying, watch out for doors and windows. Morgan and I will handle the litter box.

Kevin: Because nothing gets you in the mood for sex like cleaning out a litter box.

Madison: Ewwwwww

Today 1:47 AM: Morgan named the conversation "JULIA NEEDS TO CHILL THE FUCK OUT"

Alex: There's a cat situation?

Zoe: Yeah my uncle left his cat at the house and I'm supposed to take care of it.

Alex: Aww that sounds cute.

Kevin: Tell that to Julia.

Alex: Haha she has a weird thing about cats, right?

Today 1:49 AM: Julia named the conversation "MORGAN

NEEDS TO RESPECT JULIA'S PHOBIA OF CATS"

Kevin: How are things going at the hospital?

Alex: Lots of waiting. We won't have any more news for a little while.

Julia: Is Leah still with you?

Alex: Yeah, she's been great. She was playing with my sister, and she just left to get us food.

Morgan: So adorable.

Julia: That's a soul mate level match right there ;)

Alex: God you guys are worse than my dad.

Kevin: Is he trying to set you up?

Alex: It's so weird. Even my mom seems to like Leah. But I don't think she's thinking clearly with everything going on.

Kevin: Sorry

Alex: Julia, do you have Leah's phone number? Just in case there's an emergency. I forgot to ask her.

Julia: Just in case of emergency, huh ;) ;) ;)

Alex: Will you quit with the winky faces?

Julia: Sorry I was trying to cheer you up :(:(:(

Alex: The frowny faces are just as bad!

Julia: Okay, okay, I'm done. I'll text you Leah's number.

Alex: Thanks! Have fun doing it with a cat watching you ;)

Julia: ALEXANDER MICHAEL SONG. THAT IS A LEGITI-MATE DEMON CAT.

Kevin: Lol

Today 1:57 AM: Morgan named the conversation "JULIA'S HAVING A THREESOME WITH A CAT"

Julia

"The cat's gone, Jules."

"It's probably sitting in the hallway, enjoying my misery."

My eyes don't leave the narrow space between the bottom of the door and the carpet.

When I was eight years old, I tried to pet my neighbor's cat. At the time, I thought it was adorable. It had long gray fur, bright green eyes, and a tail as big and fluffy as a feather duster. But when I tried to pet it, the cat flipped out. It hissed and snarled and scratched my face and arms so badly I had to go to the emergency room. Although doctors determined I didn't have rabies or cat scratch fever (a real disease spread by those furry monsters), I left the hospital with a crippling fear of cats.

My aunt Elizabeth's calico.

My friend Markelle's two Siamese kittens.

The freakishly bony neighborhood stray.

I even avoid the lions and tigers (and pumas and cougars and jaguars) at the zoo because they all remind me of house cats.

And now, this stupid Demon Cat is going to ruin my whole freaking night.

I've done extensive internet research on my fear of cats, which is technically called ailurophobia. It's more common than you would think, especially for people like me who've had traumatic incidents with felines. There are types of therapy that help, but when I showed my doctor the WebMD printouts, he said my fear of cats wasn't debilitating enough to warrant treatment. I vehemently disagreed. Next time I see him I can relay my experience with Demon Cat and finally get that referral.

"What can I do to help?" Kevin sits on the bed between me and the door, so I'm forced to look at him.

"Kill the cat." I had been joking in the chat, but murder is the only way to permanently eliminate the threat.

"How about we lock the door? And push the armchair under the doorknob, so there's no way Demon Cat can get inside. Even if it magically grows opposable thumbs." Kevin laughs at his own joke. He's making fun of me, but he also used my nickname for Demon Cat so I'll let it slide.

"Fine. You move the furniture." I cross my arms, making it clear I have no intention of leaving the safety of the bed. "We also need a priest to come sprinkle holy water or burn incense or something. Get all the bad cat vibes out of here. Like an exorcism."

"Okay, I'll block the door," Kevin says, climbing off the bed. "You call up a Catholic priest at two in the morning and explain we need someone to come bless this bedroom, so we can have premarital sex. I hear priests love that."

Kevin may think I'm being ridiculous, but he does a fine job barricading the bedroom. First, he stuffs towels under the door, like you're supposed to if there's a fire. Then, he turns the lock and checks it three extra times at my request. Finally, he pushes the overstuffed armchair across the room, shoving the backrest under the doorknob to prevent anyone—or anything—from entering. I feel incredibly lucky to have scored such a perfect boyfriend. (I'm just saying, if your man can't cat-proof a bedroom, do you really want to be with him?)

"Better?" Kevin climbs back onto the bed and kisses me on the nose.

"A thousand times better, thank you."

"Can you focus on us now?"

"Absolutely. Demon Cat is dead to me."

"Good." Kevin settles into the pillows and takes my hand.

"Good," I repeat back to him.

The stress of Demon Cat dissipates and I suddenly feel awkward as I remember the pact. This is our moment. Kevin and I have done all the PG-13 stuff before, but this is new for us. We're talking full-on penis-in-vagina sex. The real deal.

Maybe I shouldn't care so much. Last week in the cafeteria, Zoe went on a rant about how the entire concept of virginity is a heteronormative construct, and I totally agreed with her. She and Morgan are way more experienced than the rest of us, yet there are threads on Reddit arguing sex between two girls doesn't count. Which sucks on so many levels.

Everyone gets to decide for themselves what fucking counts as fucking, Zoe had yelled over her tray of chicken nuggets and canned peaches.

Or we can just abolish the concept of virginity altogether, Morgan had countered.

They both made excellent points. But if I'm deciding for myself, like Zoe suggested, the whole penis-in-vagina thing kind of matters. It feels different, somehow, than everything Kevin and I have done before.

I once saw a reality show about girls who were waiting until marriage to have sex, and they were petrified their husbands would be terrible in bed. That's how I'm feeling now, except I'm scared I'm the one who will be terrible.

I'm not totally naive. I've attended a public high school

for the past four years. I read romance novels. I spent last night listening to true crime podcasts while reading a *Cosmo* article called "13 Must-Read Tips for First-Time Sex." But that's still not the same as having sex in the flesh (pun semi-intended).

"You okay?" Kevin asks.

"Yeah." I take a breath. "Just a little nervous."

"If you don't want to—"

"NO!" I shout involuntarily. I glance at the door, concerned for a moment Demon Cat heard me and might be plotting alternative routes into the room. "Sorry. I just really, really, *really* want this. I'm freaking ready, you know?"

Kevin smiles. "I really want this too."

"Just first-time jitters," I say. "How about you start?"

"Um, okay?" Kevin looks confused for a moment, but he doesn't back down. Instead, he smooths out the comforter, gently moves me so my head is resting on a pillow, and climbs on top of me, straddling my torso with both legs. He pushes my bangs out of my face and leans down to kiss me, gently at first. I kiss him back and soon I'm pulling him closer, pressing my pelvis against his. We've been here before, kind of. But the tingling is stronger than usual. It's like all the senses in my body, all the nerve endings, are sending excited messages back to my brain. Those nerve endings know this is it.

This time, we're going all the way.

The *Cosmo* article said satisfying foreplay is a must.

Basically, the more aroused you are, the better the sex is going to be. And if this foreplay is any indication, the actual sex will be mega-fantastic. We've only been at it a few minutes, and I already feel like I'm going to burst. Maybe because the stakes are so high. Or maybe because it's been weeks since Kevin and I skipped lunch to make out in his car.

I pull back and try to simmer down a bit. At least long enough to get supplies from my purse. Obviously, we need condoms for the safest possible sex, even though I'm also on birth control. (I'm the type of person who takes every precaution. Look at what I made Kevin do to cat-proof the door.)

But I've come equipped with other supplies. The *Cosmo* article suggested lube, something I'd seen in the feminine hygiene aisle but never considered using. Apparently, lube makes sex much easier for first-timers. Especially first-timers with vaginas.

I crawl out from underneath Kevin and scurry across the room to where I dropped my purse. I dig underneath my wallet and phone charger until I find what I'm looking for—a tube of premium personal lubricant and a packet of medium-sized condoms.

(I've only seen Kevin's penis a couple times and it's not like I have any other genitalia to compare it with. But when questioned, Kevin blushingly admitted that he's not that big. Which I promptly assured him was totally fine with me. A small to midsize penis is way less intimidating than trying to shove a giant thing in my body. Why is *that* a desirable thing?)

"I told you I would bring condoms," Kevin pants when I get back.

"My condoms are better. They're ribbed on both sides for maximum pleasure."

"Do we really need fancy condoms?" Kevin asks.

"You won't be complaining when you're experiencing maximum pleasure," I say. "And I brought lube."

"Don't condoms already have lube?"

"Will you trust me? I did my research."

I step out of my prom dress as Kevin pulls off his dress shirt and unzips his pants. It's like one of those frantic pre-sex scenes in a romantic comedy. I swear I even see a button fly. In one motion, I slip out of my underwear—a lacy purple thong I got from Victoria's Secret, just for tonight—and slide back underneath Kevin. I offer him the condom, and he pulls the packaging off with his teeth, which, really, is the epitome of sexy.

"Give me a sec," Kevin whispers. He lays back on top of me, pressing his face against my neck and massaging my breasts until I feel him get hard again. I moan in response.

"What's wrong?" Kevin asks. "Am I too heavy?"

"No, no. You're perfect. That's perfect. Keep going."

"Okay." Kevin gives me the condom and leans backward. I try to roll it on him in a sexy way, but all I can picture is me and Zoe in health class, giggling as we stretched condoms onto organic bananas. For the record, getting a condom on a penis is way easier than fitting it on a super crooked banana. Maybe it would have been easier if Ms. Nelson hadn't been so picky about only buying organic.

Kevin was right. The condom is pre-lubed, but this is our first time and we're going for maximum pleasure *and* maximum comfort. Additional lube is definitely required for the comfort side of the equation. I grab the tube from the nightstand and unscrew the lid. I try to squirt a dollop into my palm, but I lose control and the dollop quickly turns into a handful.

"Holy fuck that's a lot of lube," Kevin says.

"Crap, crap. What do I do?" I hold up my palmful of lubricant like a peace offering.

"I don't know. Whatever you were going to do with it before."

I massage a bit across the entire region, but my hand is slippery and lube goes everywhere—my legs, Kevin's legs, the sheets, and somehow, inexplicably, my left ear. The whole situation is slipping away from me. (Pun definitely intended this time.)

"That's so much lube," Kevin says, ever the master of understatement.

"I know, I know. But lubrication is good. Easy entry, right?"

Kevin laughs and we fumble around a bit more, our bodies slipping against one another. I lose track of what exactly is happening, but I know it feels good. After another minute, Kevin pulls up from my lips.

"Ready?" he asks.

"Yeah, I'm ready."

After a few mistaken attempts, we finally get traction. I tilt my head back, close my eyes, and open my lips to moan in response. Then it hits me. A sharp, screeching pain that far exceeds any "slight discomfort" the *Cosmo* article prepared me for.

"Ow, ow, ow. Stop! Ow."

"What?" Kevin's eyes fly open and he pulls out immediately.

The pain is gone as quickly as it arrived.

I hear Kevin comforting me.

I feel the soft caress of his hand against my leg.

But I can think of only two things. The searing pain I felt at the moment of entry. And the fact that I'm now lying in a huge freaking puddle of lube.

Zoe

"Trust me, you didn't hear her tone of voice."

Morgan has been on the phone with her mom for nearly twenty minutes. I'm in the living room, sprawled in a leather recliner, scrolling mindlessly on my phone and eavesdropping on the conversation. Morgan doesn't have a problem with me listening in. But her constant pacing around the kitchen island was making me dizzy—better to browse Instagram in comfort, I decided.

From the highly edited photos on my feed, you would think our senior prom was the perfect social event. The student council girls are holding bottles of sparkling grape juice and smiling in front of a limousine. The wholesome girls from the volleyball team are posed next to a magnolia tree in coordinating red dresses, while the less wholesome volleyball girls are pictured drinking from plastic cups in somebody's basement. The single girls are posting goofy midjump action shots with their friends, and the girls in relationships are posting serious pics of them staring longingly at their significant others. Even Julia got in on the action. I double-tap a picture of her and Kevin holding hands, her purple dress glinting as the sun sets.

It's not that prom wasn't good. It was fine. Above average, even. But all the captions declaring it the "Most Amazing Prom Ever!" or "The Best Night of My Life!" overstate its grandeur a bit. There were balloons and streamers and food and cake. A Hollywood-themed photo booth and oversize cardboard Oscars guarding the entrance. But our senior prom was hardly different than any other high school dance. If anything, the excessively fancy dresses and high heels prevented any real dancing from happening.

"I swear, I wasn't checking on her," I hear Morgan say from the kitchen. "We were looking for the cat and, like… No, Mom, it's a long story…" There's a pause and Morgan huffs in frustration. "I *was* giving her space!" she exclaims a moment later.

I tune them out and return to my phone. I've heard this conversation a hundred times before. It always goes something like this: Madison gets annoyed with Morgan.

Madison calls their mom to complain about Morgan. Their mom texts Morgan and tells her to back off. Madison makes a passive-aggressive comment, which makes Morgan upset. Morgan calls their mom to complain about Madison. Their mom texts Madison and tells her Morgan is just trying to help. And on and on the script repeats itself. It's like the water cycle we covered in earth sciences back in middle school—there's groundwater, evaporation, and condensation. And I've learned over time it's best to avoid the precipitation.

Bulldog the Cat is crouched on the coffee table, his oversize tail flicking rhythmically like he's about to pounce. But he doesn't pounce. He just stares at me with glinting yellow eyes and occasionally makes a soft squeaking sound. It's clear the cat is displeased about something, but he's not exactly communicating his needs. I shrug at him, letting him know I've done all I can to make him comfortable. I emptied a can of tuna feast into his food bowl, filled up his water, and scraped the disgusting clumps of litter from his box. It's not my fault his guardian abandoned him in a house full of sex-crazed teenagers.

Back in the kitchen, Morgan's voice has reached new levels of shrill. "I'm giving her as much space as physically possible, Mom," she whines. "But it's like…we go to the same school, we have the same friends. Am I supposed to pretend like we're not related? Do you know how absurd that sounds?"

I close Instagram, stand up from my recliner, and scoop the orange beast into my arms. "Come on, Bulldog," I whisper. "Let's see if we can get Morgan off the phone."

To my surprise, Bulldog doesn't protest. The cat relaxes, his oversize body turning into a fluffy, motionless lump. Perhaps this is what he wanted all along. Or maybe he's resigned to his fate. Cats are such inscrutable creatures.

I wander back into the kitchen. Morgan is still pacing, but she's switched to counterclockwise. I dump Bulldog on the counter. He makes a soft squawk— perhaps relief, perhaps protest—then springs off the counter and stalks down the hallway. What did I say about cats being inscrutable?

"You okay?" I approach Morgan slowly and wrap my arms around her waist. She doesn't pull away, but she doesn't exactly lean into the hug either. The embroidered spaghetti straps of her prom dress have fallen halfway down her arms, so I push them back onto her shoulders. Through the speaker, I hear Morgan's mom babbling on about some self-help book she read for book club.

"Hi, Mrs. Alvarez!" I call loudly into the phone.

"Is that Zoe?" Mrs. Alvarez asks. "Morgan, has Zoe been there this whole time? Are you ignoring her? Come on, sweetheart. We were just talking about managing priorities."

You were just talking about managing priorities, I mouth to Morgan.

She glares and tries to push me away, but I remain attached to her hip. If I don't get Morgan off the phone, she's going to spend the entire night talking to her mother. And if Morgan spends the entire night talking to her mother, I'm going to be left alone with a disgruntled feline. It's not exactly the magical prom night you hear about in movies. Definitely not worth posting on Instagram.

"Mrs. Alvarez, everything's fine!" I call into the phone. She's back to discussing her book club selection for this month. Something about the transformative power of communication. "Morgan has to go, okay? She'll call back if she needs you." I remove the phone from Morgan's hand and press the red button.

"That was rude," Morgan says.

"Ignoring your amazing girlfriend is rude too, don't you think?"

Morgan's eyebrows scrunch together, and I know she's trying to out-logic me. "You have a point," she finally says.

I lean in to kiss her. She hesitates for a moment, but then her lips meet mine and everything else fades away. Morgan's lips are undeniably perfect. They're soft and velvety with the perfect amount of bounce. If Morgan didn't get bored so easily, I could kiss her for hours. Or days, even.

But as so often happens, she pulls back and our lips gently part. Sometimes, the end of a kiss means Morgan wants to move to a more comfortable location, like the third bedroom I know is waiting for us. But more often,

Morgan pulling back means she has something on her mind. Something that must be said. Like now.

"I'm sorry. I know I'm being, like, so annoying. But I can't get over her voice. Did you hear how angry Madison sounded? It wasn't her usual frustration. She legitimately sounded like she despised me or something."

"She sounded normal to me." I can't help but sigh. I love Morgan and I usually have all the patience in the world for her twin issues—really, I do—but I can't keep having the same conversation all night. Especially not on prom night, which is supposed to be about us.

It's as if Morgan is reading my mind. "Okay, sorry, I'm done." She wipes her hands down her sides as if symbolically cleansing the worry from her system. If only it were that easy.

"We can keep talking if you need to," I say tentatively.

"No. My mom says I need to move on. You say I need to move on." Morgan smiles. "I guess I need to move on."

"I believe in you." I hold up my hand for a high five and flash Morgan a bright smile. I wholeheartedly believe she wants to stop obsessing over Madison. I can also say with absolute certainty we'll be talking about this again in an hour. That's okay though. We have all night.

"So is there a bedroom left?" Morgan raises one eyebrow.

"Of course! The last one is all for us." With my arm around her waist, we walk to the back hallway. "I haven't actually seen this bedroom before. At family gatherings, we usually stick to the kitchen. But my uncle promised three rooms with queen-size beds."

"Where were you going to put Alex and Leah?"

"Alex swore he wouldn't be having sex, so I figured they could hang out in the cinema room. I mean if you really tried, I suppose you could do it in those movie theater seats."

"Ooh, let's try there next," Morgan says.

"You're ambitious tonight." I turn the knob, and the door to the last bedroom opens with a noisy creak. "I don't know if—" I switch on the overhead lights, and the rest of my sentence gets stuck in my throat.

My arm falls from Morgan's waist as I survey the room. I would have snatched up the animal carcass bedroom in a second if I'd known the horror waiting for me behind this door. Hell, I would have rented a hotel suite for the night if it meant avoiding this monstrosity. It appears that, for some unfathomable reason, my uncle, a grown-ass adult, has created a shrine to his favorite place on the planet.

The one and only Yale University.

It's as if the home decor section of the college bookstore exploded all over the room. Yale pillows, Yale blankets, Yale beanbag chairs. Yale pennants, Yale posters, Yale lava lamp. Who knew such a thing existed? And everything not Yale-branded is the same vomit-inducing color combination. A blue-and-white shag rug, blue-and-white pinstripe curtains, blue-and-white M&Ms displayed in candy dish that is—wait for it!—blue and white. I didn't know it was possible to despise the color navy blue, but this bedroom has proved me wrong.

My chest gets tight, and I can feel bile from my stomach creeping up my throat. This room is a physical manifestation of every anxious thought, every irrational fear, every gut-clenching moment I've experienced over the past week.

I can't have sex in this room tonight.

I can't even breathe in this room tonight.

For the past thirty minutes, I hadn't worried once about my college decision. It might have been the longest stretch of calm I'd experienced all week. For a blissful half hour, my mind was occupied by the Morgan and Madison drama and the cat named Bulldog. But now, all the feelings I've been repressing crash back into my brain.

The devastation two months ago when I was waitlisted. The subsequent relief when I realized I would be going to the University of Oregon with Morgan. The shock and confusion when I got off the stupid waitlist after all. The unanswered email sitting in my inbox.

It's too much for me to handle. I slam the door shut.

"Do you know what would be fun?" I ask Morgan in an ultra-cheery voice even a stranger would identify as fake. "We should bake scones. Why have sex when you can bake scones, right? Come on."

"Uh, Zoe? Are you okay?" Morgan is staring at me like I'm spouting gibberish.

"Yup." I take Morgan's hand and drag her back to the kitchen. "This is a great idea," I say, summoning the enthusiasm of a contestant on a television baking show. "I'm fine. We're fine. Everything is going to be fine."

Alex

Leah has been gone for seventeen minutes.

I didn't know Leah before tonight. I shouldn't miss someone I barely know. But right now, I desperately need her to come back.

Everyone in my family is stressing me out. Dad is pacing around the waiting room, attempting to look busy, and occasionally saying something inane like "you ever wonder about the people who decorate hospitals?" or "the thermostat sure is working overtime tonight." And with Mom stuck in her own little world, I feel obliged to answer each of his stupid comments with a noncommittal grunt. Which only encourages him to say more pointless things to fill the silence.

Mom won't stop praying. With her eyes shut, she sways back and forth in her seat. Her hands are clasped together so tightly her knuckles have turned white. Her praying is even more annoying than Dad's pacing, mostly because indulging in religion right now feels like a disservice to Halmoni.

My grandmother is a loud and proud atheist. "You're going where?" she would ask whenever my parents dressed up for church. She hated it even more if Jenny and I were dragged to Sunday school. I know I shouldn't be angry. The prayers are really for Mom, not Halmoni. But it still feels wrong.

Without Leah here to entertain her, Jenny is now trying to take care of everyone. Just like her grandmother would. She keeps offering me coffee and rubbing Mom's back and asking Dad if he wants to play cards. That's Halmoni's go-to line. Whenever someone in the family is stressed or something bad happens on the news, Halmoni suggests a card game. Uno. Skip-Bo. Rummy. Even Go Fish. A deck of cards is her magic cure-all for any ailment. It's sweet Jenny is trying to fill her shoes, but I want to shake my sister and tell her there's no need to replace our grandmother. Not yet. Not ever.

"Are you sure you don't want to play cards?"

Jenny is perched on the chair next to me, her fingers clutching at the armrest. Her thin black hair is pulled into a sloppy ponytail, and she's wearing the same faded

YMCA T-shirt and jean shorts as yesterday. I'm not sure if she never made it to bed or if those were the first clothes she found when Mom woke her up.

"No thanks," I say. "Not right now."

"When is Leah coming back?" Jenny leans in to whisper. "Is Leah your girlfriend? I can keep a secret. I won't even tell Mom and Dad." She holds out her pinkie to demonstrate her seriousness.

"She's coming back soon," I say. "And no, she's not my girlfriend."

"I don't believe you," Jenny says.

"I'm telling the truth. We're just friends."

"Why?"

"I don't know." I rub my forehead. "I don't know if I like her as a girlfriend. And the last month of high school isn't the best time to start dating someone."

"But why?"

"Seriously, Jenny?" My sister never outgrew the "why" phase most kids leave behind in kindergarten. She knows it bothers me, but that doesn't usually stop her. Tonight is an exception.

"Fine." Jenny pouts, and I'm hoping she'll shift her attention to Mom or Dad. But she doesn't. "Are you sure you don't want coffee? I can make it. I read the instructions on the coffeepot."

"For the hundredth time, I don't want coffee."

"Mom said it was really good," Jenny says, her voice

moving into whining territory. "And you've had a long night."

"Okay, fine." I rub at my eyes. If Jenny wants to make me coffee, she can make me coffee. Even though I have no intention of drinking it. I saw Mom dump hers into a potted plant.

"Decaf or regular?"

"Do you even know what those words mean?"

"I'm not a baby," Jenny says defensively.

"Fine. You pick."

"But I don't know what you want. Are you tired? Do you want caffeine?"

"I don't care."

"I could make you one of each. Or I could do half and half. I think that works. Or—"

"Okay, okay. I'll take regular."

"Good choice."

Jenny hurries over to the coffee station. There's no way my ten-year-old sister knows how to make coffee. We don't even keep coffee in our house. But we all need something to do with our hands right now. That's why Mom's hands are clenched in prayer. Why Dad keeps riffling through random copies of *Good Housekeeping* without absorbing a single word about lemon crumb cakes.

I'm currently massaging the crumpled lottery ticket I found in my pants pocket earlier this evening, my fingers turning black from the worn-off ink. I should throw it away, but Halmoni gave me the ticket, and I don't want to jinx her surgery somehow.

Every week, Halmoni buys two lottery tickets, each with identical numbers. I always tell her buying two different tickets would double her chances of winning the jackpot, but Halmoni doesn't care so much about winning. She would love the money, of course. But what she really wants is to watch her favorite news-caster, Harry Jefferson from channel 8, announce that two people have won the Powerball. She wants Mr. Jefferson to look down at his notes with a mix of shock and amusement. "And what a funny coincidence," he would say. "Both of our winners are the same person!" Halmoni laughs uncontrollably every time she thinks about it.

But yesterday, she lost one of her tickets. She said it blew away in a gust of wind, but I bet it fell out of her pocket. She was wearing her salmon-colored sweatpants—the slouchy kind old ladies wear. They're the same pants she's worn once a week for as long as I can remember, and the velour is developing shiny bald patches. The pockets must have holes by now.

Without her twin tickets, Halmoni had little interest in the lottery announcement. She said it wasn't worth stay-ing up for the eight o'clock news. After dinner, when I was trying on my suit, Halmoni handed me her remaining ticket and told me I should use the winnings to pay for college. I said thank you and shoved it in my pocket, but I didn't bother to check the numbers. It was Friday night, so I wanted to play games online with Kevin, not stay downstairs in my suit and watch cable news. Besides, it's not like people in real life ever win the lottery.

"Here you go." Jenny has returned with my coffee. She hands me a Styrofoam cup, then sits next to me. "Try it."

I slip the lottery ticket back into my pocket and look down at the cup in my hands. It's worse than I imagined. The steaming water is a muddy shade of brown with suspicious specks floating on the surface. As soon as we get home, I'm buying a coffee maker. Then I'm teaching Jenny how to use it. She's going to be in middle school soon, and you can't be a middle schooler if you think coffee is made by dumping grounds into hot water like it's powdered hot chocolate.

"What's wrong? Did you want decaf?"

I lift the cup to my lips and take a small sip. The scalding water burns my tongue. The loose coffee grounds stick to the roof of my mouth. As I lower the cup, I force a pleasant expression onto my face. "No, this is perfect. Thank you so much."

"Oh, good." Jenny smiles. It's the first time tonight I've seen that familiar crinkle around her eyes. "Let me know if you want more, okay?"

"I will. I pinkie promise." I hold out my pinkie to Jenny. She clenches her pinkie around mine with more force than usual. We shake up, down, then up again. It's been our tradition for as long as I can remember.

I wrap one arm around Jenny's hunched back and squeeze her tight. I want her to know I'm scared shitless, too. I want her to know it's normal to be freaked out when someone you love is in danger. I'm about to say something reassuring, except without the cursing, when Mom suddenly jolts up from her seat. A short man in turquoise scrubs and a clipboard under his arm is standing in the doorway.

"Mr. and Mrs. Song?"

"Yes!" Mom flies across the room before the man has finished speaking. She doesn't bother to tell him her name is Lee, not Song, like she usually would. Dad joins them, placing a protective arm around Mom's shoulder.

"Should we go?" Jenny whispers.

"Yeah, go ahead. I'll be there in a second." I wait until Jenny has turned her back to me, then dump my cup of watery coffee grounds into the same potted plant Mom used earlier. There's a chance this plant will be dead by the end of the night if Jenny insists on further developing her barista skills.

By the time I've joined my family on the other side of the room, the man has already started explaining the situation. I hear a smattering of what he says. There are neutral phrases like "delayed getting started" and "wonderful surgical team." There are positive phrases like "great vitals" and "strong heartbeat." And then there are the scarier words. The ones usually followed by panic and confusion on *Grey's Anatomy*. Stuff like "unexpected bleeding" and "not inflating properly" and "other arteries."

Mom and Dad nod along, taking in his every word, and their faces don't look too panicked. At least not in front of the hospital person. Jenny shrinks back and soon she's standing completely behind me, clutching my left arm for support. I reach my other hand into my pocket and brush my fingers against the warm slip of paper.

The clock on the wall says it's 2:16.

Leah has been gone for twenty-five minutes.

Madison

I'm perched on the slippery edge of the bathtub, my toes curled in the shaggy bath mat beneath my feet. It's the middle of the night, my boyfriend is half-naked in the next room, and I'm on the phone with my mother.

I told Jake there was a mild family emergency, and I had to take this call. If I told him the truth, which is that I'm playing the most frustrating game of telephone with my mother and my twin sister because I said something passive-aggressive and—according to Morgan—looked at her funny, he would likely sprint in the opposite direction.

Our mom is a bit of an enabler. At least that's what Dad said during the divorce.

He told the judge he wanted a divorce because Mom was enabling an unhealthy codependency and preventing him from cultivating a meaningful relationship with his children. Mom told the judge she wanted a divorce because Dad was texting some lady named Paula all day and night rather than putting any effort into cultivating a meaningful relationship with his children. It was a bit of a he-said, she-said situation until Dad moved back to Spain with Paula, essentially proving Mom's point.

Dad wasn't completely off base. I know it's abnormal to be on the phone with my mother when my very attractive boyfriend is naked in the next room. But I'd rather have a parent who calls multiple times a night than one who calls twice a year.

Mom always says late-night chats are when she does her best parenting. She teaches night classes at the community college and prefers a nocturnal lifestyle. Even on weekends, it's usually Morgan and me who are asleep first and Mom who's awake in the living room streaming *Downton Abbey*. If this drama with my sister was happening midmorning, she would be significantly less invested.

"I don't know what you want me to do," I say. Again. "My tone may have been slightly harsher than it needed to be, but it's not like I'm going to find Morgan and apologize. At least not until she apologizes for embarrassing me in the group chat."

"Why were you embarrassed?"

"Because she kept checking on me!" I hear my volume increase, then tamp it down so Jake doesn't hear me. "In front of everyone. It's so annoying."

"This is a big night for you physically, sweetie. Your sister is worried about you. I know she can be a bit much, but it's because she cares."

"Don't you think it's a little ridiculous Morgan is more worried about me than you are? You already worry too much, but then Morgan—"

The implications of Mom's words hit me and I regroup mid-tirade. "Did you say a big night for me physically? What's that supposed to mean?"

"Well…um…" Mom starts stammering, and I can picture her blushing through the phone. And that makes me blush, which only infuriates me more. "Your sister mentioned the little agreement you and your friends made."

"Oh my fucking…"

"Sweetie, I'm totally supportive! I mean…" Mom starts stammering again. "Not totally supportive. I would be okay if you never had sex. Or at least waited a few years. But I'm not judging you. Sex can be a beautiful—"

"But. Morgan. Told. You." My whole body is trembling with fury. My toes clench and push the bath mat away from the tub. "This is my business. If I wanted to talk about it, I would have talked about it."

"Please don't make this into a big deal, Madison. Your sister saw something on the internet about the potential difficulties of people with your condition having sex. She was concerned about you."

"ARE YOU KIDDING ME?" I shout. "Are you telling me Morgan was googling things about my sex life? Dude, that is so messed up. Seriously, Mom…"

There's a knocking at the door. Before I can answer, Jake steps inside. He's wearing nothing but boxers, and there's a cigarette hanging from his lips. My heartbeat quickens, and I glance at the cell phone in my hand, suddenly worried my mom can smell smoke through the speaker. I shoo Jake away with my hand and wait until the door closes before letting out the breath I was holding.

"Mom, I have to go. Jake's waiting for me."

"Sweetie, are you upset with me?"

"No." I stand up slowly from the bathtub and stretch out my toes, first one foot, then the other. "I just wish you would've told Morgan to stay out of my business. It's embarrassing."

"Do you want me to call her back and talk about your privacy?" Mom asks, taking her enabling to perhaps the highest level ever.

"No. It's fine. I should talk to her on my own." From the other side of the door, I hear Jake laughing to himself about something. "Just not tonight, okay?"

"Of course, sweetie. I totally understand." There's a brief pause, and it's like I can feel Mom blushing through the phone again. "Be careful, Madison," she finally adds.

I sigh loudly enough for her to hear. "I always am, Mom."

I take a minute to breathe and twist my aching wrists. Then I splash some water on my face and slip back into the bedroom. There, inexplicably, I find Jake posing for a selfie with Melvin the arctic fox.

"Babe, check this out!" Jake says. "I'm taking some sick pics with Melvin." He scrolls through the photos on his phone, which all feature Jake posing half naked with an arctic fox whose expression somehow seems lewd. While the pictures are horrifying, there's probably some gross section of the porn industry where they'd be worth a few bucks.

"Isn't that bestiality?" I ask. Jake looks at me blankly. "You know, when you have sex with animals?"

"Oh! Ew, no. Melvin and I are bros. It's not like that," Jake says. "Now, the elk head is a whole different thing."

"Don't you corrupt Theodore!" I stand in between Jake and the elk with my hands on my hips. I'm mostly joking, but it's true I feel a certain kinship with the elk.

"I won't, I won't." Jake pulls me back to the bed and sits down, but being so close to the smoke makes me cough. I pull away and go stand by Melvin, covering my mouth with my sleeve.

Thankfully, Jake takes the hint. "Oh, babe, you don't have a problem with me smoking, do you? You said Zoe hates her uncle, so I figured she wouldn't mind ashes in the carpet." Jake grins, and I can feel my nerves melting away.

"I just didn't know you smoked," I say. "Cigarettes,

I mean." I'm trying to keep my voice neutral. I know smoking is bad. Everyone knows smoking is bad. But secondhand smoke is especially bad for me. Inhaling too much smoke causes flares, and I'm sure if I asked my mom, she'd happily print and laminate a list of the other fifty side effects.

"I'm not a hardcore smoker," Jake says. "Me and the guys on the team will have a cigarette every now and then. It helps us relax."

"But that's not how smoking…"

I stop talking before I finish my sentence. I was about to tell Jake smoking was addictive, it wasn't possible to have the occasional cigarette, and it would ruin any chance he had of playing professional baseball. But it's not my place to tell Jake what to do with his body. Everybody over the age of four knows smoking is dangerous. There are inch-high warnings on every pack. And Jake, despite his carefree attitude and occasional cluelessness, is not a stupid person. He took three honors classes this year and even got an A in one of them. He can solve a Rubik's Cube faster than anyone else in our grade. He's not the ignorant airhead my judgmental friends are determined to believe he is.

In other words, I don't need to lecture my boyfriend about his health. That's what Morgan would do. And I have no desire to make Jake feel like Morgan makes me feel every day of my life.

"You okay?" Jake asks.

"Nope. I mean yes, I'm okay. And no, I don't have a problem with you smoking. Though I'm slightly surprised it's not pot."

"Aww, babe. I wanted to be totally focused on you tonight." Jake says this with a dramatic flourish of the arm like he's just declared his undying love for me.

"I guess that's cute." I take a tiny step in Jake's direction.

"You guess?!" Jake crosses the room in two strides and takes my hand. "You're a harsh critic tonight. I thought I was being majorly cute." Jake pulls me back to the bed, and I lean in closer, willing myself not to cough.

"Fine, whatever." I giggle as Jake high-fives himself over my head. "I guess you're majorly cute." I snuggle closer into his muscular chest, and the scent honestly isn't bad. Jake smells more like aftershave than nicotine. "But we should go outside. Zoe may hate her uncle, but I don't want to be the subject of his wrath. The dude beheads animals." *Also because my sister would completely freak if she knew I was around secondhand smoke*, I add to myself.

"No problem," Jake says. "Wait. You know what would be dope?"

"Um, no?"

"We should go on the roof! We can go stargazing. That shit is romantic. Think about how dope it would be to do it on the roof."

I wince slightly at Jake's suggestion. Climbing on roofs

is undoubtedly dangerous and may be impossible the way my joints are hurting. And this is hardly the small, rustic cabin in the woods Zoe had been describing. Scaling the walls of such a large structure might be deadly. And what about Jake's cigarettes? Majorly cute or not, smoking on a roof has to be a fire risk.

But this time, I'm able to push away those thoughts as soon as they jump into my head. Tonight is about me and Jake. Not me and Morgan, not me and Morgan and Mom. Not even about the structural integrity of this house.

I toss my phone on the bed and grab the bag of Cheetos. "Come on," I say. "I bet you this bag of Flamin' Hot Cheetos I can find a way onto the roof before you."

Julia

My dad says I'm a hypochondriac.

Then again, my dad also says Bob Dylan is the greatest musician of all time.

He says this frequently, usually when I'm listening to Fynn Ludwig, an obscure singer/songwriter from Germany, who is actually the greatest musician of all time. Fynn follows me on Twitter. And Tumblr. And he's liked three of my edits on Instagram.

My dad may have two master's degrees and a PhD, but his obsession with some croaky old man proves he isn't always right. At least that's what I tell him when he quotes songs I've never heard in the middle of dinner.

But if I'm being a hundred percent honest, he's a tiny bit right about me being a hypochondriac. WebMD is one of my most frequently visited websites, after Facebook and Tumblr, but before Gmail. I'm notoriously bad at checking my email.

I enter my symptoms into WebMD's "Symptom Checker" feature.

Vaginal pain.

Painful sexual intercourse.

Vaginal aches.

And, for good measure, *Sex hurts.*

I press enter and my results appear.

My closest match is endometriosis—pelvic pain, painful intercourse, lower back pain. Most of those symptoms could fit me. And my back has been hurting lately. I thought it was from sitting on Kevin's beanbag chair too much, but endometriosis could make sense.

"Jules? You okay?" Kevin climbs onto the sheets that are still sticky with lube. He's re-dressed since our failed attempt to have sex, but his shirt is on backward and his hair is rumpled in a hot, I-almost-had-sex kind of way. "You've been staring at your phone for a while."

"I think I have endometriosis."

"I'm sure you don't." Kevin laughs a little, but in a sympathetic way. Normally, I hate being laughed at, but it's okay with Kevin. I know he finds my antics endearing, not stupid or annoying. He's usually even willing to discuss my possible diseases for a few minutes before assuring me I don't have a gluten intolerance or thyroid irregularity.

"Look at this." I click back to my results.

Kevin reads aloud: "Endometriosis. Vaginal cysts. Yeast infection. Pelvic Inflammatory Disease."

"Right. So if it's not endometriosis, it could be something worse. Like cancer."

"Cancer wasn't on the list," Kevin says.

"Right. But you're always telling me WebMD is unreliable. So I could have cancer."

Kevin pries the phone out of my hands and tosses it onto the duvet. "I love it when you use my own logic against me." He nuzzles into my shoulder, his warm breath tickling my ear.

"So what should I do?"

"There's nothing you can do right now. And you only have one of the symptoms, Jules. Maybe you could talk to your doctor at your next appointment."

"At my next appointment!?" I shoot Kevin a dirty look and lunge for my phone.

"Okay, okay." Kevin holds up his hands in mock surrender. "So call your doctor on Monday and see if she thinks your WebMD results have any merit."

"But I wanted to have sex tonight!"

"I understand, but what are you going to do about it now?" Kevin sighs. "Track down your doctor's home address and knock on her front door at three in the morning?"

"See, now you're contributing some valid ideas."

"That was a joke, Julia."

I sigh dramatically and turn back to my phone. There must be useful information somewhere on the internet. I will have sex tonight whether my freaking vagina likes it or not. This sex pact was my idea. I can't be the only virgin left come morning. Everyone knows Kevin and I are the strongest couple in our group. There's no way we can be the only ones not doing it.

It's more than that though. Tonight is supposed to be my final hurrah with Kevin, a celebration of successfully surviving high school together. Kevin and I are heading to different colleges in the fall (him to Reed, me to Lewis and Clark), so moments like this will be rarer. Our campuses are only fifteen minutes apart and we have every intention of staying together, but still. It's the end of an era.

"We can try again if you want," Kevin says. "Maybe go a little slower? I could have been doing something wrong. It's not like I'm a sex expert." Kevin's face lights up. "A sexpert!"

It's a bad joke, but I smile. Kevin's right, as usual. How often do you get something perfect on the first try? Basketball free throws. Origami cranes. Masters of the Hula-Hoop devote years to perfecting their craft. It took me days to keep the thing circling my hips for even ten seconds.

The trick is to reframe how I'm thinking about sex. It's

a learned skill. One that requires practice just like math or cooking or changing a tire.

"Okay." I nod seriously. "My hopes were too high the first time. If we're going to be sexperts..." Kevin laughs. "...we need more practice."

"And we have all night for practice," Kevin says, ever the supportive partner. "Also, didn't you tell me it's supposed to hurt a little the first time? Maybe our bodies were just...limbering up. Like stretching before running a race." Kevin is not known for his track prowess, but he may be right.

"That's true. My brain was probably overexaggerating."

"You can be a bit of a hypochondriac." Kevin whips off his backward shirt and flings it to a corner of the room.

"You sound like my dad."

"Isn't that a good thing? Your dad is cool," Kevin says. "Besides, doesn't Freud say we're all secretly attracted to people who remind us of our parents?"

"Ew. Can we not talk about my dad when we're trying to have sex?"

"You brought him up."

"Yeah, and I regret that now." I pull my hair into a ponytail and climb back on top of Kevin. "How can we make it hurt less? Should we use more lube?"

"I don't think that's possible," Kevin says.

He makes a good point. This bed is disgusting.

"Maybe you need to be more aroused. Hold on. I have

an idea." Kevin wriggles out from underneath me. Not difficult, considering this bed is basically a Slip 'N Slide. He finds my cell phone buried in the comforter and clicks on my Spotify. "We need some sexy music. To get you in the mood."

Kevin turns up the volume, and the luscious voice of Fynn Ludwig fills the room.

Oh, I got you baby...there isn't any maybe...when you and me finally meet...the angels in heaven above will weep.

It's his sexiest song.

"Oh my god. I love you so much." I pull Kevin back toward me.

"Are you talking about me or Fynn?"

"Mmm...you." I kiss his cheek. "But you know this song makes me feel things. Things in places. You know?"

"Can we please not talk about Fynn Ludwig making you feel things in places? That's gotta be as bad as talking about your dad."

"You started the music."

"True enough."

I bite my bottom lip as Kevin moves my hair to one side.

Seconds later, he's on top of me.

And under me.

And all around me.

This part is familiar. We've been casually fooling around in his basement for months now.

Kissing.

Touching.

Breathing.

Our bodies folded together like one of those modern art pieces in the sculpture garden.

There's just one more thing we need to try.

"You ready?" Kevin whispers.

A different Fynn song is playing: "Dangerous Mist." One of his darker tracks. It's his commentary on the school-to-prison pipeline in America. Not your classic sex music, but Fynn could sing about gonorrhea and still sound like a god.

Maybe I have gonorrhea. If I'm remembering Ms. Nelson's lecture on sexual health correctly, painful intercourse is a major symptom of STDs. I've never had sex before, but aren't there some genetic STDs? I should ask my doctor about that too. Actually, after we have sex, I should make a list of everything I need to discuss. I always blank out when the doctor asks if I have any questions.

"Jules?" Kevin kisses my cheek.

"Hm?"

"You okay?"

"Yeah. Just thinking about STDs."

"Ew, why?"

"Sorry, just my brain. What did you say?"

"I asked if you were ready to try this again," Kevin whispers.

"Oh, yeah," I whisper back. "Definitely."

Alex

It's 2:47 when Leah finally returns. She stumbles into the waiting room with five or six plastic bags hanging off each arm and a wad of napkins tucked into the strap of her dress.

"Are you okay?" I hurry across the room to relieve Leah of her load. "What took you so long? Is there any food left at IHOP?"

"So many people in prom dresses," Leah pants. "I think every high school in the state of Oregon had prom tonight. I saw Elise Hartman and Spencer Rhett and Lily Wu. And Diego Luther, who was completely stoned. He tried to hit on me three different times. It was awful."

"I have no idea who any of those people are."

I'm checking what's inside each takeout box and sorting them into piles on an empty table. Breakfast food in one stack, dinner food in another. This amount of food would be appropriate if the hospital were full of hungry families, but the only people in this waiting room besides us are two women holding each other in one corner and a balding man coughing nonstop in the other.

"How do you not know Diego Luther?" Leah asks as she produces cartons of something—soup, probably—from another bag. "He's the one who got arrested last month for possession. Not that it did him much good."

"I kind of live in my own bubble," I admit. "Freshman year, I cared about meeting new people and stuff. Now I'm pretty set in my ways."

"Did you even know who I was before tonight?"

"Umm…" I busy myself with sorting the last few Styrofoam boxes. "I recognized your name. I mean, kind of." That's a massive exaggeration. When Julia announced Leah was my mystery prom date, I spent a few minutes stalking her on Facebook. Despite our sixty-odd mutual friends, she was a complete stranger to me.

"Are you serious? Our school's not that big, Alex." Leah flips open a box of strawberry-covered pancakes and starts eating berries with her fingers. "Also, we definitely sat next to each other in English last year."

"Actually?" I stare at Leah's freckled nose and dark brown hair. I may be slightly oblivious, but I would have remembered Leah sitting next to me every day. There's no way I could have concentrated on the literary merits of *Moby-Dick* if Leah had been in my line of vision. She's the kind of girl who captures your attention.

"I'm totally messing with you." Leah cracks up, and I start laughing too. "We've never been in class together," she says. "But I definitely noticed you. And not just because you were Julia's friend."

My face grows warm, and I start rearranging the take-out boxes for no good reason. I'm not the kind of guy girls notice in the hallway. I'm the kind of guy you ask for help when your locker gets stuck or you forget to finish the calculus study guide. I sneak a glance up at Leah. She's casually eating strawberries like nothing abnormal happened between us.

Nothing abnormal did happen between you, I chide myself. *Leah probably flirts with guys all the time. And that didn't even constitute flirting.*

"Let's hand out this food," Leah says. "Does Jenny like pancakes? And what do your parents like?"

"Umm…" I glance across the room. Mom and Dad are huddled together at one end of a couch. Mom looks like she's praying again. Dad is awkwardly typing on his phone with one hand while his other hand strokes her leg. "Actually, now might not be the best time. We just found out there were complications with the surgery. Nothing horrible, but everyone is kinda freaked out right now."

"Alex!" The cheerful expression drops off Leah's face in an instant. She punches me in the shoulder and not in a playful way. "Why didn't you tell me? That should have been the first thing you said!"

"Sorry." I slip my hands into my pockets, my fingers finding the weathered lottery ticket Halmoni gave me yesterday. I know it's terrible, but I hadn't thought about my grandmother since Leah came back with the food. Leah has the kind of personality that makes you forget all the shitty things happening around you. "Everything is going to be fine," I say with a lot more confidence than I felt earlier.

Leah nods solemnly, her eyes wide. She looks like she's about to cry, and I want more than anything to go back to the fun version of Leah from a few minutes ago. I can't handle anyone breaking down right now. Because if Leah starts crying, I'll start crying. And if I start crying, well… I'd rather not.

"It's okay," I say, but a wobble in my voice betrays me. I clear my throat. "Really, it's fine."

"Alex, you don't need to be all manly. It's okay to cry."

"It's not…I'm not trying to be manly." I look at my parents, then my sister. "It's just…if I don't keep it together, then Jenny will get upset. And if Jenny gets upset…"

"Okay, I get it. I'm sorry." Leah steps toward me so our heads are practically touching. My breath catches in my throat. Even when we were slow dancing to Ed Sheeran at prom, we were never this close. I can smell the peppermint lingering on Leah's breath. "I just want you to be okay," Leah whispers.

"I'm…fine," I whisper back, suddenly hyperaware of what my own breath smells like. I've seen enough romantic comedies to know this is a classic pre-kiss move. And part of me is so enchanted by Leah I want to lean in, but I don't. Because this is a hospital waiting room and my parents are ten feet away and my grandmother's life is at risk and I am so not the kind of guy girls spontaneously kiss.

"Pancakes!" I exclaim as I step backward, tripping over a table leg. I seem to be developing a habit of shouting in the quiet waiting room, and everyone looks up at the commotion. "I mean, we should hand out this food before it gets cold."

Leah nods and turns back to the boxes. If she's disappointed at the interruption, her face doesn't show it. "What would Jenny want?" she asks, all business again.

"Well, she's ten. So anything with sugar."

"Chocolate chip?" Leah sorts through the boxes, retrieving one with so much whipped cream on top I can't even see the pancakes underneath.

"Perfect," I say. "You give those to her. I'll see if my parents want anything."

I walk across the room and hover awkwardly until Dad looks up from his phone. "How's it going?" he asks.

"It's fine." I look back at Jenny and Leah. My sister is grinning at the sudden appearance of sweet breakfast food. And then, like some kind of traveling magician, Leah pulls a yo-yo from her purse and hands it to Jenny. Soon, my sister is eating pancakes with her right hand and flinging the yo-yo around with her left.

"What's going on, Alex?"

"Oh, uh, not much." *I just almost kissed a girl for the first time.*

I perch on the chair next to Dad. If he notices my flushed face, he doesn't mention it. "I don't know if you guys are hungry, but Leah got a bunch of stuff from IHOP—pancakes, burgers, a couple salads. Whatever you want."

"Who's Leah?" Mom's eyes fly open.

"Alex's new girl—"

"My prom date," I remind Mom, interrupting Dad before he can finish his thought. Thank god he didn't see our almost kiss. I would never hear the end of it. "You met her down in the lobby? She's been hanging out with Jenny for the past couple hours? Remember?"

"Hmmm." Mom stares in the direction of Leah and Jenny, her eyes glazed over with a thin layer of tears. I had been both shocked and relieved when Mom had welcomed Leah enthusiastically, but now she doesn't even seem to remember her.

"I think we're fine without food for now," Dad says. "It was nice of you to offer though. And tell your girlfriend—"

"Friend," I correct.

"Tell Leah we really appreciate her help with everything."

"Will do." I glance back over at the girls. Jenny is staring in awe at Leah as she demonstrates some loopy yo-yo trick. I suddenly understand why she and Julia are such good friends. They've probably been to circus camp together or something.

"The surgery will likely be another hour, so if you and Leah had other plans…"

"We're fine staying here."

Once again, I find myself reaching for the lottery ticket in my pocket. I can't believe I didn't watch the winning numbers last night like Halmoni told me to. What if this had been the lucky ticket and I never knew? Wouldn't it be amazing if I could hand her millions of dollars when she came out of surgery? Not that any lottery official would be awake at this time of night. But the news she was a millionaire would surely aid the healing process. Or at least pay for her medical bills.

I pull the ticket out of my pocket and carefully unfold the paper. From my other pocket, I grab my cell phone. There are fifteen new messages in the group chat, but my friends can wait.

I open an internet browser and search for the Oregon lottery. The little spiral symbol circles and circles, but nothing changes. I check the bars in the top corner of my phone. Four out of five, which is typical for me. I shake my phone in frustration like Halmoni used to do when she first got a cell phone, but nothing happens. Of course nothing happens.

"Dad, do you have internet on your phone?"

"I've got nothing," Dad says. "I've been trying to look up your grandmother's insurance plan for thirty minutes. But the hospital is either blocking our signals or we need a new provider."

"I've been texting fine," I say. "Is there Wi-Fi I can use?"

"I don't think so," Dad says. "Are you okay? If you have any questions about Halmoni's procedure, you could always ask the nurse."

"No, nothing like that." I shove my phone back into my pocket and walk over to Leah and Jenny. Dad thinks I'm trying to get information about Halmoni's surgery. Maybe normal people would have questions in my situation, but I trust the medical professionals. Besides, I have a far less productive task in mind. Before Halmoni gets out of surgery, I need to know if, by some astronomical chance or absurd twist of fate, she won the Oregon Powerball.

"Hey, can you come here for a sec?" I pull Leah away from my sister, who protests through a mouthful of whipped cream. "Can you see if you have an internet connection on your phone?"

"Um, okay?" Leah pulls out her phone and opens Facebook. She tries to refresh the home page a few times, but nothing happens. "Nope, nothing."

"Yeah, same here. But I really need to check something

on the internet. I know this is going to sound ridiculous, but my grandmother gave me a lottery ticket randomly. Well, it's not random because she always gets lottery tickets, but she usually gets two…" I pause when I realize my rambling makes zero sense to Leah. "I just need to find internet somewhere in this hospital."

"Let me think." Leah bites down on her lip, then checks her phone again and looks back at me. Most people would have questioned why I need internet so desperately when my grandmother is in surgery. Most people would be freaked out by my weirdness. But I'm beginning to realize Leah isn't most people.

"Okay, so I've spent a lot of time in hospitals," Leah says. I look at her curiously, but she doesn't elaborate. "And hospitals are notorious for having zero internet. But there are definitely computers at the nurse's stations and in tons of offices around here."

"That sounds impossible," I say. "There's no way anybody's going to let random teenagers use a hospital computer to search for lottery numbers."

"Ah, but that's where you're wrong." A conspiratorial grin creeps onto Leah's face as she starts shoving takeout boxes back into the plastic IHOP bags. "We're not random teenagers," she says. "We're random teenagers with two hundred dollars' worth of breakfast food. And in a hospital at three in the morning, pancakes are the most valuable currency you could possibly imagine."

Zoe

"Okay. Classic English scones. What do we need?"

It's a rhetorical question. I don't expect Morgan to answer, and she doesn't. My girlfriend is sitting cross-legged on top of the kitchen counter, staring at me with both eyebrows raised. At some point tonight—I don't know when—she changed from her prom dress into a pair of plaid pajama pants and a Timbers T-shirt. If I hadn't been so distracted, maybe I would have thought to bring a change of clothes too.

But alas, I'm stuck baking scones in my three-hundred-dollar ensemble from Nordstrom like some kind of weirdo. My mom will kill me if I get dough on this thing.

Not that I foresee an occasion in the near future where my crystal studded, two-piece dress will be the appropriate attire. My mom only agreed to spend this much after the saleslady suggested we choose something "more suitable for my body type." My mom and I are alike in that way. When someone tells us not to do something, we're all the more determined to do it.

"Three cups all-purpose flour. Half a cup of white sugar. Five teaspoons baking powder. Five teaspoons? That feels like a lot. Don't you think?" This question isn't rhetorical—I would genuinely appreciate Morgan's input on the baking-powder ratio—but she still doesn't answer. "Okay, um, then we need salt, butter, one egg, and a cup of milk. That should all be doable. My uncle stays here occasionally. I mean, he left his stupid cat here after all."

I start opening random cabinets. Most of them are filled with stone dishware and fancy martini glasses, but above the microwave I find a pantry of sorts. I grab the flour, sugar, baking powder, and an unopened bag of white chocolate chips. Normal scones are too plain. An occasion like your senior prom calls for scones with pseudo chocolate.

"Hey, Zoe. Maybe we should chat?" Morgan speaks slowly, enunciating every word. It's the same kind, slightly condescending voice she uses whenever she's trying to talk Madison out of making a bad decision. "I don't know if you noticed, but for some reason, you're making classic English scones."

"Not just classic. I'm making fancy scones now." I open the refrigerator door. It's not nearly as well-stocked as the pantry. There's an entire shelf of Heineken, but my options are otherwise limited.

"Fancy scones or not, I find it odd you would decide to start baking, like, right when we were about to have sex," Morgan says.

"Okay, I found butter. But no eggs. How does a person not have eggs? And the only milk he has is almond milk. God, I hate him so much. He's not even lactose intolerant. He drinks the stuff for the hell of it. Doesn't he know the environmental impact of almond milk?" I'm failing to answer any of Morgan's questions, but it's difficult to meet her eyes.

"This feels like a something-else-is-going-on type of situation," Morgan says. "Is it me? Are you mad at me for some reason?"

"No, I swear it's not you." I sigh, fiddling with the sugar canister. There's no logical explanation for my atypical behavior other than the truth: I'm in the midst of an existential crisis about where I'll spend the next four years of my life. I'll obviously tell my friends eventually, but I want to be totally sure first. I want to show up at school wearing one of my ten Yale T-shirts or my single University of Oregon sweatshirt and confidently announce my decision.

In this moment, though, I'm freaking out and Morgan

knows something is wrong and I don't have any eggs. Really, the eggs are my problem.

"I don't believe you," Morgan says. "What did I do wrong?"

"We need to find an egg substitute." It's a response to some question, just not the question Morgan asked. "Maybe I'll text everyone. Do you remember Julia's vegan baking phase last year? Those horrifying bran muffins she gave everyone?"

I type my question into the group chat. A second later, there's a bubble next to Julia's name, and I feel a twinge of guilt. If Julia is this available to help with a baking conundrum, she and Kevin must not be having sex. And they deserve a magical night more than anyone else.

My first time with Morgan was like something straight out of a romance novel. It was last summer on the Fourth of July. Morgan, Madison, and I had made brownies, stolen a bottle of pink sparkling wine from their fridge, and were lounging on a flannel blanket to watch the fireworks. When Madison started complaining of mosquito bites and decided to head inside…well, one thing led to another. That was a whole different kind of fireworks.

It's true that I frequently complain about virginity being a pointless social construct that only furthers heteronormative conceptions of sexuality. But it's also true that I think about that night nearly every day.

"Zo, I'm here for you," Morgan says, her voice pleading.

"You can tell me what's going on."

I put my phone on the counter and look up. Morgan is leaning forward, her hands clenched together, a concerned frown pulling at her cheeks. We've been dating for two years, yet I'm still always struck by Morgan's capacity to care. Ninety percent of the time, she's worried about her sister, and understandably so. But from the second I started acting weird, Morgan has been entirely devoted to helping me. I don't know how I got so lucky.

"Is it because I was freaking out about Madison? Or because I was ignoring you when I was on the phone with my mom?"

"It's not—"

"Because I'm really sorry, Zoe. I know I've been distracted tonight, but I'm here now. Is it weird for you that I'm always, like, worried about my sister?"

"No, it's nothing like that. I swear I don't mind how close you and Madison are."

Morgan looks doubtful, but it's the truth. Maybe some girls would be jealous of their relationship, but I love how much Morgan adores Madison. And I desperately want them to work things out. Mostly because they deserve to be happy. But I would also get way more studying done without the need to diffuse sister drama.

"Will you just tell me what's wrong, then?" Morgan asks. "Or should I spend the rest of the night guessing? Because you know I will. I can be very persistent."

"I'm well aware." My phone buzzes, and I open my messages to see three texts from Julia and two from Kevin. I don't know what those two are up to, but it doesn't seem to be sex.

"Ahem." Morgan clears her throat.

I turn my phone facedown on the counter, but I still don't know what to say. I could (1) Announce straight up that I got into Yale, (2) Backtrack and explain my relief at being waitlisted in the first place, or (3) Ignore my problems entirely and ask Morgan to fly to Mexico with me. If only that were a real option.

"I'm waiting…"

I rest my head in my hands. I should have told Morgan as soon as I got the email, and she could have helped me work through these confusing emotions. Now I feel lost.

"Fine," Morgan says after close to a minute of silence. "I'll have to start guessing. If it truly has nothing to do with me worrying about Madison…is it because I didn't pick the red prom dress you liked?"

"I honestly don't remember the red dress," I say, inadvertently agreeing to Morgan's question-and-answer game. She'll never guess I got into Yale. It's been years since Yale accepted anyone off the waitlist, a fun fact everyone in my family has pointed out.

"Okay. Um…is it because my mom made an awkward comment about your cleavage when we were taking pictures?"

"No, I thought she was funny."

"Oh, I know. What if you saw all the guys grinding on their girlfriends at prom and it was a major turn-on for you and now you're reevaluating your sexuality?"

I make a gagging noise.

"Or you felt left out because we weren't dancing like that and now you think I'm ashamed of being with you?"

I shake my head.

"I'm going to get this." Morgan drums her fingers on the countertop. "You didn't get weird until we were about to do it. But there's no world in which you don't want to have sex with me..."

I laugh.

"I've got it!" Morgan leaps off the counter. "I bet it's because your uncle's room was covered in Yale stuff, and you started feeling bad about college again, right?"

I nod slowly, and Morgan's tone instantly shifts from triumph at solving the mystery to pity and concern for me.

"Your uncle's a jerk," Morgan says. "There's so much more to life than Ivy League schools. You and Madison and I are going to have the best time together. I honestly think Oregon is better for you, anyway. Remember that smart person camp you went to on campus last summer? You loved the vibe. And I don't know if you would like the East Coast. It's all, like, pretentious and stuff. Oregon is more your kind of people."

I nod vehemently to everything Morgan says, and by

the time she finishes her rant, I'm crying. She just vocalized everything I've been feeling since I opened the email.

"I'm so glad you said all that." I wipe the tears out of my eyes. "But it wasn't just seeing my uncle's creepy bedroom. The thing I haven't told you is..."

I take a moment to calm my shaking hands. Morgan stares at me, her mouth slightly agape like she can tell major news is coming.

"The thing I haven't told you is I got off the waitlist at Yale. They emailed me this week. I guess it's the first time in forever it happened, and I've been really freaking out. You know how I was set on—"

"OH MY GOD!!" Morgan shrieks—and my girlfriend is not normally a shrieker. Before I can finish my sentence, she flies across the kitchen and clutches me in a bone-crushing hug. "I'm so, so, so happy for you! Can you believe it, Zoe?" Morgan shrieks again. "It's everything you've ever wanted! All of your dreams are coming true."

My body goes limp in Morgan's embrace. Maybe I should be touched by her uncontrollable joy, but I just feel numb. Morgan is my girlfriend. She's supposed to understand my deepest insecurities. She's supposed to know me better than I even know myself. But this? The hugging and the shrieking and the laughing? This is the last thing I wanted.

Julia

"Ow. Ow, ow, ow."

Kevin immediately starts to pull out.

"Wait, no. I'm fine."

"You sure?" Kevin kisses my forehead. "I don't want to hurt you."

"Yeah, let's keep trying." Kevin starts to push back inside me. When he's halfway in, the pain comes again. A pain that is sharp and screeching. A pain that fills my vagina and reverberates up through my torso and down my thighs. It's as if there's a cement wall preventing him from going any further.

"Ow, ow, ow." I press my fingernails into Kevin's

forearms. He slides back out of me.

"What's wrong? It still hurts?"

"Yes." My eyes fill with tears. I take back what I said about sex being a learned skill. People have sex all the time, and I don't hear anything about them experiencing unbearable pain. Our species would not have survived for so many centuries if sex were this unpleasant for everyone. We're talking about a basic freaking biological function here. And I aced the AP Bio test last year. I even managed to score higher than Zoe, the queen of standardized tests.

"Darnit. Gosh freaking darnit." I tug a sticky pillow out from under Kevin's head and chuck it across the room. It hits a lamp, which falls onto the floor with a dull thud.

"Um, I was kinda using that pillow. But okay."

"Why can't I do this? This sucks."

"It's not your fault." Kevin pulls himself up, so he's sitting cross-legged on the rumpled comforter. "People's bodies work differently. We'll figure it out sometime. I'm not worried about it."

"I know." Kevin never seems to worry about anything. I wish I could achieve his level of chillness. "I just hate being bad at things. I bet Madison and Jake aren't having this problem. And Zoe and Morgan have sex all the time! It's just me. I'm the broken one."

"Well, to be fair, Zoe and Morgan aren't trying to get a penis inside them."

"You're right. I should have been a freaking lesbian."

"Not what I meant." Kevin brushes my bangs out of my face. I decided to be adventurous and get bangs for prom. I'm still not sure if I like them or not, but I love how Kevin uses them as an excuse to touch my face more than usual. "How about we do something fun to get your mind off this?"

"Like what?" I ask. "We're in a house in the middle of the woods for one purpose. There's nothing fun about this if I can't have sex."

"I brought my computer, so we could watch Netflix or something. What's that baking show you keep talking about?"

"I guess." I cover my face with both arms, so Kevin can't see the dampness of my eyes. Tonight was supposed to be perfect. It was supposed to be a night I would think back on fifty years from now. I wanted sparks and passion and the kind of fairy-tale romance I mock relentlessly but desire nonetheless. Watching people knead bread dough and perfect their Italian meringues isn't what I had in mind.

Kevin slides off the bed and retrieves his laptop. "Here." He hands me the computer. "You get it cued up. I want to clean off a little. They really should put instructions on the lube."

"Like, 'don't use all of it at once'?"

"Exactly." Kevin grabs his clothes and steps into the bathroom. I'm glad we claimed one of the bedrooms with an attached bath. I imagine Kevin running naked to the communal bathroom, his lube-covered feet sliding on the wood floors. It's not a pretty sight.

I open his computer and choose the first available Wi-Fi network. I guess when you live in the woods, having password-protected internet isn't a major concern. I type Netflix into the search bar, but I can't bring myself to press enter. I'm not the type of person who gives up. I'm certainly not going to give up on a satisfying sexual experience with Kevin. At least not right away.

I hold down the backspace key and type in a new web address.

Cosmopolitan.com.

Once, when I was little, I found a stash of Mom's magazines in the bathroom. I remember flipping through my first ever *Cosmo* and being utterly confused at the diagrams of people laying on top of each other and the toys that didn't look like toys at all. It wasn't until years later I realized with great embarrassment what kind of toys *Cosmo* was talking about.

I scroll through their list of recent articles.

"13 Post-Pregnancy Sex Positions New Moms Need."

"The Truth About Nipple-Only Orgasms."

"What You Need to Know About Toe Sucking."

"15 Simple Ways to Improve Your Sex Life."

I click on the last one. Simple is what I need. I can't even get Kevin's penis inside me; there's no way I'm advanced enough for moves like toe sucking (what?) or nipple-only orgasms (so many questions).

I skim through the list. The first suggestion is lube, which we already tried to an embarrassing degree. There are details on using sex toys, role-play, acupuncture, masturbation, yoga. But nothing to explain why my vagina is too narrow or too dry or too angry to accommodate an average-size penis. I need simpler than simple. I need one of those *Sex for Dummies* books.

"So what are we watching?" Kevin returns from the bathroom, his clothes clinging to still-sticky skin. It's going to take multiple showers for us to fully de-lubify.

"I'm reading something."

"Reading what?" Kevin climbs back onto the bed and snuggles into my arm. When he sees what website I'm on, he sighs. "Jules, you're getting obsessive."

"I'm not obsessive. I'm determined."

Kevin laughs and kisses my nose. That's my go-to line when I'm obsessing about something.

"Seriously though," I say. "I don't want to give up. I know it's a silly pact, but it's important to me. I don't want tonight to be like every other night when we watch Netflix, make out in your basement, and eat microwaved pizza bagels. I want to be with you."

Kevin doesn't respond, so I continue explaining unnecessarily. "Like, *with you* with you. In a sexual way. Never mind. You know what I mean." I bury my face in my arms. In my desperation, I'm getting awkward. More awkward than usual, that is.

Kevin exhales slowly. I know he's worried about hurting me, but I also know he'll agree to try again. He's always been supportive of my goals, whether that means cheering for me at an amateur Hula-Hoop competition or driving with me to a Fynn Ludwig concert in Portland. This time, being supportive means attempting to have sex for the third time in one night.

"Okay," Kevin says finally. "But let's try something new. Whatever we were doing before clearly wasn't working. Does that article have any advice?"

"Not really. Unless you have a thing for toes."

"Nah, your feet are kind of ugly."

I roll on my side to kick Kevin, who takes the opportunity to steal the computer away from me. He scrolls through the article.

"'Shop for new toys at your local sex shop,'" he reads. "I would rather make out with your feet than walk into a sex shop."

"At least they're encouraging people to shop local," I say.

Kevin keeps reading. "'Try adventurous sex positions.' Um, no. You went to circus camp, but I'm not an acrobat. 'Plan a romantic outing, like a couple's massage or erotic yoga.' Not going to work; it's the middle of the night. Also, I don't want to know what erotic yoga is."

"See? There's nothing helpful."

"Wait, we can do this one. 'Role-play a sexual fantasy,'"

he reads. "Perfect. What's that fantasy series you like? *The Power of Eldork?*"

"You know it's *The Legend of Elgorp*," I say.

Kevin grins. I've tried to convince him to read the Elgorp books for years. It's an eight-part fantasy series, written by the greatest author of all time, Josephine Maguire. She's no Fynn Ludwig, but Josephine is still near the top of my list of celebrity crushes. Her world-building is freaking phenomenal. She's like a new and improved Tolkien.

"Why don't we try role-playing something from Elgerp. Maybe all the fantasy stuff will distract from the pain."

"You know it's called Elgorp. And this is talking about a sexual fantasy. Like doing it in public or clowns or whatever."

"Clowns?"

"I read a thing on Tumblr once."

"Okay, but you know reenacting a scene from Elgorp would be way sexier than pretending to be clowns. Especially for you. What about when Yesmina gets kidnapped and the elves of Todrina are holding her captive? And she's freaking out and stuff, trying to break free."

"How do you..." I stare at Kevin, confused by his sudden knowledge of the Elgorp universe. He usually resists my efforts to teach him about the various bloodlines and conflicts between the provinces.

"Or what about when Tan tries to steal the golden locket from the scary mermaid people? And they surround him and start chanting?"

My mouth drops open. "Kev...how do you know all this stuff?"

Kevin grins again. "A couple months ago, I started reading the Elgorp books in secret. I wanted to surprise you."

"Oh my god!" I screech and fling myself on top of Kevin. I kiss him all over his face before coming up for air. "I can't believe you read all those books for me."

"I'm only on number five. So if you tell me spoilers, I'm breaking up with you."

"Still, that's amazing! The second book is eight hundred pages. And you hate reading for fun."

"Yeah, when I saw how long the books were, I didn't think I would get through them. But I got sucked in. The characters are so good, you know? Yesmina and Lila have to end up together, right? And I need to know if Tan is working with Queen Hayoria. Or maybe not working for her willingly, but being coerced or manipulated in some way."

"Oh my god," I breathe.

"Sorry, I really meant for it to be a surprise, but oh well." Kevin shrugs.

"No, it's just..."

"What?"

"It'll sound stupid."

"You can tell me." Kevin takes both my hands in his.

"It's just...hearing you talk about Elgorp is a major turn-on."

Kevin's face lights up. "So you want to do this? You want to try a role-play thing like the magazine says?"

"Or we could skip the acting and try normal sex again." I pull Kevin back toward me. I fully appreciate his newfound dedication to the Elgorp books, but the thought of role-playing something sounds mega-awkward, even with my boyfriend.

"No way. I have a great idea."

"Kevin…" I moan as he heads back to the bathroom.

"You know that quote? 'A fool is someone who does the same thing expecting different results'? I think Einstein said it."

"Huh?"

"I'm just saying, we should mix it up a little. Try something new." Kevin gives me a thumbs-up before shutting the door behind him.

"Um, okay?"

I thought I was the adventurous one in our relationship. I orchestrated this whole sex pact, which in my mind was the pinnacle of excitement. But now my boyfriend—my straitlaced, socially awkward, somewhat reserved boyfriend—has instigated sexual role-play. I flop onto my back, entirely unsure about the direction our night is heading.

"I'll be right back, okay?" Kevin calls through the closed door, his voice full of excitement. "Prepare to be whisked away on a fantastical adventure!"

JULIA'S HAVING A THREESOME WITH A CAT

Group Chat
3:05 AM

Kevin: Any updates Alex?

Zoe: Yeah let us know when she gets out of surgery!

Alex: It might be a while guys. There were some complications.

Kevin: Oh no I'm so sorry.

Julia: What happened? I thought these surgeries were pretty common?

Alex: It's nothing horrible. I honestly don't fully understand what's going on. I think they're having problems opening her arteries the normal way, so they have to try something else. And they got started late. We just have to wait longer before hearing anything.

Julia: Is Leah still there?

Alex: Yeah she brought a bunch of food for my family. Now we're on a quest to find yesterday's lottery ticket numbers.

Julia: Whatever gets you going ;)

Morgan: Seriously Julia?

Julia: I'M HELPING DISTRACT HIM

Julia: Sorry Alex :(

Alex: You're all helping a great deal. Including Julia :)

Julia: YAY

Zoe: This is random but what are good replacements for eggs? I'm trying to bake scones and I don't have eggs.

Julia: Is that what the kids are calling sex these days? ;) ;)

Julia: Jk. I would go with banana.

Kevin: My sister uses tofu instead of eggs sometimes because she's allergic.

Julia: You have to have a certain kind of tofu for it to work. Also, the frittata your sister made with tofu was disgusting. BANANAS ARE BETTER.

Alex: Can't you two argue about this in person?

Julia: We're in separate rooms.

Alex: Kinda hard to have sex in different rooms isn't it?

Julia: We're preparing for a fantasy sexual role-play.

Alex: Are you guys having sex based on that terrible fantasy series you read?

Alex: Actually, please don't answer.

Julia: THE LEGEND OF ELGORP IS NOT TERRIBLE.

Julia: And it was Kevin's idea.

Morgan: Way to throw Kevin under the bus there Julia.

Alex: I seriously did not want to know any of this.

Kevin: Oh my god Julia I'm going to break up with you. Stop texting this to everyone.

Madison

"I don't know, man. This looks impossible."

I'm standing on the driveway, staring at the roof, and attempting to visualize myself getting on top of it. The house is technically one floor, but there's a basement and an attic so it looks way taller than a single-story building. Also, I'm realizing, roofs look a lot steeper the second you decide to climb them.

"It's no biggie for me, babe. You know I have a ninety-mile-an-hour fastball." Jake grabs the bag of Flamin' Hot Cheetos from my hands, winds up like he's on the pitcher's mound, and flings the high-sodium snack into the air. He hoots with excitement as the bag flies across the sky in a smooth arc and disappears onto the roof of the house.

"What did you do that for?"

"In case you were worried about climbing onto the roof and carrying the Cheetos at the same time." Jake grins. "Now we have our hands free."

"I wasn't worried about the Cheetos," I say. *I was worried about my ability to scale a wall, especially when everything is starting to hurt*, I think, but I don't share that bit with Jake. "You know that's littering," I say instead. "Very impressive littering, but littering, nonetheless."

"Aw, babe. You think I'm impressive? It was a pretty good throw." Jake cranes his neck to get a better view of the roof.

"I said it was impressive littering. Emphasis on the littering."

"Come on, babe. You've got to lighten up." Jake takes one last drag of his cigarette, then drops it onto the cement driveway and grinds it beneath his foot. Only Jake would have the gall to toss a cigarette butt on the ground in the middle of a discussion about littering. "You're only in school for what? One more month? This is what high school is all about!"

"High school is about throwing Cheetos onto the roof?"

"Throwing anything onto roofs, really," Jake says, his face serious. "One time, I was at my buddy Duncan's house, and we were bored so we scattered a bunch of Mentos on his roof. You know how when you combine Mentos with Coke it makes an explosion? So the Mentos were all over the roof, and then we flung bottles of Coke up there, trying to make something happen." Jake grins. "Well, my bottles made it onto the roof. Duncan's mostly landed in the garden. He plays first base, though, so we should have seen that coming." Jake laughs at what I'm assuming was some kind of baseball insult. I stare at him, unsure of which part of his ludicrous story I should address first.

"Please tell me you were high," I say, going with the most obvious.

"Babe, come on, now. You know me." Jake pulls me in for a hug. "I would throw Coke at Mentos even if I was stone-cold sober."

"But you were high."

"Oh yeah. We were real fucked up," Jake says.

"Makes sense."

I shiver in Jake's arms as a cool breeze rustles the trees around us. Well, more like a lukewarm breeze. It's been unseasonably hot this spring—Zoe has lectured us with even greater frequency on the dangers of global warming—but I'm still outside in the middle of the night wearing a tank top and pajama shorts. I press my face against Jake's chest, enjoying the heat of his bare skin.

"Wait a second." I pull away from Jake's hug, realizing for the first time my boyfriend is wearing nothing but boxers. "Aren't you cold?" Of course, Jake didn't bother putting on real clothes before venturing outside. That would have required too much foresight.

"Nah, babe, I'm good. I've been streaking plenty of times before, so this is nothing."

I shake my head. Some tidbits are better left unaddressed. "So how are we getting on the roof? I'm assuming you can't throw me."

"Probably not," Jake says after a moment of serious consideration. "My weight limit for chucking things is around ten pounds." Jake turns to me, a look of panic crossing his face. "I'm not trying to insult you, babe, I swear. But you are bigger than a baseball. That's just science."

"I'm really not offended, Jake." I look back at the roof, which somehow seems taller than it did a minute ago. "Maybe we should forget the whole thing. Go back inside. I'm sure Zoe won't care about you smoking indoors. As long as we're careful and don't start any fires." *And as long as we open some windows for ventilation*, I think.

"We're getting on the roof," Jake says. When I don't respond, he takes my hand. "Unless you don't want to."

I bite my bottom lip. This is my opportunity to bail. I can say I changed my mind, go back inside, and have sex with Jake surrounded by dead animal heads like a normal person. Or I can take a chance, risk breaking all the bones in my body, and do it on a roof. According to Jake, this is what high school is all about.

"I'm down." I twist my wrists in slow circles, trying to relieve the dull pain that somehow feels worse outside. "How do we get up there? I'm assuming there aren't stairs?"

"No stairs," Jake says. "Roofs are kinda dangerous, so they don't want to make it easy for people to get up there. We could see if there's a ladder in the garage. But sometimes you get lucky with old houses and there's like a built-in ladder with plants growing on it."

"A trellis?"

"I don't know what it's called," Jake says. "But one time, at my buddy's house, we found this wooden grid thing attached to the side of the house. Talk about an easy roof."

"This was at Duncan's?"

"No, at Stevie's."

"How many roofs have you been on?"

"Three. No, four. Eh, three and a half."

"All right. Let's see if we find something, I guess. You lead the way." I'm usually the decision maker in our relationship, mostly because Jake is the ultimate go-with-the-flow kind of guy, but I'm happy to let him take the lead this time. As I've learned tonight, scaling roofs is his area of expertise.

"Okay. Probably around back."

We walk hand in hand around the perimeter of the house. As soon as we step off the driveway, I'm regretting not wearing tennis shoes. The dewy grass pokes through my flip-flops, covering my feet in nature gunk, and when we reach the side of the house, I'm pausing every few seconds to shake stray pebbles off my feet.

"Shh, get down." I pull Jake closer to the gravel walkway as we pass a large picture window looking into the kitchen. Inside, Zoe is doing something with mixing bowls and Morgan is hopping around with her hands in the air. It's all very strange.

"Why are we hiding?" Jake asks.

"I don't want anyone to see," I whisper. We're not doing anything wrong, technically, but I have a feeling Morgan wouldn't agree. "Come on."

Jake and I scurry past the kitchen and living room, crouching below the windows. We traipse through another patch of wet grass before reaching the side door we left slightly ajar fifteen minutes ago. Jake had wanted to go through a window to get out of the house, but I suggested the somewhat hidden side door as a more logical, but still sneaky, alternative.

"Bingo. This is our ticket to the roof, babe."

Jake points to the stone wall next to the door. Sure enough, there's a wooden trellis with green vines growing through the slats. The rickety structure seems to be warping under the weight of the plants. I seriously doubt its ability to support me. And there's no way it's strong enough to hold Jake, who proudly eats five thousand calories a day.

"That's the trellis thing I was talking about," I say. "Those are decorative. For flowers and stuff. It's really not the same thing as a ladder."

But Jake doesn't listen. With zero hesitation, he pushes a plastic chair against the wall and starts climbing.

"Oh my god, you're going to die." I cover my eyes with both hands. "Oh god, oh god, oh god. Jake, please come down from there. Let's go back in the house. We have other snacks inside. This was a bad idea. I'm sorry. I'm so, so, so sorry."

There's a scraping noise, then a muffled yell, then a thump. I peek through my fingers, terrified I'm going to see my boyfriend's broken skull on the ground in front of me. But Jake is nowhere to be seen.

"Babe, up here!" I look up. And there's Jake, standing on top of the roof. He's holding the Cheetos triumphantly in the air and there's a massive smile on his face. "Come on up and join me! The Tetris thing is really strong. I'll talk you through the whole thing."

Jake starts dancing around on the roof with a stupid grin on his face, and I burst into loud, obnoxious, uncontrollable laughter. Laughter so intense my abdomen starts to hurt, and for the briefest of seconds, the other pain fades away. I don't care if Morgan hears me. I don't care if Jake thinks I'm a lunatic. For a few short moments, I am completely out of control and it feels glorious.

"You coming, babe?" Jake calls as my laughter fades

away and I start breathing normally again.

"Are you going to help me get up there?"

"Absolutely! I've got you every step of the way. Well, I don't physically have you because I'm on the roof. But I'm with you spiritually. Wait, that's not it. That's like Jesus stuff."

"I could use some Jesus stuff," I say as I climb onto the plastic chair. I grip the trellis with both hands, and the wood feels too thin in my grasp. "Are you sure this is strong enough?"

"It held me, didn't it?"

I shrug, unable to argue with his logic. "All right, here goes."

I place my foot on the makeshift ladder, once again feeling a familiar achiness in my ankles and knees and wrists. But then I remember how incredible it felt to laugh uncontrollably with no thoughts about my exhausted body or what Morgan or anyone else thinks of me. And I know it's that feeling of freedom waiting for me on the roof.

I take a deep breath. I twist each of my wrists one more time. And I begin to climb.

Alex

There are two types of people in this world.

People who respect *Hospital Personnel Only* signs and people who do not. I belong to the former category, as do most law-abiding members of civil society. Leah, I have learned tonight, belongs to the latter.

"I really don't feel like we should be in here," I say. "Let's go back."

"Do you want to find those lottery numbers?"

"Not if it means getting arrested."

"They wouldn't arrest us for being back here. They would politely escort us back to a public waiting area."

"People don't normally say no to you, do they?"

Leah smiles sweetly at me, then places one hand on the small of my back. I wonder briefly if this is another pre-kiss gesture. Maybe I wasn't mistaken before, and she's going in for attempt number two. But this time, Leah has no romantic intentions. Instead, she uses the hand to propel me through the hospital at a speedier pace.

I stop suddenly, and Leah nearly trips over herself. "What about your party? You seemed like you wanted to go earlier. Are you sure—"

"Oh, for the love of pancakes!" Leah turns to face me, her expression somewhere between annoyance and amusement.

"For the love of pancakes?"

"Well, I normally say for the love of God, but I didn't want to offend you since you're Christian," Leah says. "Your parents have been praying all night," she adds when I look confused.

"My mom is Christian. I'm not."

"Okay, whatever. For the love of God, then. Or Satan. For the love of somebody."

"For the love of somebody what?"

"Stop asking me about the party," she snaps. "I'm staying with you, Alex. Unless you can honestly tell me you want me to leave." Leah stands with her shoulders squared and stares me down. Her face still looks angry, but there's a sparkle in her eye. I can't tell if she's just determined to be a Good Samaritan or if there's something else going on.

Either way, I can't say I genuinely want her to leave, and she knows it.

"Uh…" I stare at my feet.

"That's what I thought." Leah looks extremely satisfied with herself. "Now let's move it." She tightens her grip on the bags of takeout and once again walks with purpose through the *Hospital Personnel Only* wing.

Even without the official sign, it's clear we shouldn't be here. This hallway has none of the comforting touches of the waiting area. No magazines, no plastic plants, no pleasant paintings of kayakers paddling down the Willamette River. Just blank walls, gray-speckled linoleum tiles, and too-bright fluorescent lighting. There is an occasional cough from inside a patient room, the steady sound of machines whirring and intermittent beeping.

"See?" Leah whispers. "There's nobody here."

"What about them?" I nod toward a nurse's station at the end of the hallway. "There's no way they'll let two teenagers in formal attire wander by. We're not exactly inconspicuous."

Leah chooses this exact moment to drop a bag of takeout boxes on the ground. One of the nurses looks up from her task and squints at us curiously.

"Calm down," Leah says, gathering the fallen Styrofoam. "They're not going to stop us. We come bearing pancakes."

"I feel like you think this stuff from IHOP is some kind of golden ticket," I say. "But a bunch of soggy breakfast food really doesn't excuse trespassing, which is what this is."

"We'll only be trespassing for another minute. See those double doors?" Leah points to a pair of white swinging doors just past the nurse's station. "They lead to the NICU. The Neonatal Intensive Care Unit. You're supposed to get there through a different lobby, but I like this shortcut."

"Are you telling me we could have used a different entrance and not violated hospital policy?" I can't believe her. "Are you out of your mind? And how do you know all these secret passageways? It's like you work here." Leah doesn't answer me. Instead, she straightens her spine and plasters a warm smile onto her face. "What are you doing?" I hiss.

Leah elbows me in the stomach. "It would help if you didn't look so petrified."

I manage to make my face look normal, but my feet are firmly rooted to the linoleum. I thought we would walk past the nurses as quickly as possible while averting our eyes. Leah seems to have a different tactic in mind.

"Hey, guys," she says. "How's it going tonight?"

I expect the nurses to press a button to alert hospital security of intruders. Or at least question why two teenagers are in a restricted hallway at this time of night. But none of that happens. One woman shrugs, another says, "Same old, same old," and a man with a face mask stretched across his mouth doesn't even look up from his paperwork.

"Well, the overnight nursing team never gets enough credit in my opinion. You guys are the nocturnal super-heroes of the medical world. I mean, you're supposed to get all this work done without compromising patient care. Nobody ever appreciates how hard it is to work at this hour." Leah's voice is compassionate yet authoritative. My fears of being caught vanish. I find myself staring at her, along with all three nurses, and nodding in agreement with everything she says. "Anyway, we were passing through to the NICU, and we wanted to bring you some food. It's gotta be lunchtime soon, right?"

Leah plops all five bags of food onto the counter, and her new friends break out of their trance. Soon, they're laughing and talking and exclaiming about the new red velvet pancakes at IHOP. It's only when one of them asks who exactly we are that Leah declares it's time to leave.

"That was amazing," I whisper as Leah pushes through the swinging doors to the NICU. "You magically made them like you. How did you do that?"

Leah shrugs. "Years of practice."

"But how are we going to get the computer now? I thought the food was our golden ticket. You gave all of it away."

"Alex, Alex, Alex." Leah sighs. "The food was to get us through the hallway. That's not our golden ticket in here."

"Then what is?" I ask.

"I am." Leah adjusts the straps of her dress and smooths

her curls behind her ears. "Follow my lead, okay?"

Leah walks decisively to the nurse's station. I trail behind her like a lost toddler.

"Hi, do you have a moment?" If I thought Leah was kind to other nurses, she's a whole new level of amiable with this woman. "My name is Leah Sonnenfeld. I was wondering if Alison or Lisa are working tonight? They're close friends of the family, and I wanted to say hi."

"Everyone is pretty busy right now," the nurse says. She starts tapping on the keyboard, then her fingers pause. "I'm sorry, what did you say your name was, honey?"

"My name is Leah. Leah Sonnenfeld."

The woman looks up from her computer with renewed interest. "You said Sonnenfeld?" Leah nods. The nurse scoots backward, jerking her rolling chair so quickly she almost falls over. "I'll get Alison right away! Lisa isn't in until the morning, but I know she would absolutely adore seeing you. Is your father here by any chance? Let me see if Dr. Dunlop is still around..."

The woman rushes down the hallway, shooing away another man who tries to speak with her. Everyone else in the vicinity has quieted down, and they're staring at us with looks of reverence. Well, they're looking at Leah that way. I'm feeling pretty invisible at this point.

"Why do they treat you like you're famous?" I whisper.

"You know what they say," she says with a wry smile. "It's all about who you know." A look of disgust suddenly clouds her face. "Oh god. Please don't tell anybody I said something so douchey."

"Your secret is safe with me."

My eyes dart around this wing of the hospital as I try to understand what's going on. Here, the walls are painted a festive shade of green and there are outlines of pine trees stenciled up and down the hallway. This nurse's station is covered with plastic flowerpots and stuffed animals, unlike the barren desk on the other side of the double doors. The nurses in this section of the hospital are wearing mismatched combinations of rainbow scrubs, and some even have cartoon stickers on their tops. But whenever I make eye contact with one of them, they look away or suddenly busy themselves with an empty clipboard.

"Seriously, will you tell me what's going on?" I whisper. "Are you some kind of hospital celebrity?"

"In a manner of speaking," Leah mutters back.

"How? What? How?"

Leah nods to an acrylic sign hanging on the wall.

The Peter Sonnenfeld Neonatal Intensive Care Unit.

"Wait. Is that you? Is this hospital named after you?"

"It's named after my brother, not me. And not the whole hospital, just this wing."

"Why didn't you…How did you…" My brain can't decide which question to ask first.

"You said you needed a computer to help your grandma," she says. "And we happened to be in a place where people knew who I was." Leah's face is bright red. "If you tell anyone at school about this, I'll kill you."

"Well, we've already established I don't know anybody at school, so no worries there. And I'm really not judging you." I stare at the sign featuring my prom date's last name. As if this night could get any weirder. "I'm trying to connect the dots. So your brother..."

"Leah! It's been so long." A very pregnant woman in magenta scrubs comes around the corner. Her face lights up at the sight of Leah.

"Alison!" Leah drops my hand and rushes over to hug the woman. "I'm so happy to see you again. When are you due? Oh my god, you're going to be the best mom." I thought Leah was lying when she called the nurses close family friends. But Leah is chatting and laughing and hugging this woman like she's a legit relative. And not a random second cousin you see at Christmas, but like a sibling or an aunt. I walk over and hover awkwardly next to their reunion. It takes a few minutes, but Leah finally remembers I'm there.

"Alison, I want you to meet Alex. He was my prom date."

"Oh my goodness." Alison drops Leah's hands and surveys me from head to toe, rumpled suit and all. I feel more than a little self-conscious. "Nice work, Leah," she says with a wink.

"Actually, we were hoping you could maybe do us a favor," Leah says. "Alex's grandma is in surgery right now, and he really needs to find a computer with internet. I know this is unusual and it's kind of a complicated situation, but you know how terrible coverage is here."

Alison waves her hand. "Say no more. I'll get you set up with a laptop and an empty room right away. As long as you've got some pictures of your baby brother for me. How old is he now? Four? Five?"

"He's turning six this summer," Leah says.

"There is no way," Alison says in mock outrage. "There is no way my little peanut is all grown up."

The two of them continue gabbing like old pals while Allison grabs a computer from the nurse's station, a ring of keys from a filing cabinet, and some bottles of water from a refrigerator in the break room. They talk about Leah's little brother and how he's reading at a second-grade level, about Leah's younger sister who recently became a level six gymnast, whatever that means, and about how her parents are renovating their vacation home in Martha's Vineyard.

I feel like I've slipped into some alternate reality where my prom date is a famous A-lister and I'm her trophy boyfriend who tags along to movie premieres. Except instead of red carpets, it's the NICU at Johnson Memorial Hospital. And instead of a movie premiere, we end up in an empty room no bigger than my closet.

"Are you okay by yourself for a minute?" Leah asks. Alison is turning on the computer and plugging it into a wall socket. "I'd like to say hello to some other people. That will give you time to look up the...stuff."

"Yeah, no worries. I'll be here."

I wait until Leah and Alison wander back down the hallway, still in the midst of a very personal conversation. Then I turn my attention to the open computer. I'll get to the lottery numbers in a moment. Right now, before she comes back, I need to find out exactly who Leah Sonnenfeld really is.

Julia

"Close your eyes!" Kevin calls from the bathroom.

"Um, if we're doing some weird role-playing scenario, I'd rather keep my eyes open."

"No, I'm not ready yet," Kevin says. "I need to get something from the closet, and I don't want you to see my costume yet."

"Your costume? How in the world are you making a costume?"

"Let's just say we chose the right bedroom." Kevin pauses. "Are your eyes closed?"

I dutifully fold my arms across my eyes. "Yup." The bathroom door swings open, and Kevin's bare feet pad across the carpet. I hear him rummaging around the closet. "Are you sure you should be looking in there?"

"Zoe said it was okay if we trashed the place," Kevin says. "Going through a closet is five levels below vandalism."

"You know Zoe's just saying that. She's going to be freaking out about cleaning everything in the morning."

"Aha!" Kevin apparently found whatever he was looking for. "Are your eyes still closed?"

"Yeah." I wait until I hear the bathroom door shut before opening my eyes. "Can you at least tell me what character you're doing? I need to mentally prepare for whatever weirdness is about to happen."

"Do you really have no patience?"

"Have I ever?"

Kevin sighs. "I thought we could do the scene where the elves kidnap Yesmina."

"So you're an elf, and I'm Yesmina?" I ask.

"Yeah. I always pictured Yesmina looking like you. Because she's supposed to be the most beautiful Magloo woman ever, and you're the prettiest human woman ever."

"Awww." Thankfully, Kevin is in the bathroom, so he doesn't see me blush. If any other guy had said that, it would have sounded like a line, but Kevin's enough of a dork to get away with it. He may tease me about reading and rereading Elgorp, but we both know who the biggest nerd in this relationship is.

I climb out of bed and wander over to the full-length

mirror next to the closet. It's only when I'm face-to-face with my reflection that I realize I'm still naked. Once you've been naked for a few hours, the shock value dissipates. I kind of get why nudist colonies are a thing.

I do see a bit of myself in Yesmina. I mean, my skin is pale and splotchy, not purple and shimmery, and my hair is dirty blond, not "the color of frozen flames." Still, in terms of general physique and demeanor, we're a decent match. Give me some Hollywood-level special effects, and it could totally happen. Unfortunately, I don't have access to special effects or whatever weird costume materials Kevin found in the bathroom. What I do have, however, is my prom dress.

I pick up the pile of lavender silk and shake out the wrinkles. When you don't have purple skin, a purple dress will have to do. I slide back into the dress, discarding the sticky boobs I meticulously attached to my skin earlier tonight. Yesmina is too free-spirited to ever wear a bra, and my boobs are still tender from the first time I peeled off the cups. My curls deflated a long time ago, but I twist my hair into a loose braid and use a bobby pin to wrap it around my head like a haphazard crown. This may be the strangest thing Kevin and I have ever done, but at least I'll look good.

I'm admiring myself in the mirror when I hear a weird noise. "Kev, is that you?"

"Is what me?"

"Those sounds. It's like scraping or something. It might be coming from the roof."

"Probably some animal," Kevin says. "Pretend it's a Yacka."

I laugh to myself. Yackas are small, opossum-like creatures that inhabit the hidden woods of Todrina, but they're notorious burrowers who would never dare climb on a building, especially one inhabited by other beings. I don't tell Kevin any of this though. I want to encourage, not dampen, his love of the Elgorp universe.

"Okay, you ready?" Kevin asks.

"Yeah." I run back to the bed and clear my throat to make my voice deeper than usual. "I mean...come forth at your own peril!" I try to sound confident and wise like Yesmina does when she's facing a foe. Look the part, be the part—that's my motto.

The door creaks open, but I don't see anything at first.

"Uh, Kev?" I walk around the side of the bed. That's when I see him.

Kevin. My soul mate.

He's kneeling on a pair of oversize tennis shoes with a brown, terry-cloth towel wrapped around his chest. He's trying to create the illusion he's three feet tall, but I can see his sock-clad feet sticking out behind him. His face and arms have been sprinkled with some kind of green powder, turning his skin the color of rotten celery.

It's the least sexy thing I've ever seen. I clap my hand over my mouth.

"Are you Yesmina, protector of the bronze goblet?" For

some unfathomable reason, Kevin is talking in a squeaky, Minnie Mouse voice. I collapse on the bed, unable to control my hysterical laughter.

"Kevin!?" I start coughing as I choke on my own spit. "Is this a joke? You're joking, right?"

Kevin glares at me, then speaks again in his high-pitched voice. "I do not joke. I am the Head Elf of Todrina! I am here to kidnap you."

I sit up and take a few deep breaths, willing the laughter to stop. Kevin is serious about this whole role-play thing, so I need to get it together. I summon my confident Yesmina voice. "Okay, elf boy. Why are you so short? And why is your skin green? Did you accidentally eat a poisonous mushroom and fall ill?"

"Huh?" Now Kevin is the one breaking character. "I'm supposed to be an elf. I thought elves were short and green."

That causes another bout of laughter. "Come on, Kevin," I say as I struggle for breath. "I love you, but you're mixing up elves and dwarves. And possibly baby ogres. Or maybe leprechauns. Elves are tall and graceful, not short and green."

"Well, what about Santa's elves?" Kevin asks. "Those elves are short! And they wear green outfits, at least."

"Christmas elves are different from mythological elves."

"Then Christmas movies have been spreading misinformation," Kevin grumbles. He ditches the shoes and stands at a normal height. The towel clings to his skin like he's Jesus or something. "So I'm just a guy with green eye shadow all over his body?"

"You're wearing eye shadow?"

"I found makeup in the bathroom. I thought I was being creative." Kevin frowns.

"Aww, I'm sorry," I say, though my sincerity is undercut somewhat by the occasional involuntary giggle. "You do look like a fantasy creature, just not an elf. Actually, you kind of look like Yoda."

"Is Yoda sexy?" Kevin asks, his voice hopeful.

"Not in the slightest."

He groans. "This was a dumb idea. I'm sorry. We should pretend this never happened." Kevin sits on the bed with me, his shoulders slumped in defeat.

"It's not your fault," I say. "You just didn't know what an elf looked like before. Now you know."

"So you want to try again?" Kevin asks.

I nod. I really do want to keep trying. Partly because I need to successfully have sex at some point tonight, and *Cosmo* was probably right about spicing things up. But also because I ruined Kevin's sweet gesture by laughing at him. The last thing I want is to make him feel insecure.

"Here." I hand Kevin the laptop. "You google what a fantasy elf looks like. And I won't laugh this time, okay?"

"You promise?"

"I totally promise. But you have to wash off the green eye shadow. You look like you're suffering from a strange skin disorder, which really isn't a sexy vibe." I sink back into the pillows as Kevin returns to the bathroom. It's hard not to point out the smudges of green makeup on the back of his neck, but I resist the urge.

"I'll be fast," he says.

"No worries. I'll be texting."

"Updating everyone on the thrilling details of our sex life?"

"Obviously."

I hear Kevin sigh as he closes the bathroom door, and I briefly worry he resents me telling our friends so much. I tend to be an oversharer in every aspect of my life, but this is decidedly more intimate, even if we haven't gotten to the actual sex part yet.

"Do you mind me texting the group?" I call.

Kevin pokes his head out of the bathroom. He has made no progress on de-greenifying whatsoever. "Not really," he says after a moment of thought. "I mean, is it any different than you telling Zoe and Zoe telling Morgan and Morgan telling Madison and then Madison telling you her mom's opinion in the group chat? This way it all happens faster. And I'm in the loop."

"Plus, I'm providing crucial entertainment for Alex while he's at the hospital."

"I'm sure he appreciates that. If my grandmother were in the middle of surgery, I would definitely care about the details of my friend's sex life."

"I know you're being sarcastic, but that is exactly the kind of entertainment I would desire in a difficult situation."

Kevin laughs, revealing a streak of green on his teeth. It's too much for me to take. I pull a pillow over my face to muffle my laughter. "Go wash your face, elf boy," I yell through the pillow.

Zoe

I have always considered myself to be a logical person. I take the time to consider all viewpoints, evaluate my options, and come to an informed, well-researched decision.

When I wanted a puppy at the age of eight, I put together a PowerPoint presentation featuring five pro-puppy arguments and twenty-four subarguments. We had a golden retriever puppy named Puddles three days later.

When I took the SAT, I developed a test-taking strategy to optimize my time per problem and delineated a foolproof method for choosing between equally correct answers. This test-taking strategy yielded me a near-perfect SAT score and eventual admission to Yale University.

Which is the cause of my current angst. But still.

My point is, logic and rationality have served me well.

It's not that I don't have emotions. I experience as many meltdowns and moments of gloom as the next person, probably more. But I pride myself on understanding where my emotions are coming from and analyzing how I can most easily return to a less volatile mindset.

So naturally, when I experience a wave of emotional distress that is completely unfounded, has no rational explanation, and shows no signs of dissipating, I get a tad freaked out. Okay, I get majorly freaked out. Which is why I'm aggressively whisking a bowl of smashed banana and almond milk into a liquidy puree.

"My girlfriend is going to Ya-a-ale, my girlfriend is going to Ya-a-ale."

Morgan is dancing around in circles, her arms raised above her head, singing in an obnoxiously high-pitched voice. In any other situation, I would find her antics adorable. It's not often Morgan is this unequivocally joyful. But right now, I'm infuriated.

I wanted Morgan to be sad. I imagined she would fake a smile, but then her lip would start quivering and she would burst into tears. She would tell me she was proud of me, of course, but she desperately wanted me to stay in Oregon. She would say she couldn't imagine her life without me, that a long-distance relationship was too much to handle. She would beg me to choose her, not Yale.

I start scooping flour into my bowl of banana goop, not bothering to measure a damn thing. White powder flies everywhere, but Morgan doesn't notice.

I hate myself for allowing these thoughts into my brain. There was a zero percent chance of Morgan ever saying something so ridiculous. I wouldn't be dating her in the first place if she were a quivering lip girl who would selfishly demand I give up an Ivy League education for her.

What's more, I don't want to be the kind of girl who wants that kind of girl. I'm a strong, open-minded, independent feminist. But right now, against all the habits of rational thought I have spent my life cultivating, I wish my girlfriend weren't being so supportive. Not when support means she's overjoyed about me moving across the country.

I pour a decent amount of sugar into the bowl, then add a pinch of salt and a teensy bit of vanilla. All I have left is baking powder, but I should definitely measure the rising agent if I want these scones to be edible. Five teaspoons still seems like a lot.

"Come on, Zo! Why aren't you dancing with me?" Morgan spins up to the counter and tries to grab my arms. I pull away and look for a measuring spoon instead. "I still don't understand why you're making scones," Morgan says. "You seem, like, depressed or something. This is a time for celebration."

I slam kitchen drawers as I search for a tiny spoon. I just

need to talk to Morgan. I can tell her how conflicted I've been this week. I'll explain how her super-giddy reaction hurt my feelings. I'll reveal I still might want to attend the University of Oregon. We'll return to the land of reason and make a pro-con list. Nothing makes me feel better than a good pro-con list.

But when I look up at Morgan, the moment has passed. She's dancing back across the kitchen, skipping through the dining room, and making an excessive amount of noise. I sigh and return to my scones, realizing I almost forgot the white chocolate chips. Maybe the addition of candy will redeem this bowl of mush. I try to ignore Morgan banging around in the living room.

"What's that sound?" Morgan yells.

"Um, you?" I dump all of the chips into the bowl. My mood tonight definitely warrants an entire bag of faux chocolate.

"It's not me." Morgan jogs back into the kitchen, grabbing the edge of the counter to steady herself. "It sounded like it was coming from the roof."

"I don't know then." I slowly fold the white chocolate chips into the dough.

"Wait, there it is." Morgan points to the ceiling. Sure enough, there's a faint scratching noise and the occasional thud.

"Probably a squirrel," I say, turning back to my scones.

"I think it's too loud to be a squirrel. But then again,

you just got into Yale, so maybe I should trust you." Morgan laughs to herself, then resumes twirling around the house. "I can't believe I'm officially dating the smartest person in our class! Did you know nobody else got into an Ivy this year?"

Tears well in my eyes, but I wipe them away. I wish Morgan would shut up and never talk about Yale again. Is she that eager for me to leave? I clench my eyes shut. It's too many emotions at one time.

I think back to earlier tonight when Morgan was ultra-fixated on Madison. I had been slightly perturbed the drama between the twins was complicating our prom night. But now I have all of Morgan's attention, and I hate it. At this moment, what I need is space. Space to process the shitstorm of anger and guilt and resentment and confusion swirling through my brain. And space to bawl my fucking eyes out.

So I do the unthinkable.

"Maybe Jake and Madison climbed onto the roof." I can't believe I'm manipulating my girlfriend. I feel slimy even uttering those words, but I keep talking. "Jake could have convinced Madison. Maybe they wanted to have sex up there or something."

This is what happens when logic and rationality fail me. I start spouting ludicrous bullshit just to get a moment alone. If any of our friends were to do something wild like climbing on top of a roof, it would be Julia and Kevin. But even Julia would think twice about scaling a house at three in the morning.

"No way," Morgan says immediately. But then, in true Morgan fashion, she starts to second-guess herself. "Do you think Jake is that reckless? Even if he is, do you think he could have persuaded Madison to do something so stupid? Although..."

There's a loud clunking noise and Morgan looks back at the ceiling. She lowers her voice. "I've always suspected Jake was a bit of a pothead. I know we have the occasional drink or whatever, but do you think he smokes weed?"

Despite the circumstances, it's a struggle not to laugh. Most of us don't suspect Jake smokes weed. We know with absolute certainty he does. The entire baseball team does. I'm pretty sure he smokes normal cigarettes too, but that would be too much information for Morgan to handle.

"Yeah, he definitely smokes." I'm not even trying to rile her up further. It's just the truth.

"I knew it, I knew it, I knew it." Morgan paces back and forth, wringing her hands. "I promised I wouldn't get involved, but what if she's actually in danger? Then it's, like, my obligation to see if she's up there, don't you think?"

"You could go outside and check on her," I say, my voice cracking. Morgan doesn't notice the tears slipping down my face. Of course she doesn't. My girlfriend has two extremes—focusing on me and obsessing over Madison. And I intentionally flipped the switch. I'm a terrible human being.

"Okay, I'll be just a minute," Morgan says.

"Only check the roof. Don't go into their bedroom or anything. I don't want Madison to get upset." I realize for the first time my selfishness could also ruin Madison's night.

"I won't," Morgan says. "I'm just going to step outside, see if anything's up there, and come back in. Actually, I may have to go down the driveway a bit because of the angle of the roof. Right? Or maybe I'm overthinking this. Anyway, I'll be right back. Is that okay?"

Morgan doesn't wait for my response.

Which is good because I'm already on the floor crying.

Alex

The Sonnenfeld Center for the Arts opened its doors today, welcoming students from throughout the area. The center offers art classes for both children and adults and functions as an all-in-one hub where artists can create, display, and sell their work.

Michael Sonnenfeld, local real estate developer, business owner, and philanthropist, oversaw the project from start to finish.

"There's a growing market for this type of development," Sonnenfeld said in an interview earlier this year. "But it was also about giving back to the community that raised me. When we invest in arts education, Oregonians thrive."

The project experienced a few roadblocks in its early stages. The riverfront land had been unofficially used as a park by locals, despite the lot changing hands many times over the past decade. This led to a zoning dispute that culminated in a contentious protest last September.

"In the end, the people of this community came together to support the arts," Sonnenfeld said. "Our children deserve the best. And that's what I intend to give them."

Local artist twenty-year-old Alyssa Linden has been anticipating the grand opening for weeks: "I can't believe my work is in a real-life gallery. It's surreal. I'm going to be teaching classes there too. I only wish this place had been around when I was a kid."

For more information or to register for classes, visit sonnenfeldartscenter.com.

There's no way.

I read the article for a second time. Then a third.

Surely there's another wealthy man named Sonnenfeld somewhere in this city. Just because Leah is the first Sonnenfeld I've ever met doesn't mean it's not a common name. As Leah pointed out, it's not like I socialize much.

I click on another article. *City Greenlights New Luxury Condominiums from Sonnenfeld Properties.* It's about the hideous high-rise downtown.

Then another. *Potential Senate Bid from Real Estate Mogul Michael Sonnenfeld?* Because more millionaires in government is just what this country needs.

My hands are shaking as I click on the next one. *Johnson Memorial Renovates NICU After Generous Donation.* I had been holding on to a tiny sliver of hope, but this article confirms what my brain already knew. Michael Sonnenfeld donated a large sum of money to this very hospital after his son—Leah's little brother—was born prematurely and spent three months in the NICU.

I lean closer to the screen, squinting at the photo underneath the article. The caption reads: *Michael Sonnenfeld; his wife, Elise; and their oldest daughter, Leah, at the ribbon-cutting ceremony.* When I look back to the grainy image, there's no doubt about it. My girlfriend is standing next to her parents, holding a ridiculously large pair of scissors.

Shit. Not my girlfriend. Nobody said anything about Leah being my girlfriend. Well, other than my father, sister, and all of my friends.

But if a relationship had been possible fifteen minutes ago, it's not now. There's no way I can date the daughter of the millionaire who destroyed Halmoni's favorite park.

My grandmother devoted the last two years of her life to lobbying against this arts center. She and her friends fought valiantly to protect their park—including almost getting arrested when the police showed up at a peaceful protest. For months, our conversations around the dinner table were about Halmoni's hatred of this building project and the millionaire behind it. She referred to him exclusively as a nappeun nom, which is basically the worst thing my kind-hearted grandmother will say about another human being. My parents would try to calm her down:

"You and your friends can find a different park," Dad said over and over.

Mom would argue, "An arts center is nice. Good for the kids."

At first, I didn't understand Halmoni's anger. Like my parents, I figured an arts center would benefit the city. But the more I listened to her, the more I realized she was right. Her park was a place where elderly people from all different backgrounds gathered to walk every morning. It was where musicians—actual local artists—could practice during the summer. It was where Halmoni took me to watch the goslings grow up every spring.

The news article didn't mention the goslings. Or the parade of retirees in tracksuits carrying homemade picket signs. Or—and this is the part that fills me with rage—that the so-called community education classes cost two hundred dollars apiece.

For a while, I thought we would win, but I should have known better. A millionaire clearly has more power than a bunch of geese-loving grandmas. One by one, the protestors found other parks for their morning walks. Eventually, even Halmoni gave up the cause, though she still gripes about the nappeun nom a few times a week. I can't betray her by dating his daughter.

Nope. Not dating. I have to stop doing that.

I pull out my phone and start texting Julia. She's the one who set me up with Leah, and this feels like the kind of thing she should have warned me about. My friends knew how invested my grandmother was in fighting the arts center. Kevin and Zoe even came with me to a protest.

The door swings open, and Leah walks in. The second I see her smiling face and dazzling prom dress, my commitment to staying calm disappears.

"Your family is super rich!" I declare as soon as the door clicks shut behind her.

"Dammit." Leah's shoulders slump. "I knew this would happen. I told myself, Alex is probably super weirded out by how the nurses are treating you, and he's going to google you the second he gets internet. And then I thought, there's no way he'd do something that absurd. But you googled me, didn't you?"

"Well, um. Yes?" Now I'm the one who's embarrassed. When Leah says it, I realize how creepy it is to google your prom date when she's in the next room. But I still need answers.

"Is this your dad?" I turn the computer to face her. "Is he really the nappeun nom who kicked the elderly women out of their park?"

"Yeah, to build an arts center." I stare at Leah, incredulous. She didn't deny the part about stealing a park from a bunch of kind old ladies. "Are you really complaining about a place where children do art?" Leah stands with her hands on her hips, posturing for a fight. How do I explain what this park meant to my grandmother without sounding pathetic?

"There were geese in that park!" I know it's a feeble argument, but watching the goslings grow up with Halmoni is one of my fondest childhood memories. On Saturday mornings in the spring, we would buy doughnuts at the grocery store and eat them in the park. Halmoni would teach me phrases in Korean, and I would name the baby geese things like Quackers and Beak Face. I know it sounds dumb, but I always imagined taking my own kids there someday. But thanks to Leah's dad, those happy memories have been snatched away from my future children.

"Geese, Alex? You're angry because of geese?" Leah sounds half-confused, half-exasperated. "Why do you care about geese? They're supposed to be the meanest animals."

"So because they're mean you get to destroy their natural habitat?"

"Nobody destroyed the river. Or the riverbank. Or any actual parks."

I glare at her.

"All right, let me collect my thoughts," Leah says when it's obvious I'm waiting for her to explain. She takes a deep breath and makes a huge show of calming herself down, but I can tell she's trying not to smile. Part of me is relieved she's not furious about my googling, but the other part of me wonders how she can be so lighthearted about this. I'm certainly not joking.

"As the daughter of a…What did you call my dad?"

"A nappeun nom," I say. "It means a terrible person."

"Yeah, I got that from context clues," Leah says, and I have to smile a little. There's something about her that makes me feel happy, even when I'm trying my best to remain pissed off. "Just because I'm related to him, doesn't mean I think like him."

"So you were against the arts center?"

"Well, it's complicated."

"OH MY GOD!" I stand up as dramatically as I can, shoving the table aside.

"Shhh." Leah giggles. "You're going to break the computer."

"You tell me you're not like your father, and then you say you agree with him? Which one is it?"

"I'm saying he's my dad." Leah sighs, looking thoughtful now. "Yeah, I felt really guilty when all the old ladies started protesting. And I was furious when he called the police on them. Seriously, I was so embarrassed that I faked having the flu so I could skip school. But it was an empty lot, Alex. There's an actual park right down the street. And it's kind of a cool place."

"The classes are a billion dollars!"

"Art stuff is expensive." Leah shrugs. "Look, I try to stay out of his work things. I know a lot of people don't like him…" Leah nudges me in the shoulder. "…but what am I supposed to do?"

"You could not hold the giant scissors at the ribbon-cutting thingie!"

"Well, someone did their research." Leah glares at me. "I'll have you know that giant scissors are awesome. Also, that was for the hospital. Surely you don't have a problem with saving the lives of little tiny babies?" I don't have a response to that, and she knows it.

"Look, I'm sorry about your geese. I really am." Leah pushes me back into the chair and leans on my shoulder, softly stroking my arm with her fingers. I can feel the heat emanating from her face, and I'm struck by the overwhelming desire to kiss her. There's no way I'm misreading this interaction. I may be oblivious, but I'm not a total dolt. Still, I keep my lips to myself. I'm reassured Leah isn't evil, but what would I tell Halmoni? That my first kiss was with the daughter of her mortal enemy?

Leah and I sit in companionable silence. I close my eyes and lean into her embrace while she hums quietly to herself. It sounds like she's singing a lullaby, but one I don't recognize. "Did you even check the lottery numbers?" Leah asks after a while.

"I totally forgot." I'm fishing the paper out of my pocket when I feel my phone buzz. I check the notification immediately. "It's from my dad," I whisper.

"What is it?" Leah jumps up. "Is the surgery over?"

"Yeah, they just finished. He didn't say how it went though." I look at Leah. At this moment, I'm grateful to have someone by my side who can share my panic. Even if she is my grandmother's enemy. Even if she probably has a gigantic trust fund. "We have to get back there. Right now."

"Okay, let's go."

"But what about the lottery ticket? I have to know if…"

"I'll check the ticket." Leah propels me to the door. "You go back through the secret hallway. I'll be there in a minute."

"But normal people aren't allowed in that hallway. I mean, it's not like my family owns the hospital. Maybe I should go the long way."

"Technically, my last name being on the building doesn't give me permission to trespass." Leah winks at me. "Do what I did before. Act like you belong and ignore anyone who says otherwise. And never be afraid to name-drop. Now, go!"

Leah pushes me into the hallway and shuts the door behind me. I feel an overwhelming urge to second-guess myself and ask a nurse for instructions on the proper way to get back to the surgical wing. But Leah's right. There's no time for hesitation. I didn't see Halmoni before she went into the surgery, and I'm the only person in the family not there now.

Leah and I may come from different worlds, but it's time for me to be a little more like her. I need to become a person who doesn't respect *Hospital Personnel Only* signs.

JULIA'S HAVING A THREESOME WITH A CAT

Group Chat

3:46 AM

Alex: JULIA BETHANY HARMOND

Julia: What did I do?

Alex: LEAH'S DAD BUILT THAT ARTS CENTER!!

Julia: I'm aware of that fact.

Morgan: Literally everyone is aware of that fact.

Julia: Wait, did you NOT know her dad was Michael Sonnenfeld? Haha that's pretty common knowledge.

Alex: How does everyone know this stuff except for me?

Morgan: Maybe because you spend your weekends playing

video games instead of socializing?

Kevin: Hey now. Don't blame video games. I knew who Leah's dad was.

Alex: THEN WHY DIDN'T YOU TELL ME!?

Kevin: Calm down. You're texting like Julia.

Julia: Kev, will you hurry?

Morgan: How are you two still not in the same room?

Julia: Because Kevin is taking forever to fix his elf costume. Obviously.

Alex: ISN'T THERE SOME KIND OF BRO CODE ABOUT THIS?

Julia: A bro code would be like Kevin can't have sex with Leah. It has nothing to do with divulging whether or not someone's father is a millionaire.

Kevin: I promise not to have sex with Leah, bro.

Morgan: I'm sorry, can we backtrack to why Kevin is fixing his elf costume?

Julia: I'm not about to have sex with an anatomically inaccurate elf.

Morgan: Right, because THAT would be weird.

Julia: Exactly. I'm only into wholesome elf sex.

Today 3:52 AM: Morgan named the conversation "WHOLESOME ELF SEX"

Alex: Julia, how are you so chill about this? Do you not remember how upset my grandmother was when her park got destroyed? There were protests!!

Morgan: There are other parks nearby, right?

Alex: NOT WITH THE GEESE.

Julia: You really need to chill. Her dad gave a bunch of money to the hospital. And her whole family works at the food bank on Sundays. He's the good kind of millionaire.

Alex: THE GOOD KIND OF MILLIONAIRE?? Julia, you're the president of the Young Democrats club. Do you hear yourself??

Julia: Treasurer, actually.

Alex: JULIA

Julia: ALEX

Alex: HOW DO YOU SUPPORT THIS ARTS CENTER?

Julia: Because it's cool? Look, I'm sorry about the geese. I really am. You know how much I appreciate water birds. But the arts center is fun. Morgan and I are taking a fiber arts class this summer.

Kevin: What in the world is fiber arts?

Morgan: Don't throw me under the bus! I'm with Alex's grandma.

Julia: I'm with your grandma too! All I'm saying is the arts center is nice. And so is Mr. Sonnenfeld. Just because he's super rich doesn't mean he's some kind of alien.

Alex: Um, it kind of does.

Kevin: Lol

Morgan: Just an FYI, if you want a chance with this girl, you probably shouldn't call her dad an alien.

Morgan: Also, does anyone hear anything on the roof?

Julia: You could call Leah an alien if you were doing some

alien sex role-play. You could use the green makeup Kevin found.

Morgan: I feel like Leah could be into some wholesome alien sex.

Kevin: I wouldn't recommend it. My skin feels itchy.

Kevin: I meant I wouldn't recommend the green makeup. I can't speak to alien sex. Or any kind of sex for that matter.

Julia: WELL MAYBE WE COULD HAVE SEX IF YOU WOULD FINISH YOUR FREAKING COSTUME

Today 3:57 AM: Morgan named the conversation "WHOLESOME ALIEN SEX"

Madison

"My turn." Jake shoves a handful of Cheetos into his mouth and chews loudly, spewing reddish-orange dust everywhere. "Thomas Jefferson, JFK, and Teddy Roosevelt."

"In this scenario are they all alive and semi-young?" I lean back on my elbows.

"Yeah. Imagine those dudes in their prime."

"Okay. Well, Thomas Jefferson was terrible, so I would clearly kill him."

"Good choice."

"This is a hard one," I say, my voice whiny. "I can't imagine them not old."

"Hey, you gave me a bunch of Pokémon, and I had to imagine them not…what do you call it?"

"Animated?"

"Exactly."

"Okay, okay. Give me a second."

I'm usually a fan of Fuck, Marry, Kill, but this round is just proving how little I remember from US History. Though I am impressed Jake could name three presidents other than George Washington.

"I think I would fuck JFK," I say. "Even back in the day, everyone agreed he was hot, right? So then I would marry Teddy Roosevelt. All I remember is they named the teddy bear after him, so I'm imagining him being cuddly. That's solid husband material right there."

"You wouldn't marry JFK?"

"Hey, you said there was no judgment in Fuck, Marry, Kill." I throw a Cheeto at Jake in protest.

"Like you weren't judging me for wanting to fuck Pikachu," Jake says.

"Because Pikachu is a baby! That's gross."

"Babe, we've been over this. Who is the Pokémon expert on this roof?" I begrudgingly point at Jake. "A Pikachu is like a certain breed of dog. So there are grown-up Pikachus and baby Pikachus. I would fuck a grown-up one. Consensually, obviously. Also, in Gen 2 there is a legit baby Pikachu named Pichu, which totally proves the classic Pikachu isn't a baby."

"I only understood twenty percent of what you just said."

"That's because you didn't spend enough of your childhood playing Pokémon," Jake says.

"I spent very little of my childhood playing any kind of games. I didn't have time. I was always dancing."

"Oh yeah, I forgot you're a dancer. That's sick."

"I *was* a dancer," I correct Jake. "I was a hardcore ballerina. I danced twenty hours a week and went to professional intensives every summer."

"You were gonna go pro?"

"Nobody would say it like that, but yeah." I laugh. "It's kind of like baseball, I guess. You can go to college for dance or you can audition for companies right away. That was my goal."

"So why'd you quit?"

"Long story."

"Could you hold your leg behind your head like those circus people?" Jake asks.

"Like this?" I swing my leg toward the sky in a graceful arc and pull it to my face until my knee touches my nose. "Used to be a lot easier, but I've still got it."

"That is so fucking dope."

"Thanks." I release my leg, much to the relief of my hamstrings.

I lie back on the roof, resting my head in my hands. It's been cloudy and rainy for the past week, but tonight is perfectly clear. I've never been one for stargazing or appreciating nature in any capacity, really, but even I have to admit the view up here is spectacular.

Being on the roof is not romantic, despite what Jake said. Mostly because every part of my body is chilly, and coldness is not a sexy feeling. But the way the stars sparkle against the darkness, reaching into every corner of the sky...it's inspiring. It makes me feel invincible, which isn't a feeling someone like me gets to experience very often.

"So why'd you quit dancing?" Jake asks again.

"You're unusually persistent tonight." Jake is a bit like an overeager puppy. If he's doing something annoying or talking about something I don't like, I can usually distract him with the human equivalent of a Milk-Bone.

"You don't have to talk about it." Jake shrugs. "But it seemed like you wanted to."

I've discussed those years of my life with Jake, and he's kind enough not to push me. I obviously told him about my lupus as a courtesy, but he hasn't mentioned it since. He sees me for more than just my diagnosis. Or he forgot our conversation entirely. Either way, Jake is a welcome respite from the lupus-obsessed people in my life. Sometimes it's better to keep the past in the past. But there's something special about lying on this rooftop with Jake next to me and billions of stars overhead that makes me want to answer him.

"When I was younger, I was dancing six days a week,

so it was normal for me to be tired and achy. I didn't think anything of it. But then it got a million times worse. I could barely get out of bed, everything hurt all the time, stuff like that."

"That's when you got Lumos," Jake says.

"Lupus." I smile. Jake does remember our conversation. "But yeah. It felt bad suddenly, even though I may have had symptoms for a while. It took more than a month for the doctors to diagnose me, and I was in and out of the hospital all that time. After that, I was so busy with follow-up visits and catching up on schoolwork that I missed a ton of dance."

"So you left?"

"Not quite yet. I still wanted to be a ballerina. So once my lupus got manageable, I insisted on going back. My mom was freaking out. She thought it was too soon. But I didn't care." I shiver as a cold breeze sweeps across the roof. Jake scoots closer, so I can lean against his shoulder. I've never talked about my last day of dance with anyone, not even Morgan.

"I pushed myself really hard in class like I used to," I continue. "I should have taken a break, but I wanted to prove I could do it. As it turns out, I couldn't. When I got home that night, all of my symptoms came back, even worse than they were before. I was taken to the hospital in an ambulance. It was humiliating."

"I'm really sorry," Jake says.

"Eventually, my doctors cleared me to take a recreational class, but that felt worse somehow. Not to brag or anything, but I had been really good. I couldn't picture myself in a ballet class with girls who weren't as serious as me. So I quit."

"Wow. So you never danced again?"

"Nope." I don't tell Jake about all the times I sneak into the basement to do barre exercises and inevitably start sobbing. That feels too personal to share even under the stars.

"Do you still get tired when you do physical stuff? Or are we good?" Jake asks. I elbow him in the ribs. Only Jake would use a traumatic story about my chronic illness as a segue to sex.

"We're good," I say, massaging the joints in my hands. "But I'm not sure if we're good on the roof."

"Aw, babe, why not? I thought we were gonna join the mile-high club."

"First of all, the mile-high club is for airplane sex. We're maybe twenty feet off the ground. And there's no such thing as the twenty-foot club."

"We could start one," Jake says with a wink.

"Second of all, I'm cold, which means you must be freezing. You're covered in goose bumps." I take the opportunity to run my palm across his chest. Even with the goose bumps, Jake is ripped. "And third of all, the condoms are still in the house."

"Shit. We remembered the Cheetos, but not the condoms."

"Both important, but…"

"Yeah." Jake gets onto his knees and surveys our surroundings. "Okay, let's hop off this roof, sneak back inside, find the condoms, and then get busy."

"Hop off? Your plan for getting off this roof is to hop off?!"

"Not literally. I meant hop off as a…What's that phrase from English?"

"A metaphor? A figure of speech?"

"Exactly," Jake says. "I figured we'd go down the way we came up. Sound good, babe?"

"Uh, yeah?" I stare off the edge of the roof, suddenly remembering how much easier it is to climb up a ladder than to climb down. And that's with a real ladder, not a precarious vine-covered trellis. "You have to go first," I say. "I want you there to catch me if I lose my footing or something."

"Of course, babe. I've got you." Jake crouches down and walks carefully to the edge of the roof, using his hands for support. "And if you do slip, just let yourself fall. If you try to catch yourself, you might break your wrist. It's better to be bruised all over."

"Wait," I say, a bit of movement catching my attention.

"Babe, I'm kidding! If you fall, I'll be there to catch you. That was more advice for myself. I can't be fucking up my pitching arm right before summer."

"No, I'm serious." I point to the orange lump stalking across the roof. "That has to be the cat from inside, right?"

As if on cue, the cat hisses at me and flips its tail.

"How did it get up here?" Jake asks.

"I assume the same way we did. Cats can climb, right?"

"He's a fucking Spider-Cat."

"We must have left the door open," I say. "Damn. Zoe will be so pissed at me if I'm the reason the cat gets lost. We have to get him off the roof before anyone notices he's missing."

"Okay, fine. We hop off the roof, get the cat inside, and *then* we get busy. Deal?" Jake crawls toward Spider-Cat, who sprints to the other side of the roof.

"I don't think we can just grab him."

"No shit." He sighs. "Let me try this one last time. We figure out how to catch a cat, catch the cat, hop off the roof, leave Spider-Cat inside, find the condoms, and *then* we can have sex."

I nod.

"I'm just saying, doing it on an airplane would have been way easier."

Zoe

My uncle has terrible taste.

The Yale bedroom was bad, sure, but his kitchen floor is truly hideous. I don't even know what it's made of—stone, tile, some kind of plastic compound?—but it's massively ugly. Who would want an olive-green floor? And not just any olive-green floor. This stone/tile/whatever is spotted with gold flakes. Like he's the fucking Marie Antoinette of central Oregon. It's disgusting.

The floor is also disgusting in a literal sense. Now that my outright sobbing has subsided to a few stray tears and the occasional sniffle, I'm aware of the thin layer of grime coating the floor. And my body. You'd think someone who can afford gold flakes would also hire a cleaner. Or perhaps a life coach to help them be less of an asshole.

I know this isn't my uncle's fault. Yes, he's a terrible person in every conceivable way. But he's not the reason I'm crying. Hiding the truth from my friends, intentionally causing my girlfriend more stress, applying to my uncle's alma mater to please my family—every bad decision along the way has been thanks to Zoe Blackwell. I deserve to be sprawled on the floor, drawing frowny faces in the dust with my fingertips. My prom night is one big frowny face.

I also know wallowing isn't a productive means of handling negative emotions. I don't lack self-awareness. But right now, my options are finishing my scone dough, wallowing on the floor, or addressing my problems in a mature fashion.

I choose wallowing.

The front door flies open, banging against the foyer table with a velocity that's sure to leave a dent. A blubbering Morgan appears in the doorway. "You were right," she sobs. "Madison and Jake are on the roof." She slams the door behind her and joins me on the floor of the kitchen. "I heard their voices and saw them walking around, so I know it's them. And Jake was naked, which can only mean they're going to have sex on the roof."

"Wait...what?" I stare at Morgan. Her skin is red and splotchy and her eyes are shiny with tears. It's like looking into a mirror. An incredibly unflattering mirror. "I said those things so you would…I mean, I don't think they're actually on the roof."

"I'm telling you," Morgan says, half hiccupping, half sobbing. "They're naked up there. Like, no wonder Madison hasn't been talking in the group chat. She's too busy trying to die."

"Listen, I have to tell you something. I did a horrible thing." I sit up, tucking my bare legs underneath my butt. My girlfriend is on the verge of a panic attack because of my lie. I can't let that happen. It's time to admit I'm an awful human being.

Morgan looks at me in confusion. "Are you crying, too? Why are you crying?"

I take a deep breath. "Here's what happened. And please don't immediately break up with me."

"Zoe, what's going on?" Morgan turns to face me, taking my dust-covered hands in hers.

"I was being completely irrational." I feel the need to start this confession by acknowledging my utterly bizarre behavior. "When I told you about Yale and you were super happy, I felt betrayed. I wanted you to be sad or at least conflicted. I thought you would ask me to stay."

Morgan opens her mouth, but I keep talking before she can react.

"And I know I'm a hypocrite. I think it's dumb when people follow their significant other to college because odds are they're going to break up within a few months.

The rational part of my brain wholeheartedly believes that. I mean, I'm not about to argue with statistics. But it still made me sad you didn't fight for us."

"Zo—"

"Wait, I'm almost done." I tuck a few strands of tear-soaked hair behind my ear. "When you were celebrating and being super happy, all I wanted to do was cry. So I made up something ridiculous about Jake and Madison on the roof. I knew you would go outside and leave me alone for a few minutes. It was stupid and manipulative. Especially with how sensitive you are about Madison. I feel really guilty."

Morgan cocks her head slightly to the left as she waits for me to finish. I'm usually able to read her emotions, but this time I'm at a loss. Her face is a blank canvas.

"So yeah. That's all. You can talk now." I mime zipping my lips shut. Morgan smiles, which fills me with relief, but she doesn't speak right away.

"Okay," she says finally. "That was a lot of information. I feel like we should discuss each of your points in an organized manner."

"God, I love you so much." Morgan narrows her eyes at me. "Sorry, I'm not talking right now." I rezip my lips and motion for her to continue.

"Well, first of all, Madison and Jake are absolutely on the roof. I mean, I think it's weird you made up a story to get me out of the house, but you were right."

"But that's not possible," I say. "There's no way—"

"Do you think I can't see?" Morgan snaps. "I will swear on literally anything. I saw my twin sister on the roof with her naked douchebag boyfriend. I may be a little obsessive, but I'm not delusional. Or blind. You can go outside and look for yourself."

"Sorry. I believe you." I stare at the kitchen ceiling, trying to imagine Madison and Jake doing it right above us. It's not a comforting thought. "I don't understand how they got up there," I say. "Messing around on a roof, especially at nighttime, is super dangerous."

"Why do you think I'm freaking out!?" Morgan wails.

"Sorry, sorry, sorry. I'm not being helpful at all."

Morgan chokes out a laugh. She slides so we're both facing the refrigerator, then lies down on the floor, pulling me with her. I can feel the grime clinging to my arms and back, but I'm not in a position to complain. Together, we stare at the fancy beams on the ceiling.

"Are you going to dump me?" Morgan asks.

"What are you talking about?" I scramble to my elbows, sending dust flying. "Of course not. You should be the one breaking up with me after all this."

Morgan props herself up, and I can see tears creeping back into her eyes. "Well, you got mad because I didn't beg you to stay in Oregon with me. Which only a selfish and controlling person would do, by the way."

My skin grows hot. "Yeah, sorry again," I mutter.

"But from what you just said, it's like you assumed going to Yale would be the end of our relationship," Morgan says. "When I didn't think that for a second. Like, I know you're right. The odds are stacked against a long-distance relationship working. But why don't you think we could beat the odds? It's like you don't even want to try."

"Morgan, I'm so sorry." Half a second later, tears are pouring out of my eyes again. I didn't think there could be any liquid left in my tear ducts, but I guess I've been wrong about a lot of things tonight.

For a few minutes, Morgan and I cry together on the floor. She's hugging me and I'm clutching her and our makeup is an unbelievable mess. As the tears finally slow, I realize there's one more thing I need to come clean about.

"Listen," I sniffle. "There's something else." I drum my fingers against the floor. This feeling has been floating around the back of my brain for months now. Maybe even years, if I'm honest.

It's like how every little kid wants to be an astronaut. Flying around in space and visiting other planets sounds cool when you're a kindergartener who doesn't understand that (1) Space travel involves years of intense training, (2) Only the best of the best actually travel into space, and (3) There's a chance your mission will end in death and destruction. Going to Yale was my impossible, little-kid dream. When it was far away, it was easy to commit to four years at a strenuous school in Connecticut. Now that I've been accepted, I feel like I'm hurtling across the solar system toward who knows what and all I want is to come back home to Earth.

"What's wrong?" Morgan looks panicked. "See, this is why I think you're trying to break up with me."

"No, no." I take a deep breath. "It has nothing to do with you." This feeling may have been eating at me for a while, but expressing it out loud feels like a giant leap. "It's not that I didn't think our relationship would work if I went to Yale," I say, choosing my words carefully. "It's that I don't know if I want to go to Yale at all."

"What do you mean?" Morgan asks, like she can't even comprehend the words coming out of my mouth.

"I know I'm supposed to go to Yale. I know it's been my dream since I was five years old. And I know I've annoyed everyone by talking about it constantly." I'm on the verge of breaking down again. "But now it all feels wrong. I don't know what to do. And I'm freaking the fuck out."

Julia

"I've done my research this time," Kevin calls from the bathroom. "Are you ready to have sex with an elf?"

"Please don't ever repeat those words," I say.

"If you insist."

Honestly, the thought of Kevin as an elf is kinda hot. Elves are by far the sexiest fantasy creatures. I know some people are into mermaids when all they know is the Disney version. Legit mythological mermaids are terrifying. It's not all seashell bras and singing crabs. Elves, however, are more appealing to me. They're smooth and graceful, often with a mysterious or sinister aura. Plus, they're super smart, and I value intellect in a partner, human or otherwise.

"All right, m'lady. Are you ready to be kidnapped by a sexy elf?"

"So ready."

The door opens again. This time, I can see Kevin. And believe it or not, he actually looks like an elf. He's replaced the brown towel with an off-white sheet tied around his body. It's a little toga-esque, but there are probably elves somewhere in Roman mythology. His black hair has been plastered into short spikes with a *lot* of gel, and he wrapped little rubber bands around his ears to make them pointy. My only critique is his skin still has a greenish hue, but I decide to let it slide. He looks pretty freaking elf-like.

"Are you Yesmina, protector of the bronze goblet?" Kevin even changed his voice. The Minnie Mouse squeak has been replaced by a softer, more lyrical tone. "Answer me, lady!"

I play along. "Yes, I keep the goblet for the sword master of Abedebio. But the elves of Todrina will never touch its power."

"Ah, but in that you are mistaken!" Kevin takes a few steps toward me, then halts. "What do we do now?" he whispers.

"I thought you were going to kidnap me," I whisper back. "Also, it ruins the whole fantasy vibe if we stop to think about what we're doing."

"Okay, but how do I kidnap you? Should I hide you in the closet?"

"You're a pretty terrible kidnapper if you tell me your plan," I say.

"True." Kevin adjusts his ear bands. I realize they must hurt, and I appreciate his dedication. "Is this turning you on yet?"

"Not really? But I think we should keep trying. You put too much effort into your costume to give up now. I'll try to get more into it."

"Okay, me too. But hold on a sec."

I think Kevin's going to continue with his elf monologue, but then he suddenly steps forward and presses his lips against mine. It's the same lips and the same general kissing technique, but he's more assertive than usual. Like being a make-believe elf has given Kevin newfound confidence. I lean into the kiss, wrapping both my arms around Kevin's waist. It's fiery and passionate and sexy, like something straight out of a fantasy novel. This is the kind of role-play I can get behind.

Soon, I'm fumbling with the sheet wrapped around Kevin's body as I attempt to undo the knot and find his skin underneath. Kevin removes his arms from my back and reaches around to help me. For a moment, I think he's going to untie the knot, but then he changes course. He gently twists both my arms behind my back and wraps a strip of cloth around my wrists.

"What are you doing?" I remove my lips from his. I'm mega-confused by this new kind of foreplay.

"Why, I'm taking you prisoner, my darling," Kevin says in his sultry elf voice. He tightens the cloth, tying multiple knots to keep my wrists firmly in place. And I don't know if it's Kevin's commanding elf presence or this new way he's kissing me, but I start to get why *Cosmo* suggested role-play in the first place.

"Ohhh, smart...I mean...I demand you untie me at once! I am the great Yesmina, protector of the bronze goblet, daughter of Lady Jammes, keeper of the Icharoo Estate! I will not be held captive by some lowly elf, no matter how attractive I happen to find him!"

"Unfortunately, you don't have much choice in the matter," Kevin the Elf says. "I doubt your guards will find you in the dark hills of Todrina." With a sneaky smile, he scoops me off the floor and tosses me onto the bed. Seconds later, he's on top of me, kissing my neck and running his hands through my hair. I squirm in response, unable to do much making out with my hands secured behind my back.

"You must untie me," I pant into Kevin's ear. He instantly stops everything he's doing. Right as I was starting to get excited too.

"What's wrong? Are you okay? Did I hurt you?"

"No, *elf boy*, I was in character. I'm supposed to protest being kidnapped."

"How was I supposed to know?" Kevin asks.

"Good point," I say. "We need a safe word, so you know if I really want you to stop." I remember seeing a *Cosmo* article from a while back. It was written for people experimenting with more intense stuff like BDSM that can get dangerous without clear boundaries. But if a safe word will keep Kevin in character, I'm in. "We need something we wouldn't say in normal conversation."

"Um, okay." Kevin pauses. "How about pigeons?"

"Pigeons?"

"Yeah. You never talk about pigeons while we're making out."

"So?"

"So it's the perfect safe word."

"Right, but why pigeons?"

"Because it fits all of your criteria," Kevin says. "I'm just trying to be helpful. We could use ostrich. Or hummingbird."

"Do you have a thing for birds I should know about?"

"No. If I had sexual feelings toward birds, then it would be a terrible safe word because I could randomly moan something about pigeons."

"Okay, okay. Whatever. Pigeons is fine." The tingling I was feeling is starting to fade, and I need it to come back. "Will you please start making out with me again?"

Kevin climbs back on top of me, and we resume our elfish foreplay. Kissing and squirming and panting and rolling. It's so intense I forget all about the kidnapping scenario until the cloth binding my wrists gets caught on the bedpost. I protest again.

"I demand you untie me," I say in my best Yesmina voice. This time, Kevin doesn't stop. Instead, he amps up the intensity, flipping me over so I'm lying helplessly on top of him. "My guards will find me here, and they will seek vengeance on you and your elf clan! They will search all five corners of Elgorp if that's what it takes!"

"Well, then, I suppose we should make sure they don't find you," Kevin the Elf says. He rolls off the bed and lifts me into his arms once more.

"Stop!" I shriek. "Where are you taking me?"

"To a place only I know about. A place where you will never be found!"

Kevin opens the closet door and switches on the light. He pulls a couple blankets onto the ground, which is really quite considerate for a kidnapper, and places me in the cushioned nest. Then, with one eyebrow raised, he closes the door. I hear the lock click.

"Come back! I demand you come back!"

"Ah, but you are locked in this dungeon for all of eternity."

Part of me wants to tell Kevin the elves of Todrina don't live in castles with dungeons, but I don't want to kill the mood. So I continue to play the part of Yesmina. Quite magnificently, if I do say so myself. "Not the dungeon! It's so dark and scary," I cry out, writhing on the pile of blankets.

As my eyes adjust to the darkness, I survey my

surroundings as Yesmina might. The board games stacked against the back wall would be chests of forbidden treasure. The neckties dangling from the hanger above me could be bloodthirsty serpents. Perhaps the piles of shoes are the remains other prisoners who have long since perished in this forbidden land.

"Uh, the lock isn't working."

"You must help me," I cry out in fake desperation. "The serpents will eat me alive! They do not know I am the chosen one. Their quest for blood knows bounds."

"No, Jules. The lock came off the door."

"And what will befall my people back home?" I'm totally getting into character now. It's like Yesmina and I are one and the same. Maybe I should do theater in college. I store that thought in the back of my brain as I continue my impassioned monologue. "There are people who depend on me for their very existence. My family will be devastated! I swear to you, if my guards do not find you, my family will. They will avenge my death!"

"Julia, seriously—"

"They will declare war against the elves of Todrina! Your lands will be ravaged. Your people will be lost. They will—"

"PIGEONS!" Kevin yells. "For the love of god, Julia, pigeons."

"Huh?" I sit up on my pile of blankets. My senses are heightened, and I feel a wetness between my legs. All I want is to have Kevin in this closet with me, his elf arms wrapped around my body, as we make love to each other in our fantasy land. "What about pigeons?"

"Pigeons is the safe word, remember?"

"Right. What's wrong? Was that too much fantasy? Wait, did I give away any spoilers?"

"No, Julia. I'm fine. It's the closet."

"What about the closet?" I climb off the floor and reach for the doorknob. It doesn't turn.

"The lock broke," Kevin says. "I think you're trapped inside."

Alex

The whole walk back to the waiting room, I feel myself deflating. Without Leah, the forbidden route is just another hallway. Long, white, and empty with no nurses to question my presence.

I should have brought Leah with me. Even her worried chatter would help me escape from the thoughts that come as I walk by myself. Leaving her to research lottery numbers was utterly pointless. Halmoni has undoubtedly forgotten about her lone ticket, and it's not like she has any chance of winning. The whole lottery thing was a futile attempt at distraction when I should have been sitting with my parents and sister, waiting patiently for the surgery to end.

Every muscle in my body tenses as I get closer to what could be devastating news. Or miraculous news. There's no clear way to decipher my dad's message. He definitely wouldn't tell me something bad via text, a sobering realization that fills my throat with bile. But he also wouldn't elaborate on good news if he was busy talking to doctors. So I have zero clues about my grandmother's well-being. And gut instinct isn't helping. All my gut is communicating is a strong desire to vomit.

By the time I arrive in the waiting room, any remaining happiness from my adventure with Leah has disappeared. I'm back in the same brightly lit room with the same stained carpet and the same fabric couches. I'm back to waiting.

Jenny is asleep on one of the sofas with her legs curled to her chest, her breath catching in tiny snores. Mom sits next to her, stroking her head and reading a magazine, while Dad speaks in hushed tones to the receptionist.

"Ji-hoon," Mom says, calling me by my Korean name. She smiles and beckons me over.

All the tension I've been holding in my back and shoulders melts away. That's not the fake, teeth-only smile Mom uses when salespeople come to the door or her boss comes over for lunch. It's her actual smile. The smile Mom tries to avoid in photos because she hates the tiny space between her front teeth and the wrinkles on either side of her mouth.

She would only be smiling her real smile if Halmoni was okay.

"What's going on? How's Halmoni?"

"She's out of surgery," Mom says in mixed Korean and English. "The doctor says everything went well. We can see her when she wakes up."

"She's not awake yet?" The pitch of my voice rises, and I can feel my back muscles turning into knots again. "How long has it been?"

"Your grandma's doing fine, Alex." Dad walks across the room to join us. He places one hand on my shoulder. "She's waking up from the anesthesia. It takes a little while, but we should be able to visit her in ten or twenty minutes."

"What about Jenny? Does she know?"

"Let your sister sleep," Mom says. "She has dance tomorrow. We'll wake her up when it's time to see Halmoni."

"You think she's capable of dancing after tonight?" I ask.

"She has rehearsal for her duet," Mom says. "If she doesn't show up, Oaklynn's mom is going to try and turn it into a solo for Oaklynn."

"But she's going to be exhausted, and—"

"Let's discuss the dance situation at home," Dad says, cutting me off. I slump back in my armchair. With the news of Halmoni's recovery, Mom seems back to her normal self. That means Jenny will absolutely be at her duet rehearsal with Oaklynn tomorrow. That also means any interaction between Leah and my mother will be significantly less positive. Maybe I should text Leah and tell her to wait in the car. Or even tell her to Uber home and offer to meet up with her tomorrow. My nosy father, however, has other plans.

"Tell us all about Leah," Dad says with a not-so-subtle wink. "Did she leave already?"

Mom's ears perk up at the sound of a girl's name. "Who's Leah?" she asks, her eyes narrowing.

"Alex's new girlfriend," Dad says.

"She is *not* my girlfriend." I turn back and forth between my parents to make sure they're both getting the point, but Mom still looks horrified and Dad still looks pleased with himself. "And she's still here. She ran into some people she knew." I'm not ready to drop the Leah-is-the-daughter-of-Halmoni's-archnemesis bomb quite yet. If ever.

"Have I met her?" Mom asks.

"You've met her twice now," I say slowly. Next to me, my father is having a hard time controlling his laughter. "Down in the lobby you were hugging her and crying and calling her my girl…I mean, my friend? Do you remember?" Mom shakes her head. "And she was the one who brought the food. The pancakes Jenny was eating?" Mom looks at me blankly. I knew her behavior had been slightly peculiar, but I figured she would at least vaguely remember Leah's existence.

"Speaking of which…" Dad looks around the room.

"Is there still food? Didn't Leah bring a bunch of bags?"

"Um...the food was part of a business transaction," I say.

"What do you mean business transaction?" Dad asks.

"What's the nature of your relationship with this girl?" Mom waves off Dad's question with a flick of her wrist. She evidently believes her line of inquiry is more important than Dad's hunger. "I don't think you should be dating a girl we haven't even met. Do you know her family? What are they like? Are you sure you want to date someone right before you leave for college? Where is Leah going to college? A good school or no?"

"We're really, really, really not dating," I reassure my mother. Her stroking of Jenny's hair has grown notably less gentle. "Julia fixed us up for prom. But it was totally a one-time thing."

I try to remember the other ten questions Mom asked about Leah, but all I can think about is the last one. Where is Leah going to school next year? Has she mentioned that at all? There are plenty of people going to the University of Oregon like me, but not everyone. Leah's parents certainly have the money to pay for an expensive out-of-state college. What will it mean if Leah is going far away to school? Actually, I can answer that one easily. Leah and I will go our separate ways like we always planned. What I don't know is what will happen if Leah is staying here. That's the real question.

"Well, she's very pretty," Dad says, glancing toward the door.

"Wait, *that's* Leah?" Mom asks, her eyes following his.

"You seriously don't recognize her?" My dad is laughing again. "She's been around all night, Michelle."

I look up. Leah is standing in the doorway of the waiting room with a massive smile on her face. She's bouncing up and down on her toes and waving me over.

"She looks a bit like a young Judy Garland," my dad is saying. "Or an old Judy Garland if your reference point is *The Wizard of Oz*."

"Okay, Dad, whatever." I wipe my sweaty palms against my pants. The exhilarating combination of excitement and anxiety I experienced while running through the hospital is back.

"I'm going to talk to Leah," I say. "And I swear we're not dating, so can you please treat her like she's a normal friend?" I glance back and forth between my parents, not sure which I trust less. At this point, an inquisition from Mom might be more tolerable than Dad reminiscing about actresses from the 1940s.

"I've been perfectly civil all night," Dad says. I glare at him because that couldn't be further from the truth, but I'll take what I can get.

I stand up, smooth the wrinkles in my pants, and walk over to Leah. By the time I reach the doorway, her grin has doubled in size and she's legitimately jumping in the air.

"Guess what?" she whispers excitedly.

I mean to say *what?* like a normal person would, but a different question tumbles out of my mouth. "Where are you going to school?" I ask. "Next year, I mean. What college are you going to?"

"Huh?" Leah stops hopping. "What are you talking about?" She shakes her head. "No, we have to do my thing first. It's way more important. So it took some time to find the right website and the correct drawing number." Leah's face is flushed and she's back to bouncing. "And when I looked up the numbers, I couldn't believe it. But I double and triple and quadruple checked it, I swear." Leah grabs my hands. "Alex. Your grandmother won the lottery!"

"Mr. and Mrs. Song?" A nurse steps into the room. "Your mother is awake if you'd like to see her."

"Come on, let's go." I tug Leah toward the nurse. "I have to see Halmoni." It's only then my brain finishes processing Leah's words.

"Wait, are you for real?" I drop her hand and lower my voice to a whisper. "Did you say my grandmother won the lottery?"

Madison

One limb at a time. That's all I can think about.

I unwrap my left hand from its ironclad grip on the trellis. The joints in my fingers ache like they've been stuck in that position for hours when it's actually been less than a minute. I find a new wooden rung at eye level and clench it with all the energy I've got, which is not much energy at all.

I shakily exhale. Time for my left foot.

On the porch below me, Jake is being less than helpful. "You've got this, babe! Ouch! Fuck, fuck, ouch, fuck. Spider-Cat won't stop scratching me. Oww…fuck. Babe, will you hurry? We've got to get him inside."

After twenty minutes of sweet-talking Spider-Cat

and trying to convince him broken twigs were treats, I had been ready to give up. That was when Jake tackled the cat. No warning, no strategy—he just leaped across the roof and had the cat in his arms before it could react.

Of course, there was plenty of scratching and yowling after that—the scratching came from Spider-Cat, the yowling from Jake and his new captive in equal measure— but Jake managed to descend from the roof with a squirming cat in his arms. It was an impressive display of physical prowess rivalling any superhero movie. If only I had an ounce of that ability in me.

I tune out Jake's dramatics and focus on the task before me.

I slowly and deliberately slip my left foot off the trellis. My ankle is throbbing with the dull pain I always feel at the beginning of a lupus flare. I stretch my ankle in slow circles, a movement that sometimes helps soothe the achiness, but my joints are beyond ankle circles now. My toes clench a section of trellis a few rungs down. I'm thankful I decided to abandon my sandals on the roof. They were only ten dollars at Target, and I need all the traction I can get.

"Ow! I'm trying to help you, you stupid cat. Did you want to be stranded on the roof all night? Fuck! Babe, this thing is digging its claws into my chest. Why is it so pissed at me?"

Now, my right foot. This one finds a new foothold more easily. For whatever reason, my left side always hurts worse than my right. Whenever I explain this to my doctor, I can tell he doesn't believe me. "That's highly atypical of lupus patients," he always says. But I'm the expert on my own body, at least that's what my mom tells me. And I believe my left arm and leg always get the achiest.

"Babe, you're super close," Jake calls. "It's an easy jump!"

I risk a glance at the ground. This whole time, I've kept my eyes trained on the wall in front of me, but now I can see I'm about halfway down. Still, the ground feels impossibly far away. A jump from this distance may be easy for Jake, but for me? My bottom lip trembles as a single tear slips down my cheek. I want to be furious at myself for my own incompetence in simple climbing and my stupidity for getting up on the roof in the first place, but being furious requires energy. Instead, I just feel defeated.

"Owww! Babe, can you help me? Spider-Cat just clawed at my face. FUCK! OUCH!" I hear a thump underneath me. "Oh no. Shit, shit, shit. Babe, he got out of my arms. I'm sorry, but I swear he was aiming for my eyeballs. Madison!?" With the cat no longer in his possession, Jake switches his attention to me. "Are you okay up there?"

"I can't do it." My voice cracks. "I'm going to fall."

"No, you're not!" Jake calls. "It looks far, but I swear it's an easy jump. You just gotta go for it, babe. I've got you."

It's an easy jump, I think to myself. *If Jake can do it, so can you. You used to be a ballerina! A jump like this is no problem.*

But my hands and feet stay firmly attached to the

trellis. My whole body starts quivering. Even this tiny leap feels impossible right now.

"Come on, Mad! Take a deep breath and jump."

I nod. The mechanics of a jump are simple.

Loosen your grip on the trellis.

Bend your knees, and propel yourself away from the wall.

Land in a plié, so your legs absorb the shock of the fall.

Just like a grand jeté.

I repeat the steps in my head a second time. And then a third. Finally, I take a deep breath and launch myself off the trellis.

Everything feels right when I'm in the air. But then it goes wrong. I don't have time to plié and absorb the shock of the fall. Because the second my feet touch the porch, my body crumbles into a heap of limbs.

Falling even a short distance should be painful, but I don't notice. Everything already hurts, so what's a little more agony? No, I don't feel the pain. But I feel everything else.

Sadness.

Embarrassment.

Stupidity.

Anger.

It's like clockwork. The moment something in my life is happy, my body sabotages me, leaving me in a pathetic heap. I shouldn't have climbed onto the roof with Jake. I knew from the moment he chucked those Cheetos up there. But I couldn't resist the allure of trying something new, of being daring and adventurous. It's the opposite of who I usually am, and I liked the idea of living as the anti-Madison for a change. But what goes up must come down. And this time, I've come down hard.

"Babe, are you okay?" Jake rushes to my side. "What's going on? Talk to me." I can feel his hot breath on my face and his palm pressed against my forehead like he's a concerned mother checking her toddler for a fever. I keep my eyes squeezed shut.

The last time I fell like this was five years ago. It was field day, a compulsory daylong activity in the spring when the entire middle school gathered outside for relays, obstacle courses, and complicated challenges involving buckets of soapy water and oversize sponges. By the seventh grade, field day was anything but cool, and we mostly spent the day mocking the immature activities we were forced to try. But I secretly loved field day. I always won the jump rope contest, and Morgan and I were an intimidating three-legged race team.

I knew something was wrong the second my alarm woke me up. I was feverish, my joints hurt, I was wobbly on my feet, and I had the worst stomach pain of my life. But I couldn't miss field day. I lied to my mom and Morgan, downplaying how miserable I felt. Just a cold coming on, I figured. Nothing to worry about. I'm pretty sure that was the last time Morgan believed anything I said about my health.

As I trooped outside with my fellow seventh graders into the sweltering heat, I started to feel faint. I should have given up, called my mom, and gone to the doctor at that very moment, but admitting weakness has never been one of my strengths. Instead of telling anyone how I felt, I painted my face, donned a red bandana, and was paired with Thomas Reeder for a preliminary round of the three-legged race. Thomas and I didn't have the practiced precision of me and my twin. We immediately toppled over into the brown grass. I remember Thomas tugging on my arm, telling me to hurry and get up, saying, "We'll get a bad grade if we don't pretend to try."

He didn't realize every muscle in my body was trying— and failing—to move.

Five years ago, when I lay crying in the grass, consumed by the pain, I was scared and confused. My body had never failed me before. Not when I started on pointe shoes. Not when I danced through daylong rehearsals. It was terrifying not to understand why. It got even worse over the next few weeks as I bounced from doctor to doctor, trying to figure out what was wrong with me. None of them had an answer until, finally, an even worse flare put me in the hospital.

Now I know the name of my disease, the symptoms I should expect, all the preventive measures I'm supposed to take. It's not scary anymore. It's fucking infuriating.

"Madison, you've got to talk. Tell me what's going on." Jake tries to lift me to my feet, but I stay slumped on the ground. Gravity is too powerful a force to fight at the moment.

"I'm fine," I say. "Nothing broken, I don't think."

"Okay, good," Jake says. "Are you sure you're all right? Because we've got to find this cat. Can you see it in the grass over there? It hasn't gone far. But I was thinking maybe we get some tuna or cat treats or something to lure it back to the house. The cat is pretty strong, so I think the key is to outsmart him."

"Don't worry about the cat," I mumble. Jake doesn't hear me.

"Now, me and Spider-Cat have a pretty rocky relationship at this point. I mean, he did try to scratch my eyes out. So you should be on the front lines of our rescue mission. I'll be pulling the strings behind the scenes, so Spider-Cat doesn't get suspicious."

"Forget the cat," I say again.

"Huh?" Jake kneels on the porch next to me.

"Forget the cat," I say. "You need to help me get inside."

"What's going on? You said nothing was broken." Jake looks me up and down as if he's realizing for the first time there may be other issues associated with falling halfway off a roof.

"I'm having a flare," I whisper, tears spilling over onto my cheeks.

"A what? Huh? What's going on?"

I squeeze my eyes shut, so Jake doesn't see me cry. For

the first time in a long time, I wish Morgan were with me instead of Jake. She wouldn't ask stupid questions. She would help me get into bed. She would bring me water and anything else I wanted. She would listen to me talk about my feelings while we watched *Finding Nemo*. She would drive me to my rheumatologist on Monday and everything would be better.

"A flare," I say to Jake. "It's when all your lupus symptoms get worse, basically. Achiness, fatigue, headaches. Just a lot of pain."

"What caused it? Do you need to go to the hospital?"

"A lot of things can cause flares," I explain. *Like over-exertion, not getting enough sleep, eating crappy foods, and ignoring early symptoms.* Essentially, this whole night has been one big lupus trigger, but I don't say that to Jake. "No need for the hospital. Just help me get inside."

"No problem." Jake scoops me into his arms and stands in one smooth motion.

"I thought you said you couldn't lift me."

"I said I couldn't throw you onto the roof. Lifting you is a piece of cake." I try to laugh, but my smile turns into a grimace. I bury my face against Jake's chest as he carries my limp body toward the door.

"Uh, babe?" Jake pauses in the doorway we enthusiastically snuck out of an hour ago.

"Hm?"

"What about Spider-Cat?"

"Don't worry about him," I say.

"But, babe, indoor cats can't survive in the wild. They can't hunt because they don't have claws or whatever. And if Spider-Cat has a bad sense of direction, he could get stranded out there in the woods."

I try to roll my eyes, but even that small gesture of annoyance hurts. Literally, the last thing I care about right now is rescuing a cat, but Jake seems to have grown attached to the animal that nearly gouged his eyes out.

"I'll text everyone," I say. "Someone else can look for the cat."

"You're going to tell them we left the cat outside?"

"Yeah, maybe not." My sister would completely understand me prioritizing my own health over the well-being of a roof-climbing cat. Honestly, she would be willing to murder a cat if that could somehow help me. But I don't want to get Zoe in trouble. I may not understand why she's been in a funk the past few days, but something is definitely up with her. She might not be so forgiving if I lost her uncle's cat.

"Just get me inside," I say, my voice trembling. "I'll text them…something. I'll say the cat got out, but I don't know how."

"Are you sure?" Jake asks.

"Please," I say. "I just need a bed."

WHOLESOME ALIEN SEX

Group Chat

4:23 AM

Alex: My grandma is out of surgery! The doctor says everything went well. We'll be able to see her in a few minutes
after she's woken up.

Morgan: That's wonderful! So happy the surgery went well.

Kevin: Oh thank god. Tell her we said hi!

Kevin: Also, Julia says yay!

Kevin: Julia says I didn't use enough exclamation points.
She wanted 25 of them, but that seemed excessive.

Morgan: Why can't Julia type her own exclamation points?

Kevin: She's trapped in a closet. The lock broke and we can't get her out.

Morgan: Literally what the FUCK have you two been doing?

Kevin: It was a dungeon situation. Don't worry about it.

Kevin: Jk. Julia says you should all worry about it because she's stuck in a closet. Imagine 17 exclamation points.

Zoe: Can you slide her phone under the door?

Kevin: Good idea.

Morgan: Who could have predicted Julia and Kevin would be having the kinkiest sex.

Zoe: I'm zero percent surprised.

Julia: I AM BACK IN THE WORLD OF CYBERSPACE. HALLELUJAH. THAT WAS A ROUGH TEN MINUTES.

Morgan: You're still in a closet, Julia.

Julia: Being stuck in a closet without a phone is a whole different experience than being stuck in a closet with a phone.

Kevin: Is anyone good at doorknobs?

Zoe: Just break down the door. I don't fucking care.

Kevin: I'm not going to break your uncle's door, Zo.

Zoe: That's too bad for me.

Alex: Sorry, got distracted. There is some craziness going on here. I'm kind of freaking out. But thank you for all the kind thoughts, wishes, etc. I'll tell my grandma all of you were thinking about her.

Julia: Craziness with Leah? ;) ;) ;)

Alex: No, Julia. Craziness with my grandma.

Kevin: Everything okay?

Alex: Yeah. More than okay. We're not completely positive, but we think she might have won the lottery. Kind of.

Morgan: What?

Kevin: What??????

Julia: WHAT IN THE FREAKING WORLD!?!?!?!?

Alex: Yeah it's unreal. But honestly it'll probably only cover her gas bills now that she and her friends have to drive further to a good park. I'll see what Leah has to say about that.

Julia: OH MY GOD

Alex: What?

Julia: Your grandmother just got through surgery and won the lottery and you're still upset Leah's dad built an arts center?

Alex: So?

Julia: SO YOU'RE CLEARLY IN LOVE WITH THIS GIRL.

Zoe: Yeah it's very obvious.

Morgan: Alex is in loooooove.

Alex: You guys are acting like six-year-olds.

Morgan: So are you.

Julia: OOOOOHHHHHH

Kevin: If you're rich now, can we go on a cruise?

Julia: No, he needs to take Leah to Paris or something.

Madison: Sorry didn't have my phone so I missed stuff. Jake and I saw the cat outside but idk how to get it so can someone help?

Madison: Zoe the cat is outside

Julia: ZOE THE CAT!!!

Madison: Zo?

Kevin: Idk why she's not responding. I'll go tell her.

Madison: Thx

Zoe

"I don't understand what changed," Morgan says. "Yale has always been your dream."

"I don't know. Maybe it still is. I don't know." I'm off the disgusting floor now and furiously kneading scone dough with freshly washed hands.

"But you always know," Morgan says. "You go through life like it's one big geometry proof. You have logical explanations for everything. You're, like, the most decisive person I know."

"Well, then I guess I'm broken." I slam the dough down on the counter. I'm working this dough within an inch of its life, but I have to keep occupied. These scones are going to be inedible if they ever make it into the oven.

"I didn't mean that." Morgan glances at her phone. "Oh my god, Julia's stuck in a closet. That's hilarious."

"She could not be any more on brand," I say.

Morgan taps away at her phone as mine continues to light up with new messages. I wipe the stickiness off my hands, so I can respond as well. I don't want our friends to know I'm in crisis. The last thing I need is more people running around waving Yale banners.

"Okay," Morgan says as the incoming messages slow down. "What is your gut telling you? Like, what feels right?"

"I don't know how to listen to my gut. Where do you learn that sort of thing?"

"You just feel it." Morgan shrugs. "That's how I make decisions."

"Well, all I *feel* is myself freaking out." I'm now poking the dough with the pointy end of a wooden spoon. It's quite therapeutic, though I'm not sure it's doing much for the scones. "I don't think I have a decisive gut."

"Okay, then forget the gut thing," Morgan says. "You should make this decision in a way that makes sense to your brain. Let's make a pro-con list. Reasons you want to go to Yale versus reasons you want to go to Oregon. But you have to stop stabbing the scones."

"You're the best girlfriend ever," I say. "You know there's nothing I find sexier than a pro-con list."

"You have mentioned that on multiple occasions." Morgan smiles. "Do you have paper or something?"

"I can do one better." I toss my wooden spoon into the sink and run down the back hallway to the garage.

Last year, Uncle Ross decided to host a game night for all the local Blackwells. It got uncomfortably competitive when he lost badly at Pictionary—really, there is no way what he drew was a platypus—and there hasn't been a game night since. Knowing my uncle, though, there's no way he threw away the pricey whiteboard we drew on. Sure enough, I find the Pictionary easel under a heap of cobwebs. I wipe the wooden structure clean with a spare beach towel and lug it back to the kitchen.

"Ta-da!" I present the whiteboard to Morgan with an arm flourish.

"That's amazing," Morgan says. "This house literally has everything."

"Except for practical things like eggs." I remove the magnetic marker from the board and toss it to Morgan. "You're in charge here. Help me pick a college based on logic and reason."

"I'll do my best." Morgan divides the board with a purple line. On the left side, she draws a blob with a triangle protruding from one end. On the right, she draws a blob with a bunch of little lines poking out of it.

"What in the world?" It looks strangely like Uncle Ross's platypus.

"This is a duck. For the Oregon Ducks." Morgan adds a couple wings and an eyeball to the first drawing. "This is for the Yale Bulldogs." There's no way to redeem the pokey-line blob, so Morgan writes "dog" in tiny letters underneath it.

"Well, Oregon wins for best mascot for sure," I say.

"Are you sure you don't just hate bulldogs because of your uncle's cat?"

"No, I only like fluffy dogs," I say. "But all ducks are cute."

"Got it." Morgan writes "better mascot" under the Oregon header. "What about academics?"

"Um…well, Yale has smaller class sizes. And a lower student-to-faculty ratio. And a better statistics program."

"Good, good." Morgan adds all those to the Yale column. "What about location?"

"Oregon has rain, but Connecticut has snow. Rain is a little better, but they're mostly even." Morgan draws a cloud with snowflakes on one side and a cloud with raindrops on the other. It's abundantly clear a career in the visual arts is not in her future. Though she'd give my uncle a run for his money in Pictionary.

"What about campus life?" Morgan stands, marker poised, waiting for my assessment.

Last summer, when we were on the East Coast for a family wedding, my dad and I spent a day touring the Yale campus. Well, it was supposed to be me and my dad. But when Uncle Ross found out we were going to his favorite place on earth, he created a car pool and recruited most of my cousins to come along too. I spent most of our tour shushing the younger kids and begging my dad to stop singing the fight song. There wasn't room left in my brain for interesting tidbits about campus life. I try to compare the bits I remember with everything I know about the University of Oregon.

"They're different, obviously. But both would be equally good."

"Seriously?" Morgan glares at me. "You expect me to believe you have no preference? I know you've been researching these schools since you were five."

I stare at the whiteboard. While the process of making a pro-con list is undeniably enjoyable, I can't think of anything for Morgan to add to either column. At home, I have a plethora of spreadsheets and quizzes saved on my laptop. I have a section of my bookshelf devoted to college catalogs. Morgan's right. I've been weighing the advantages and disadvantages of various universities since middle school at least.

"Come on, Zo." Morgan taps her marker impatiently. "What else goes on the list?"

"Maybe I should find one of those comparison charts online." I reach for my phone.

"You don't need to google anything." Morgan slides both our phones across the counter, out of my reach.

"You've been researching this stuff all year. These are supposed to be *your* pros and cons, not what some blogger thinks."

"Fine, fine." I cross my arms. "Well, Yale is a better research institution. And more students study abroad. But it's really competitive, which may not be a good thing. Oregon has a really good football team—"

"Which you don't care about," Morgan interjects.

"But there's good school spirit. And a lot of community engagement."

Morgan adds both of those to the list, then turns to me with crossed arms. "What are their rankings?" she asks. "On those national college lists?"

"That's a silly algorithm." I know exactly where Morgan is going with this, and it's not helpful. "They manipulate those numbers, and it's all about prestige. I don't care how elite the school is."

"Yeah, but what are they?"

"Yale is number three. Oregon is 104." I sigh. "At least the last time I checked."

"I think we can assume the rankings haven't dramatically changed." Morgan writes the numbers on the board in bubble letters, then draws a bunch of stars next to Yale.

"You're trashing Oregon for no reason," I snap. I need to get back to kneading my dough. Or poking it with a wooden spoon. List making is supposed to make me feel better, but I'm just getting frustrated.

"I'm not trashing anything," Morgan says. "I'm going to Oregon, so I obviously like it."

"But you're supposed to be helping me make a logical decision, and you're being completely biased!" Fuck it. I grab the dough and start pounding it against the counter.

"Oh my god." Morgan throws the marker on the floor. "I'm the one being biased? Seriously, Zoe?" Morgan glares at me and starts reading through our list in a sarcastic voice. "Yale has better classes, better teachers, better opportunities, and is the number three school in, like, the whole country. Oh, but I'm sorry. You don't like the mascot!"

I thought I was out of tears, but they're back again. I throw the dough into its bowl and reach for a paper towel to dry my eyes. "Why are you being so mean about this?" I sniff back a sob. "This is why I feel like you want to get rid of me."

"I'm not trying to be mean." Morgan's voice is quivering now too. "You asked me to help you make a rational decision, and there's no rational world in which the University of Oregon is a better school than Yale. That's all I'm trying to say."

"You *do* want me to move to Connecticut!" With each passing second, I feel myself losing more and more control. This is why humans aren't supposed to stay awake all night. Nothing good ever happens at four in the morning.

"I'm not trying to get rid of you!" Morgan shrieks back. "You're the one who has to be Little Miss Logical all the time. I'm the one who said to listen to your gut, remember? What do you want from me?"

"I don't know what I want from you! If I knew, I wouldn't be FREAKING out!"

Morgan and I face off across the kitchen island. I'm gasping for breath. She's rubbing at her eyes. In two years of dating, we've never fought like this. Our disagreements are resolved through calm, well-mannered conversation. Not hysterical shouting.

"Hey, um, sorry to interrupt…"

"WHAT!?" Morgan and I both shout. I whirl around to find an uncomfortable-looking Kevin hovering in the doorway. "Sorry, Kev." I try to lower my voice and make my face look semi-normal. "How long have you been there?"

"Longer than ideal," Kevin says.

"It's okay." Morgan comes around to stand next to me and places her hand on my back. Even that small touch is comforting. "What's going on?"

"Have you seen your phones?" Kevin asks. "Madison texted."

"Not in a while." I retrieve my cell phone from the end of the counter. Sure enough, there are seven more missed messages.

"Is Madison okay? What's happening?" Morgan's hand clenches at my dress.

"She and Jake saw your uncle's cat outside," Kevin says. "Madison is fine, but the cat may not be."

Julia

It took most of the night, but I'm finally adequately aroused.

Which sucks.

Because I'm stuck in a closet by myself listening to Kevin wiggle the doorknob on the other side. I could satisfy the tingling myself, but that's not what tonight is supposed to be about. The whole point of the pact is to do sexy things *with* my boyfriend.

"This sucks so much," I yell to Kevin.

"At least you have your phone."

"I don't want my phone. I want you."

"I'm working on it, Jules."

"I know." I huff in frustration and drum my feet against the carpeted floor. I'm behaving like a toddler, but the reality is that I'm stuck in Zoe's weird uncle's closet. What other way is there to act?

"Do you have light in there?" Kevin asks. "Can you try the door from your side?"

"Ooh, you're smart." I turn up the brightness on my phone, then feel around on the wall until I find a switch. "Bingo!" A bright fluorescent light floods the closet. I'm no longer Yesmina, protector of the bronze goblet who is being held hostage in a dungeon with slithering serpents and forbidden treasure. I'm just Julia. And Julia is cold, annoyed, and, unfortunately, still a virgin.

"Try to open it from your side," Kevin says. "My latch thingie is stuck."

"Is that a euphemism for some kind of sex move?"

"What?! No, I'm trying to get you out of a closet. Sex is not on my mind right now."

"That's unfortunate for you."

"Can you please check the door?"

"Hold on." I press down on the handle, but it doesn't budge. And on this side of the door, a key is required. "Why would you put this kind of lock on a closet?" I ask. "It's like this house is made for legit kidnappers."

"I know. It makes no sense. Maybe they installed it backward or something."

"I'll text Zoe to see if she knows about a key." I retrieve

my phone from the floor. "Oh shoot," I say, reading the last few messages in our group chat.

"What's up?"

"Madison saw Demon Cat outside. And Zoe's not responding." I text Zoe again using all caps. Some may find my electronic communication style obnoxious, but I firmly believe capital letters are the optimal way to express my enthusiasm.

"There are too many things happening," Kevin says. "Okay, can you hang here for a few minutes? I'll go tell Zoe about the cat and ask for a key."

"But I'm cold." I know Kevin can't see me pouting, so I try to make my voice as whiny as possible.

"You're in a closet, Julia. Put on a coat."

"Fine, whatever. I'll be marginally self-sufficient."

"I'll be right back, okay? I love you."

"Love you too," I say. "Oh, and make sure they know I'm not the one who let out Demon Cat. If I had wanted to kill him, there would have been blood involved."

But Kevin is gone.

I poke around my confined space. Technically, this is a walk-in closet, considering I managed to walk inside and get stuck, but it's not a giant one. In three steps, I can get from the door to the back wall.

I start searching the built-in shelves for a coat. This closet has a peculiar combination of clothing. A basket full of mismatched toe socks, a few sweatshirts, the odd pair of jeans, and a top hat. Zoe said her uncle lives here part-time, but I can't imagine what kind of life he leads with this selection of apparel.

I select a navy-blue sweatshirt reading "Yale Alumni Association" from the closest pile. I don't love the idea of wearing some old guy's sweatshirt, but it's better than freezing to death. While I'm at it, I grab a pair of neon yellow track pants. As long as I've got the time, I may as well get out of this dress entirely. I'm confident we won't be resuming our Elgorp role-play anytime soon.

After changing into comfier clothes, I add a few more blankets to my makeshift bed and flop onto my stomach. There's nothing new on my phone, so I open Spotify and turn on the saddest song Fynn Ludwig has ever written, "Ode to Alexis." It's about Fynn's relationship with his ex-girlfriend, and the melody is breathtaking. But even Fynn's mournful crooning can't console me right now.

I feel like a failure.

I planned the most perfect night of all time and every single thing went wrong.

What if this is a sign my relationship with Kevin is doomed?

What if I'm one of those losers who peaked in high school?

What if the rest of my life is nothing more than a series of failed attempts to succeed at basic human functions?

WHAT IF I'M STUCK IN THIS CLOSET FOR

THE REST OF MY EXISTENCE ON EARTH!?

I grab a pair of combat boots and throw them across the tiny room. They hit the wall with a satisfying clunk.

"Jules, you okay?" Kevin knocks on the door.

"No, I'm upset. So I'm throwing shoes at the wall."

"Well, good thing you're handling this rationally," Kevin says. "Listen…"

"There's no key?" I recognize the defeat in his voice immediately.

"I didn't get a chance to ask," Kevin says. "Zoe and Morgan were fighting and it was super awkward, so I wanted to get out of there. I did tell them about the cat though."

"Hm." Usually, this type of gossip would perk me up. Anyone who says they don't enjoy gossip is clearly lying to themselves. But not tonight.

"What's going on?" Kevin asks.

"What do you mean?"

"Well, you had no interest in the latest news about Zoe and Morgan, and you have that depressing song on loop. I do know you, Julia."

"I suppose." I turn down the volume on my phone. I hadn't meant for "Ode to Alexis" to get stuck on repeat, but it's fitting.

"So what's going on?" Kevin sticks one finger under the door and wiggles it around. I reach out my own finger to meet his. It's almost romantic.

"I'm upset everything fell apart. I know it's stupid, but I wanted tonight to be perfect so badly. I wanted to end high school with a bang. Literally." Kevin laughs. "It's just...tonight was supposed to be a night we would tell our grandchildren about in sixty years. You know?"

"For starters, I don't know why you're convinced our grandchildren will want to hear about us having sex. That's weird. Did your grandparents ever talk to you about sex?"

"Ew, no. But I'm saying—"

"But this is a way better story anyway," Kevin says, cutting me off. "We dressed up like fantasy characters. You got stranded in a closet with no key! There's no way you're ever going to forget tonight."

"It's not just about the story."

"Then what is it?"

"I guess I wanted reassurance we would be okay next year. I thought having sex would make everything more official."

"I get that." Kevin forces his whole hand under the door. It's stuck at an awkward angle, but I grab it appreciatively.

"You do?"

"Yeah. I mean, I don't agree with you, but I understand why you feel worried." There's a brief pause. "Julia, we're as official as anyone our age could possibly be. I even offered to get you a promise ring."

"Which I turned down because promise rings are a creepy symbol of female oppression."

"My point is I'm all in. And I'm pretty sure you are too."

"I definitely am." I squeeze Kevin's fingers.

"Ow. Hold on. I need my hand back." Kevin wiggles his fingers out from under the door. I know he's still there, but I miss being able to touch even a tiny part of him. "Listen, if you are that eager to have sex, we can rent an Airbnb again tomorrow night."

"I have to study for calculus tomorrow night," I say.

"Okay, so maybe not tomorrow. But we have every single night this summer."

"Aww, you would rent an Airbnb every night this summer for me?"

"Until I ran out of money. Which would be immediately."

"Maybe Alex's grandma can bankroll our sex plans. If she actually won the lottery."

"There's no way that's true."

"I don't know. I kind of believe it."

This time, I stick my hand under the door. It's horribly uncomfortable and there's a chance I could sprain my wrist if I stay in this position too long. But then Kevin tickles my fingers, which is so adorable it justifies the pain.

"Are you feeling better?" he asks.

"I mean, I'm still a virgin in a closet and there's a demon cat on the loose, so not ideal."

"True, I suppose."

"But I'm with you." I smile as Kevin squeezes my hand. "So I'm more than fine."

Madison

"You good now, babe?"

I close my eyes to keep tears from rolling down my cheeks. If only it were that easy.

Jake carried me inside, deposited me on the bed, and handed me my phone so I could text my friends. Even the smallest act of moving my thumbs on the keyboard was painful. And, of course, Zoe and Morgan chose this moment to not be glued to their phones, so I had to keep texting until Kevin volunteered to go find them.

"Well if you're feeling better…"

I never said I was feeling better, I want to scream. But if I scream, I'll cry. And I refuse to cry in front of Jake.

"…maybe you and I could move on to something more fun, if you know what I mean."

The only fun I want to move on to is sleeping. But I can never sleep when my lupus is this bad.

"We could put on a show for Theodore, if you know what I mean."

I crane my neck just enough to see Theodore's lifeless eyes staring down at me with pity. This dude gets it. If only he weren't dead, he could tell Jake to shut his fucking mouth and bring me some green tea with a splash of coconut milk.

"We can make tonight a grand slam, if you know what I mean."

"Jake," I moan. "Every dead animal in this room knows what you mean."

"Oh, dope. Okay, let me hit the bathroom, and then we can knock this one out of the park…" Jake winks at me. "If you know what I mean." He saunters over to the bathroom, and I sink even farther into the bed.

I don't usually mind Jake's obliviousness. In fact, I enjoy his optimistic outlook on life. I admire how he doesn't let the little things (or the big things) get him down. But Jake's obliviousness is only endearing up to a point. And that point passed when I collapsed in a heap on the back porch.

I shift my body, attempting to roll onto my side, but my limbs are leaden and totally uncooperative. I squirm around, trying desperately to find a comfortable position, but it's like I'm lying in quicksand. The more I try to move, the deeper I sink into the mattress.

"All right, babe, let's take this batter to the dugout." Jake laughs at his own joke. "Eh, I don't know if that one worked. What do you think?"

I force my head off the pillow, so I can get a better look at Jake. His boxers are still on, thankfully, but his skin is shining somehow. I have a feeling he lathered lotion or oil all over himself as some kind of pre-sex ritual.

Never in my life have I been less interested in having sex with Jake. Even if I could move my body. In fact, I'm struggling to remember what it was about him I found appealing in the first place. I would happily give up sex for the rest of my life if I could have just five minutes of relief.

"No," I say.

"Yeah, you're right. My earlier ones were better."

"No to the sex. And they've all been terrible."

"Huh?" Jake walks over to the bed, his forehead knotted in concern, like he's seeing my exhaustion for the first time. "Are you sure you're feeling okay, babe? You don't look so good."

"No shit," I mumble.

"What did you say?"

"Listen…" Moving is still difficult, but I twist my neck to face Jake. "This is an intense lupus flare. There's no way I can do anything physical."

Jake stares at me, and I'm nervous for the briefest of moments that he's going to act like every terrible guy I've ever heard about. That he's going to push me to do something I don't want to do. Or throw a fit and break up with me.

But Jake doesn't do either of those things.

"Aw, no biggie, babe." Jake lies down next to me and nuzzles his forehead into my arm. "Climbing on the roof was a lot. We can do something chill."

"Thanks." I exhale slowly, grateful Jake responded appropriately.

See, I imagine myself saying to Morgan. *He's not the most emotionally sensitive dude in the world, but he's not the asshole you think he is.*

Then, I cringe because I know exactly how Morgan would respond. *Wow, not an asshole*, she would say. *I'm glad you have such high standards, Madison. Good for you.*

It's a conversation we've had before.

"What can we do to make you less lupus-y?" Jake asks.

"There's not an easy way to make it go away." I let my eyes sink shut again. "Sometimes I'll try to stretch or do a little yoga. Taking a bath usually helps relax my muscles a bit. But honestly, I just need to rest. It sucks, but yeah."

"I've got it!" Jake springs into an upright position, painfully jostling my arm in the process. My eyelids are heavy, but I force them back open to look at Jake. "My buddy Duncan is throwing an after-prom party. We can go there!"

"What are you…?" Any generosity I was feeling toward Jake disappears.

"He's got this dope Jacuzzi in his backyard. It's like a bath but better. It has these awesome jets to massage your back, your butt, whatever needs massaging." Jake jumps off the bed. "It'll be like, POOF!" He waves his fingers in the air. "No more pain."

I glare at him.

"Babe, I swear, it's like floating on a bubbling cloud. I felt like a whole new person."

"Any chance you were smoking while in this Jacuzzi?" I ask.

"Oh yeah, we can definitely make that happen. Duncan's got a decent stash."

I have no words for Jake, so I close my eyes again and let the mattress consume me.

"What do you say, babe? Should we hit up Duncan's?"

"Yes, Jake," I say, my voice thick with sarcasm as I snuggle into my pillow. "Let's go to Duncan's after-prom party. My lupus will be cured by morning."

"I don't know about curing anything," Jake says. "But I'm pumped you're down. You're gonna love Duncan. Actually, while you're chilling in the hot tub, maybe I'll find some Coke, and we'll make that Mentos experiment work for real. I could tell you were doubting me." Jake starts running around the room, fetching various articles of clothing and humming a tune that sounds like "Yankee Doodle."

He's not trying to hurt you, I tell myself. Jake is merely uneducated on the various side effects of autoimmune diseases. That's not his fault. I just have to be straight with him. Tell him I can't go the party, I need to sleep, and he needs to leave. Potentially forever.

My eyes flip open as that thought enters my brain.

Do I want to break up with Jake?

Should I break up with Jake?

I'm certainly not planning on marrying him. Or even continuing this relationship once he leaves for San Diego in the fall. But I always assumed we would have the summer together at least. We would watch every Marvel movie in chronological order, go on late-night McDonald's runs, and drive to the coast on the weekend. We would have a heart-felt, amicable breakup the week before he left for college. I would eventually feel strong enough to sleep with him.

"Almost ready," Jake calls. His humming has now turned into singing. I have no idea where "Yankee Doodle" came from, but he's enthusiastic even if he doesn't know the words. I don't know the words either, but I'm quite sure Yankee Doodle did not have a farm.

I drag my arms across the sheets until I'm clutching the bony knobs of my knees. It's five seconds of effort. I can do five seconds of effort.

With a grunt, I pull myself into a seated position, propped up on the headboard. My body aches as angry muscles adjust to the new position, and I briefly close my eyes to absorb the pain.

"Hey, Jake," I say.

Jake stops in the middle of an *E-I-E-I-Doodle-O* and looks at me. "What's up?" he asks.

In this moment, I feel like I'm stuck in that Robert Frost poem we read last semester. Two roads diverge in the woods or whatever.

Down the first road is Duncan's house, a Jacuzzi full of stoned baseball players, and another failed Mentos experiment. I can force myself to function for the rest of the night, spend a pleasant summer with Jake, and enjoy the memories of my first boyfriend for the rest of my life.

Down the second road is a summer spent alone, an awkward breakup I'm barely conscious for, and the most pathetic possible conclusion to my life as a high schooler. I could lie to my friends, say Jake and I had a wonderful night but decided to part ways before things got too serious. But I'll still have to live with the memory of my disastrous prom night.

"Were you going to say something?" Jake asks.

Of course, there's a third option. The most rational choice, perhaps. I can tell Jake the truth—I need to sleep, he should go to Duncan's alone, I'll call him in a few days. But there's a reason the traveler in the poem didn't stay at the crossroads for all of eternity. Robert Frost was a smart dude. He knew choosing nothing sucks even worse than choosing the wrong thing.

"Mad, you still down?" Jake asks again.

"Yes," I say, this time without any sarcasm. "Let's go to a party."

Alex

"What are you talking about? There's no way my grand-mother won the lottery. The odds are…" I can't think of a word to describe how impossible winning the lottery is. "…bonkers. The odds are just plain bonkers."

"First of all, you should definitely use the word *bonkers* more. It's charming." Leah hands me the lottery ticket. "And you're right. She didn't win the whole jackpot, but she had every number except one."

"Oh." I feel my chest deflate the tiniest bit. I knew what Leah was saying was impossible, but I couldn't help getting my hopes up a little. Everything else tonight has been unreal, so who's to say winning the lottery is out of the question? "You really shouldn't say she won the lottery, then. I guess it's a cool coincidence with the numbers, but—"

"Alex, she won fifty thousand dollars."

"Wait, what?!"

Leah motions for me to keep my voice down. Across the lobby, my family is waiting for me to join them, so we can visit Halmoni. My dad is propping up Jenny, who's still half-asleep, and my mom is glaring at what she perceives to be a romantic conversation between me and Leah.

"You win the jackpot if you get every number," Leah whispers. "But you still get money if you have most of the numbers right. I didn't believe it at first either because I saw a news article about someone else who won the fifty-thousand-dollar prize with the exact same combination of numbers. But I double-checked the rules, and sometimes people get issued the same—"

"Someone else had the same numbers?" I ask.

"Yeah, it's weird, right? Some kid found this lottery ticket on the street, and he won fifty thousand dollars. He was only thirteen, so he can't technically…"

I stop paying attention to Leah's words because I know she's telling the truth. Halmoni had purchased two identical lottery tickets, like she does every week. If some kid found a ticket on the street worth fifty thousand dollars…well, that means Halmoni is fifty thousand dollars richer too. This will certainly score her an interview with her favorite balding news anchor, though not for the reasons she planned.

Of all the weeks to lose the second lottery ticket! Once she's out of the hospital, I'm taking her shopping for new pants without holes in the pockets. Her wardrobe could use updating anyway.

"Alex, are you coming?" Dad's call cuts through the quiet of the waiting room.

"Yeah, sorry. Give me a second."

"It's family only," Mom adds in a voice that's both informative and that special brand of passive-aggressive only my mother can pull off.

Leah looks at me, confused. "I thought your mom liked me."

"I told you that wasn't going to last," I say. "She finally came to her senses and realized you were a girl."

"Aw, that's a shame." Leah and I share a brief smile, but then my mom clears her throat, interrupting the moment.

"Look, I need to see Halmoni, so if you want to go home and sleep." Leah shakes her head. "Or if you had other plans or something…"

"Alex, it's five in the morning. Nobody has plans at this hour. I'll be right here."

"Thanks."

Leah nods.

"No, seriously. Not just for staying, but for…" I can't express how much having Leah here tonight has helped me. With her by my side, I've managed to somewhat keep it together. Not only that, but I actually had fun sneaking through the hospital, bribing nurses with breakfast food, and arguing about commercial real estate. It may not have been sex in the woods, but my prom night has been memorable in its own way, thanks to her. "I'm really glad you were here and…"

Mom clears her throat again. One glance behind me confirms that everyone in this waiting room is staring at us.

"Just…thanks." I lean toward Leah until our faces are inches apart. I guess this could be considered my own pre-kiss move, but now's not the time for that. I certainly don't plan on having my first kiss with my parents watching from across the room. Instead, I wrap both my arms around Leah in a tight hug. She reciprocates, resting her cheek on my shoulder and placing her hands on the small of my back. Her hair smells like coconut.

We hold each other for a few seconds, then separate. "See you in a bit." I squeeze Leah's hand one last time, then hurry to join my parents. Dad is grinning with a maniacal look in his eyes while Mom stares, her lips parted in shock. Thankfully, Jenny is out of it or I'd be faced once again with her "is she your girlfriend?" inquisition. I'm sure my parents would love to pursue a similar line of questioning, but right now, Halmoni is everyone's priority.

I trail after my family past a different *Hospital Personnel Only* sign. This hallway is just as bright and sparse as the one Leah and I snuck through, but there are twice as many nurses milling about. Perhaps it's the daytime crew arriving to relieve the overnight team. The nurse we're following pauses next to an open door. Inside, I can barely make out the outline of a metal hospital bed.

"Your mother is in this room," the nurse says. "Most patients recovering from this type of procedure are quite tired, but she's been unusually chipper." Dad and I exchange a look. That's zero percent surprising. "But still, you should take it easy. She needs lots of rest."

I shuffle into the room behind my parents. While Dad settles a sleepy Jenny into an empty armchair, my eyes turn to Halmoni, lying on the bed under a light sheet. She looks older than I remember from even a few hours ago. Her eyes are sunken under papery lids and the wrinkles in her face seem to have deepened. Her frail eighty-year-old body looks so vulnerable when it isn't covered by a bright velour track suit. There are tubes coming out of her nose and arm, and the bright line on a silent machine jumps with every beat of her heart. I hang back as my parents approach the bed.

"Umma?" Mom strokes her mother's forehead with the back of her hand. "How are you feeling? The doctors said you were very strong."

Halmoni stays silent for a moment, and I'm beginning to doubt the nurse's assessment of her well-being, let alone her chipperness. But then her eyes flicker open, she takes in the sight of Mom, Dad, me, and Jenny, curled up in an armchair, and she smiles.

"What does everyone look so worried for?" she asks, her voice raspy but strong. It's the same old Halmoni.

Mom chokes out a part-laugh, part-sob, and the nervous tension in the room disappears. It's only been an hour since the doctors finished operating on her heart, and she's back to cheering everyone up, like always. Mom starts fussing over her blankets, asking, "How are you *really* feeling?" over and over again, and shushing Dad when he tries to discuss her insurance.

I want to tell her about the winning lottery ticket, but I need to get my parents out of the room. They'll obviously know eventually, but Halmoni deserves to hear the news first. I lean down to give her a hug, pausing to whisper in her ear, "Can you get Mom and Dad out of the room for a second?"

Ever since I was little, Halmoni has been my co-conspirator, lying to my parents about how many cookies I'd eaten or claiming it really was a demented raccoon who broke the porch swing. She responds with an imperceptible nod, then coughs pathetically. "I'd like some extra pillows," she says. "And perhaps some Jell-O if the dining hall is open."

"Of course," Dad says. "I'll get it right away."

"Wouldn't it be faster if Mom got the pillows and you got the Jell-O?" I interject. "I'll be right here," I add when Mom looks nervously at her own mother.

"Sure," Mom says. "What kind of Jell-O?"

"One of each," Halmoni says. I clamp my mouth shut to keep from laughing until both my parents are out of the room.

"Guess what!?" I exclaim at the first possible moment. I don't wait for Halmoni to respond. "You won the lottery! Not the whole thing, but fifty thousand dollars."

My grandmother looks justifiably confused. "I didn't buy tickets yesterday," she says.

"But you did the day before. Remember how you lost one—"

"One was stolen," she corrects me.

"Right, one was stolen. But you gave me the other ticket. And it won! It had every single number except for one."

Halmoni closes her eyes and leans back into the pillow. I worry she's feeling sick again or she's overly depressed about losing the second ticket. Maybe springing this news on her in the hospital wasn't my best idea. But when Halmoni's eyes open again, they're sparkling.

"It sounds like you won the lottery, Ji-hoon." She smiles.

"No way. It's your ticket."

"What's an old lady supposed to do with fifty thousand dollars?"

"What am *I* supposed to do with fifty thousand dollars?" I counter.

"Pay for college without all the loans. You can tell your parents to thank me."

"I mean, after taxes I could only afford a year or two. Even at a state school. College keeps getting more expensive."

Halmoni sighs. "What is this world coming to?" It's her favorite thing to say when she's reading the newspaper or watching Harry Jefferson on channel 8. "Speaking of money," Halmoni says. It's an awkward segue, but not particularly unusual for my grandmother. "How's the rich girl?"

"What are you talking about?"

"The daughter of that nappeun nyeosok."

My heart stops beating for a second. "How...how did you know?" I sputter.

Halmoni laughs. She's enjoying my current state of shock. "You all came over to take pictures in the yard."

"But how did you know Leah?"

"The nappeun nyeosok likes using photos of his family to convince people he's a community man. I recognized her the minute I saw her."

"Oh no. You're going to judge Leah. Not that it matters because we're not dating, but you really shouldn't judge her. She's such a good person. I've only known her for a few hours, but I can tell. I know you hate her dad, but Leah can't control what he does. Besides, he did give a bunch of money to—"

"Ji-hoon, calm down." Halmoni holds up her hand, dragging a hospital tube along with her. I stop my pointless monologue. "The girl seems lovely."

"Really?"

"Really." Halmoni's eyes flutter shut. I can tell she's struggling to stay awake. She rests with her eyes closed for a few seconds, then opens them and smiles at me again. "I hope you had a wonderful time at prom together."

"We did. Leah's actually been here all night. She's in the waiting room."

"She's here in the hospital?"

I nod.

"Then what are you doing sitting with an old lady? You need to fix your priorities, Ji-hoon."

"I promised I would stay with you."

"Your parents will be back any second."

"What if it takes a while to get every color of Jell-O?"

"Your sister's here."

"Jenny hasn't moved in thirty minutes."

"Stop arguing and go be with your girlfriend," Halmoni says through a yawn.

And for the first time tonight, I don't correct the terminology. My grandmother closes her eyes once again and her lips twist into a smile. "You only have one prom night," she says as she drifts off to sleep.

Madison

Well, I chose the wrong metaphorical road. I know this immediately.

In fact, I'm surprised Robert Frost himself didn't come back to life and knock me over the head with his typewriter. Or notebook. Or computer, possibly. I always assume the poetry we read in English is written by dead white dudes, but I could be wrong. Maybe Robert Frost is relaxing in a penthouse somewhere at this very moment, judging me from afar.

I should have changed my mind when it took me five minutes to get out of bed.

Or when Jake needed to support most of my weight as I hobbled to the car.

But tonight, I seem to be immune from making good decisions.

As a result, I'm sitting in the passenger seat of Jake's disgusting car, my forehead pressed against the cool glass, watching as my breath paints circles of fog on the window. Jake has transitioned from singing "Yankee Doodle" to rapping something about bitches and balloons. At least there's no longer a patriotic farm to contend with.

Everything hurts—my wrists, my ankles, my fingers, my back. And now my head is throbbing. Usually, if I get enough fluids, I can avoid the lupus headaches, but tonight is not my lucky night. Between all the roof climbing and making out, I forgot to hydrate.

"Have you ever played Pro Bowling?" Jake asks suddenly.

"No." I don't move my forehead off the window.

"Duncan has a Xbox in his basement, so we can play if you want. It's the best bowling game ever created in my opinion. I'm crap at actual bowling, but I'm basically a god at the video game version. It's all about choosing the right ball."

I wonder what would happen if I opened the car door right now. Just pushed it open, unfastened my seat belt, and leaped out of the car. Or toppled out, given my current condition. We're only going thirty, maybe thirty-five miles an hour. I might sustain some minor injuries, but the pain of a sprained wrist would be nothing compared to the agony of this conversation.

"Wait, I totally forgot you're a dancer! We should play Just Dance instead. You would totally destroy me. Don't get me wrong, I can bust a move, but you're a legit ballerina. That's some next-level shit. Although, maybe it's like me and how I suck at actual bowling. Sometimes real skills don't translate to Xbox skills."

My phone is in my purse. If I'm subtle, maybe I can text without taking the phone out of my bag. I saw a documentary once about this girl who was kidnapped, but she managed to text a random number and that person called the police. I'm sneaking one hand into my purse when I realize how utterly ridiculous I'm acting.

Jake isn't a kidnapper. He's a kindhearted dude who happens to be annoying the shit out of me right now. All I have to do is summon a bit of courage, tell Jake to turn the car around, and potentially break up with him for good.

No biggie, as Jake would say.

"Yo, do you mind if we stop for some food? The gas station is right up here."

"What?" I turn my head so my temple is resting against the glass.

"You know I've gotta eat five thousand calories a day, babe. And I don't want to show up at Duncan's and eat all his food. That would be rude to his mom, you know?"

"Sure," I say. "No problem."

"Sweet." Jake pulls into the gas station and parks his car

diagonally between two spaces. I think it's inconsiderate to take up more than one parking space, even when it's the middle of the night, but that's not my problem right now. "You can stay here. I'll be so fast, you won't even notice I'm gone."

I lean my head back, basking in the silence of Jake's absence. For the first time tonight, I'm alone, and it's glorious. I'm slouching down in my seat, eyelids heavy, when the reality of my situation sinks in.

I'm alone. Totally alone. Which means I can leave this car and never get back inside.

The logistics—or lack thereof—don't concern me. Neither does the joint pain I feel as I unlock the car door and step outside. For once, I'm absolutely certain of myself. It's like Robert Frost himself is holding up a neon sign reading, *This is the Right Road, You Indecisive Loser!*

I hobble down the sidewalk toward the entrance. One foot at a time, like on the trellis. Twenty seconds of effort, and I've made it. The sliding doors open to welcome me inside, and the middle-aged woman behind the counter grunts to acknowledge my presence.

It's hard to believe that five hours ago, I was scouring this same convenience store, picking out snacks and condoms in preparation for the best night of my life. Maybe that was where this whole lupus flare began. It was those damn trans fats Morgan is always harping about.

There's no sign of Jake, so I shuffle down what appears

to be the Pop-Tart aisle. Believe it or not, I've never had Pop-Tarts. When I was little, my mom strictly prohibited sugary breakfast food. And ever since I've been capable of buying my own snacks, first my dance regimen and then my stupid disease prevented me from trying all the good stuff. But now is as good a time as any. And I've always secretly envied people who are confident enough to eat food in the grocery store and then pay for the empty package at the checkout.

I consider the new strawberry milkshake flavor but decide the classic brown sugar cinnamon is better for a Pop-Tart virgin like myself. I grab the closest box and ease my body onto the tile floor. The cashier either doesn't notice or doesn't care as I rip open the package and take a bite of my first ever Pop-Tart.

"Madison?" Jake appears at the end of my aisle, his arms loaded with a six-pack of Diet Coke, a canister of beef jerky, and a bag of potato chips. "What are you doing?"

"This doesn't even taste like brown sugar," I say through a mouthful of Pop-Tart. "This tastes like cardboard."

"What are you doing? Are you okay?" Jake drops his food on the floor and rushes to crouch next to me. "Babe, why are you eating Pop-Tarts on the ground? What's going on?"

"I can't believe this is what I've been missing," I say.

"Babe, you're scaring me a little. Are you feeling okay?"

Jake removes the Pop-Tart from my hand, breaking me out of my breakfast pastry induced trance. "You're talking about Pop-Tarts a lot."

"You were talking about bowling a lot." It seems the only natural retort.

Jake sits next to me. "I knew I was talking too much," he says. "I could tell you felt bad, and I thought maybe distracting you would help. With some chill conversation, you know? But that was dumb of me. I'm sorry. I've been trying to help, but I'm sucking. Stupid Duncan and his stupid Xbox."

I appreciate that Jake accepted the connection between virtual bowling and Pop-Tarts without question, but it's unfair of me to blame him. None of this is his fault.

"No, listen to me." I take Jake's hands. "You're not stupid. Anyone who says that is wrong." My mind flashes back to all the negativity my sister has directed at Jake over the past year. I seriously hope he didn't notice her frequent eye rolls and muttered comments.

"Dude, you have zero experience with lupus, and you tried your best to help me tonight. I appreciate that so much. I was the one making bad decisions. I should have told you straight-up when I started feeling like shit." As if to prove my point, my body slumps farther into the shelves of nonperishable goods.

"I can do better," Jake insists. "I want to help you. Tell me exactly what I'm supposed to be doing. You could make a list if you want. I'm good at lists. Well, sometimes I get distracted if the list is boring, but I won't this time. Not if I can help you." I stare down at my knees. Jake has finished eating my Pop-Tart, so I grab the second one from the foil wrapper. "I'm serious, babe. Tell me what you want me to do."

"I want you to leave." My whisper is barely audible.

"Huh?"

"I want you to leave," I say a little louder. "I just…This is…" I take a deep breath and summon all the courage the Pop-Tart aisle has to offer. "I'm going through a lot right now, and I need to be by myself. And with my friends. It's nothing about you, I swear."

"Of course. Let me take you back to the house, and we can talk tomorrow." Jake doesn't hesitate for a moment, and that makes what I'm about to say even harder.

"No." I force myself to swallow the lump growing at the back of my throat. "What I meant is I think we need to break up. I'm sorry. I like you a lot, but this isn't right for me anymore."

"You're serious right now? You want to break up?" The mixture of bewilderment and sadness on Jake's face is so sweet it's heartbreaking. He really was the perfect boy-friend. He just isn't anymore.

"I'm so sorry." A couple of tears drip down my nose. If I had any energy left, I would be bawling right now. It's unfortunate, really. I'm ending my first real relationship in the Pop-Tart aisle of a convenience store and all I can summon are a few stray tears.

"I don't get why. Is it because you're feeling bad?"

I shake my head. "I swear it's not only my health. I think this flare just made me realize things I was already feeling. I mean, it's not like we were going to keep dating in college, right? This is just a couple months sooner."

"I guess that's true," Jake says. "I'll miss you this summer."

"Me too."

"Though me and Duncan will have more time to perfect the Mentos trick." Jake laughs to himself. It's a sad laugh, but I'm relieved to know our breakup won't stop him from climbing roofs. Jake is still Jake.

We sit together on the floor of the convenience store in silence. He rubs the top of my head, which is kind of weird, but mostly sweet. I nibble on my Pop-Tart and move my ankles in slow circles.

"Come on." Jake gets to his feet and offers me his hand. "I'll drop you off at the house."

Once again, I shake my head. "Just leave me here."

"Babe...uh, I mean...Madison. There's no way I'm leaving you in a sketchy gas station. Especially when you're all lupus-y."

"It's really okay," I say. "My sister is already on her way." It's a blatant lie, but it might as well be true. All it would take is one text to Morgan, and she'd be here in an instant.

"I can drive you. It's seriously no problem."

"Please, just go." I rest my head on the metal shelf behind me. "I'm really fine. Morgan will be here any second." Jake glances between me and the door. He's trying to work out which is the correct choice, and I love him for that. "How about I text you when she gets here?" I offer.

Jake nods and exhales. He starts shoving the packages he dropped onto random shelves. I guess he'll be raiding the refrigerator at Duncan's house after all.

"See you around," he says.

"You too."

"Good luck with college and life and everything."

"Same. I hope all the baseball stuff works out for you."

"Thanks. I hope you start dancing again. It sounds like it made you happy."

"Uh...yeah, maybe."

Jake reaches down to pat my head. I guess since we're not boyfriend and girlfriend anymore, he's resorted to interacting with me like I'm a dog. "See you around," he says again.

"Yeah. Totally."

Jake pauses for another moment. Then he smiles, tosses me an unopened box of strawberry milkshake Pop-Tarts, and walks out of my life forever.

Zoe

"Fuck, fuck, fuck, fuck." I pound my fist on the counter. "We have to find that fucking cat."

"I can't believe Kevin walked in on us fighting," Morgan says. "You know he's going to tell Julia."

"How could this have happened? Did you leave the door open when you went outside?"

"And you know Julia is going to tell everyone." On the other side of the counter, Morgan is pacing.

"Wait, actually..." I think about who sent the first text about the cat being gone. "Madison and Jake were on the roof."

"Do you think it would be weird if I stopped by Julia

and Kevin's room? And asked them not to tell anyone else? I don't want Madison getting stressed out…"

"Morgan, priorities!"

"Huh?" My girlfriend looks confused by my outburst. "Oh, you mean the cat?"

"Yes, I mean the cat. I obviously mean the cat. And not to automatically blame your sister, but it was definitely her and Jake."

"You can't say anything!" Morgan's eyes widen, and she grabs my wrist. "Please don't be mad at her. I'm sure she didn't mean to."

"I'm not mad at anyone." I can feel my eyes filling with tears again. I'm an unstoppable crying machine tonight. At this point, somebody could blink at me the wrong way and I would burst into tears. "We have to find this cat. I can't…" I suck in a mouthful of air. "I can't imagine telling my uncle I lost his cat."

Morgan hands me a dishtowel, which I blow my nose into. She makes a disgusted face, like that wasn't exactly what she expected me to do with the towel. "But, like, cats are good at this kind of thing," she says. "Tons of cats live outside and come home all the time."

"THIS IS AN INDOOR CAT!"

"Okay, okay. I just don't understand why you're freaking out so much. You hate your uncle. And his cat."

"He's still my uncle!" I can't believe how underwhelmed Morgan is by the gravity of this situation. She's the most protective person I know, yet she seems perfectly content to let this cat die a gruesome death on the side of the road.

"But you've been calling him an asshole all night."

"I've obviously been displacing my conflicted feelings about Yale onto him!" Only after shouting this at Morgan do I realize my analysis is spot-on, as per usual. Uncle Ross is certainly irritating, but he's irritating in a "let's complain about how weird Uncle Ross acted during Thanksgiving" kind of way, not a "let's murder Uncle Ross's beloved pet and not feel guilty about it" kind of way.

"Losing this cat is a huge fucking deal, okay?! I can't possibly tell my family I lost his pet and…" *And tell them I don't want to go to Yale.*

My unfinished sentence hangs between us.

After a few seconds, Morgan nods. "You're right," she says. "Let's find the cat. I can worry about the other stuff later."

"But how do we find a lost cat at five in the morning?"

"Don't freak out," Morgan says. "Look on the internet. This happens all the time."

I grab my phone and type "find lost cat outside" into Google. Morgan uses a paper towel to erase our pro-con list and instead writes "How to Catch a Cat" on top of the whiteboard.

"What does it say?"

"Way too many things. Everyone thinks they're an expert at catching cats." I scroll through the various pieces of advice from veterinarians and seasoned cat-owners. "If you go after the cat, you're supposed to avoid making any loud noises or yelling their name—"

"So maybe you should stop wailing."

"You should be taking notes," I snap. I appreciate Morgan's input, but snide remarks aren't helping. "Bulldog is likely too far gone for a footrace." I scroll through more comments. "People also suggest sprinkling cat treats and litter outside to lure the cat back by scent. And you're supposed to search your house because it could be hiding under a bed or something."

"But Madison said she saw the cat outside." Morgan adds the other suggestions to the whiteboard.

"Then we skip that step. And you're supposed to do stuff like making flyers and notifying your neighborhood association, but that should be our last resort."

"Agreed." Morgan pops the cap back on the marker. It's a comforting sound, one that indicates the satisfying conclusion of a list-making session. I'm just hoping this list will be more helpful than our disastrous Yale versus Oregon exercise.

"Why don't you give me food, and I'll scatter it outside?" Morgan says. "Then maybe we can get some flashlights and go searching."

I nod and fetch the basket of cat supplies from the pantry. There are natural salmon treats, dental treats, lickable wet treats, chicken jerky treats, and something called "beefy tender sticks." I feel sick to my stomach. If my uncle has *this* many cat treats, I can't imagine how he's going to react when he learns I lost his precious Bulldog.

"Great." Morgan takes the basket of treats from me. "Do you want to get other stuff that smells like home, maybe? Like dirty socks or a cat bed or something."

"Yeah, good thinking." At least Morgan is now fully invested in this search-and-rescue mission. I start down the hallway, but Morgan grabs my hand.

"Should we talk about…" She bites her bottom lip.

I shake my head. "It's too many things at once. Can we find the cat first?"

Morgan nods and drops my hand. She's the kind of person who likes to talk through everyone's emotions and resolve conflict as quickly and as thoroughly as possible, but I can't handle producing any more tears right now. Also, I think we proved having important conversations on zero sleep is not a wise choice for our relationship.

I run down the hallway and knock on the master bedroom door. "Come in!" Kevin calls. I open it slowly, hoping I don't interrupt anything. Thankfully, nobody is in the bed, though the sheets are rumpled and suspiciously wet looking. Kevin is sitting on the carpet, his back against the closet door.

"Wait, is Julia still in the closet?" I ask.

"Julia is STILL in the closet," a very agitated Julia yells from behind the door. Kevin slides one finger underneath to comfort her. It's endearing in a pathetic sort of way.

"Okay, well, that works, actually. Can you maybe slide some of my uncle's clothing under the door? Like dirty socks or something. We're hoping the cat will recognize the scent."

"Ew! That is the most disgusting thing I've ever heard."

"Julia, please."

"Fine." She sighs dramatically from inside the closet. "I think I saw a hamper." I hear rummaging and then a distressed moan. "Ew, ew, ew. This is so gross. Why are feet so disgusting?"

"You have a sock?" I ask.

"Ew, yes." Julia shoves a grayish sock under the door. Kevin pulls it out the other side and quickly tosses it to me. I dangle the sock from my fingers, trying not to think about why the fabric is damp. Julia has no such reservations.

"So gross," she moans. "I need to sanitize my entire body. Can you believe people actually have sock and foot fetishes? I think I have a foot anti-fetish. If you want to kill a sexy vibe, hand me a gross sock, you know?"

"Julia, while I'd love to stay and chat about weird fetishes with you…"

"Please don't encourage her," Kevin says.

"…I need to focus on the cat right now. I'll figure out the closet door as soon as we get the cat, okay?"

"Of course," Julia says in an exasperated voice. "Leave Julia trapped in a closet with a hamper full of smelly socks.

I'm obviously totally fine in here."

"Great, sounds good." I wave goodbye to Kevin and head back down the hallway.

"I WAS BEING SARCASTIC!" Julia shrieks after me. It's comforting to know I'm not the only one losing my mind.

The kitchen is empty, so I slip on my shoes and go outside, being careful to shut the front door behind me. Although it's possible that leaving the door open may be the optimal choice at this point. But is giving Bulldog the chance to wander in for treats and then return to the great outdoors a good idea? I realize my powers of rational reasoning are utterly useless when pitted against an indoor cat in the outside world. I'll see what Morgan thinks.

I spot my girlfriend at the end of the driveway. She's staring at her lit-up phone screen. "How's it going with the treats?" I ask as I jog toward her. The early-morning air is chilly but refreshing. I feel like I've been cooped up inside for way more than five hours. "Also, do you think we should leave the door open?"

Morgan shakes her head forcefully, causing limp curls to fall in front of her face. This isn't her expressing an opinion on the door issue.

"Hey, what's going on?" I ask.

"Madison is stranded at a gas station. Jake fucking left her there. We need to get there, like, right away."

"Wait, what?"

"Jake. Left. Madison. At. A. Gas. Station." Morgan spits out each individual word. Her jaw is locked, and I know she's imagining all the ways she can throttle Jake. "We need Kevin's keys." Morgan starts running back up the driveway. I have to sprint to keep up with her.

"Wait!" I place my hand on her shoulder.

"What?" Morgan stops suddenly and whirls around to face me. The anger distorting her features is at an intensity I've never seen before.

"What about the cat?" I know as soon as the words have left my mouth how terrible they sound. I try to explain. "I mean, obviously you need to help Madison, but I should stay to find the cat."

"Seriously, Zoe?" Morgan shakes her head. I take a step backward, hurt by her indifference. Obviously, a cat isn't as important as Madison, but that doesn't mean it's totally unimportant either.

"Whatever," Morgan says. "Kevin and I will go get Madison. You stay here, rescue your precious cat, and get Julia out of the fucking closet. I can't deal with her complaining anymore."

Morgan drops the bags of cat treats and storms inside. I stare at the chicken jerky, salmon treats, and beefy tender sticks scattered at my feet. I can't help but feel like I got the more difficult task.

WHOLESOME ALIEN SEX

Group Chat

5:04 AM

Alex: Hey are you guys still at the house? Is it okay if I come over after I drop off Leah?

Julia: Can you bring a tool kit with you?

Alex: Why?

Julia: BECAUSE I'M TRAPPED IN A FREAKING CLOSET.

Alex: Still?

Julia: YES. NOBODY CARES ABOUT ME.

Kevin: It's not like we haven't been trying.

Today 5:08 AM: Julia named the conversation "NOBODY CARES ABOUT JULIA"

Morgan: Julia, we're trying to deal with a cat situation. Can you please chill?

Julia: I CAN HELP WITH THE CAT! JUST GET ME OUT OF THE CLOSET!

Morgan: You would be zero help. You hate cats.

Julia: I HATE THE HELPLESSNESS OF CAPTIVITY MORE.

Morgan: Kevin, can you please entertain your girlfriend?

Kevin: This conversation is more entertaining than anything I could come up with.

Alex: Nobody answered my question.

Kevin: What question?

Alex: Are you guys still there? Is it cool if I come over in a little while?

Kevin: Of course!

Julia: ONLY IF YOU BRING A CHAIN SAW.

Morgan: Julia I am literally going to break down that door and smash your phone to pieces.

Julia: THAT WOULD BE A SMALL PRICE TO PAY FOR FREEDOM.

Alex: Hahahahahaha

Kevin: Lol

Madison: Hey guys I need some help

Morgan: What's going on?

Madison: I'm at a gas station by myself and I need a ride. It's the one off exit 9 that got robbed

Morgan: Are you okay?

Julia: There was a robbery!?!

Madison: Yeah just need a ride back to the house

Madison: Sorry I meant yeah I'm okay. There wasn't a robbery. I meant it's the gas station we talked about earlier

Morgan: What's going on? Where's Jake?

Madison: I know this is going to sound bad so please don't freak out but he left to go to his friend's house but I told him to leave because I was going to go but then I was feeling sick and we broke up and I wanted to be alone and I knew one of you would be able to come get me okay?

Morgan: You feel sick?

Madison: Yeah.

Morgan: What's the pain at?

Madison: Idk 8

Morgan: We'll be there right away. Don't try to move. If it gets worse, call 911.

Madison: Thx

Morgan: Kev, can you drive me?

Kevin: I'm on my way.

Madison: Sorry to mess up everyone's night

Kevin: You didn't mess up anything.

Morgan: Be there in 5 minutes.

Madison: Love you guys

Julia: So

Julia: Not to be that person…

Julia: But I wanted to point out that I'm still in the closet.

Julia: And if this house caught on fire right now, I WOULD DEFINITELY BURN TO DEATH.

Julia

I text the group chat again, but nobody responds.

They're probably crying and hugging and enjoying a sentimental moment in the middle of a Quik Mart. Or was it a 7-Eleven? It's totally unfair. Not only did Kevin and I fail to have sex tonight (and it was my sex pact!), but now I'm missing the emotional moment everyone will remember for years to come.

"Julia? Julia!"

"OH MY GOD! Who are you? How are you back so quickly?!"

Someone is yelling from across the house, but I can't tell who. My brain switches from my visceral fear of missing out to my earlier concern about fire and finally lands on the very real and scary possibility of kidnapping. What if some strange person has invaded the home? What if they were targeting me specifically, and fate handed them the perfect opportunity? Or what if this entire night was an elaborate setup to trap me in a confined space?

But then the voice responds and it's Zoe, not a kidnapper. "Morgan and Kevin went without me. I need to find that fucking cat. Maybe I was rude, but whatever. It's not like …whatever."

"What are you talking about?"

"Nothing." Zoe pauses, but I know from experience it's a pre-explanation pause so I don't interrupt. "Morgan and I have been fighting all night," she says finally.

"Yeah, Kevin mentioned you guys were arguing."

"Fantastic. Morgan will be thrilled." Zoe's voice is bitter.

"It's not like I told anyone," I say quickly. Zoe is my only hope at escaping this closet before sunrise, so I need her on my side. "I've been stuck in here for hours. And Kevin didn't say anything specific."

"No, I don't care at all. It was one of the stupid things we were arguing about. Morgan was more concerned about people overhearing our fight than finding the cat." Zoe slaps her palm against the closet door. "Whatever. Let's get you out of there."

"Did you have a particular plan in mind?" I ask.

"Because we've tried everything. Jimmying the lock, doing that keycard trick, pulling really hard."

"It's just a door lock, not a deadbolt, right?" Zoe asks.

"I think so."

"Cool. Let's bust off the doorknob, then. I'll be right back."

I immediately see flaws in Zoe's plan. First, there's no way to remove the knob without causing some serious damage to the door. Zoe may have been glib about destroying her uncle's house earlier in the night, but she's as much of a rule follower as I am. And second, I highly doubt Zoe has the physical strength to bust through anything. I couldn't do it, and I've attended a strenuous circus camp two summers in a row.

"I've got a hammer thing!" Zoe declares a few moments later.

"Uh, yeah. Zo, I don't know if this is the best plan."

"Are you standing away from the door?"

I shuffle to the back of the closet. "Now I am."

"Good. One…"

"I'm really fine being in this closet a little longer."

"…two…"

"Let's calm down. Maybe look for a key."

"THREE!"

I squeeze my eyes shut and cover my head like you're supposed to in a tornado. There's a guttural scream followed by a noisy smash and the sound of wood splintering.

Zoe whoops with excitement and I peek through my eyelashes. Where there used to be a shiny gold doorknob, there is now an empty hole. And where there used to be a perfectly pristine door…well, the door is still intact if you ignore the shards of wood on the ground.

"Zoe?" Through the opening, I see the rhinestones on her dress sparkling under the overhead light. "You okay?"

"Oh my god." Zoe hooks her fingers through the empty hole and pulls the door open. Her eyes are shining and she's panting. "That was exhilarating. I've never done anything like that before."

While Zoe proudly hefts her hammer and surveys the destruction, I scurry out of the closet. The first thing I see is my water bottle on the bedside table. I didn't realize I was parched until this moment.

"Oh my god…" Zoe is picking up pieces of the door, her face looking significantly more alarmed than it did before. "I can't believe I actually destroyed the door. What did I do?"

This is precisely the outcome I tried to warn Zoe about, but that's not what she needs to hear right now. "Is your uncle going to be really mad?" I ask between gulps of water.

Zoe hesitates. Then she shakes her head firmly. "No. As long as we find the cat, he'll be fine. The door is collateral damage. If we don't find the cat…"

"You're moving to a foreign country anyway?" I finish.

"Exactly."

While Zoe changes into more appropriate cat-hunting attire (I suggested a pair of her uncle's ugly sweatpants might be more functional than her super-expensive prom dress), she catches me up on Morgan's research. I try not to laugh when she describes the "how to catch a cat" list on the whiteboard. The two of them don't even realize how adorably perfect they are for each other.

"We've already scattered treats by the door, so I vote we use the flashlights on our phones and search the property," Zoe says. "I know you're weird about cats—"

"I have a perfectly rational fear of cats," I correct Zoe.

"No. It's absurd. Cats are the least scary animal on the planet." I open my mouth to correct this gross mischaracterization of the pure evil cats represent, but Zoe holds up her hand to stop me. "So you can be a lookout. If we see the cat, don't try to approach him. I feel like you would scream and ruin everything."

"Yeah, you don't have to worry about me willingly approaching a cat."

With our phones in flashlight mode, Zoe and I creep into the backyard. Morgan's internet search said we need to be super quiet, so we tiptoe around like we're the ones hiding from the cat, not the other way around. I see now why Zoe was eager to have company for this expedition. Even with the porch lights shining, it's a bit spooky out here. There's a thin strip of grass surrounding the house, but beyond that is forest. Legitimate forest. We're talking the giant pine and fir trees you see along the highway, not the baby maple trees scattered in the suburbs.

"Here, kitty! Here, kitty, kitty, kitty." Zoe's singing to the cat in a baby voice that would be creepy even if we weren't alone in the middle of the woods.

"I thought we were supposed to be quiet," I whisper. Zoe is shining her flashlight underneath the porch and sticking her head into all the little nooks. I'm focusing more on open expanses of grass. I don't want Demon Cat to launch itself at my face and claw me to death. The idea of kidnapping scared me, but cat mauling is the kind of stuff I have nightmares about.

"We just don't want to scare it," Zoe says. "But I have to call him somehow."

"Was he wearing a collar?"

"Yeah. It was navy blue, I think. Who am I kidding? It was definitely navy blue. But I don't know what information it had on it."

"Got it." I'm squinting at the tree line, searching for any sign of movement. I'm concerned the next step in this search and rescue mission will involve venturing into the forest. I was joking on our ride here about us walking into the plot of a horror movie, but the joke's not feeling so funny now.

"Actually, I think there might have been a little bell on the collar."

I take a few more steps toward the tree line, straining my ears for any unusual sounds. That's when my foot touches something rough. My whole body recoils, and I'm petrified I just stepped on a turtle. (I saw a post on Tumblr about the declining turtle population in this part of the country, and the last thing our ecosystem needs is me accidentally murdering one of the few remaining turtles.) But then my flashlight reflects off a tiny piece of metal, and I feel even worse.

I reach down and pick up a collar. Navy blue with a little bell and a heart-shaped tag reading "Bulldog the Cat."

My first thought is that Bulldog is an incredibly stupid name for a cat.

My second thought is that Zoe is mega-screwed.

Alex

I reach over and turn the knob from heat to air-conditioning. But as soon as cold air starts blowing, I'm freezing. It's that in-between temperature where cool air is too cold and warm air is too hot, but you need some kind of airflow to combat the humidity. I switch the knob back to heat.

I can sense Leah watching me. Of course, I can't look at her to confirm my hunch because that would make everything more awkward. I attempt a sideways glance, but my peripheral vision has never been great. I see the outline of Leah's body sitting in the passenger seat but can discern no details to help me assess the situation.

"It's a left up here," Leah says.

"Oh, you live in Wessex Gardens?"

"Yeah."

"That's a nice neighborhood."

"Uh-huh."

I wince. What a subpar conversational exchange. Everyone knows Wessex Gardens is the wealthiest subdivision in town. What if Leah thought I was trying to insinuate something negative? I find the amount of money her parents possess slightly disconcerting, but I don't want Leah to know that. I risk an actual head turn. She's staring out the front windshield, her lips pursed in a slight frown. Or maybe a smile. It's hard to tell in the dark.

I have no idea what happened to the easy rapport we had in the hospital. The joking and the banter all felt natural when my grandmother's life was at stake, but now I can't come up with anything to say. We covered the details of Halmoni's condition and her reaction to the lottery ticket on the walk to the parking lot. But the second we buckled in and started driving, an unbearable silence descended on my Subaru.

"You can pull in here," Leah says.

"Right here?"

"Yeah. The entrance is up ahead."

"This is the country club."

"I know. I used to take swim lessons here."

I follow Leah's instructions and turn into the dark

lot. I have my choice of parking spots, so I select a space between two streetlights. After another glance at Leah, I shift the car into park. I don't turn off the engine though. That much silence might kill me.

"Why are we in a parking lot?" I ask.

"Sorry," Leah says at the same time.

"Wait. Why are you sorry?"

"Because of the parking lot. I know it's weird. It's just…my mom wakes up early, and I was worried about her seeing a random car outside. I thought it would be nice if we could talk for a few minutes without my mom getting nosy."

"That makes sense."

Except it doesn't make sense. We've had the past twenty minutes to talk, and the only words we've uttered have been about left turns and subdivisions. My phone is vibrating nonstop in my pocket, but I don't want to be rude and check my messages when Leah and I are in the middle of…whatever this is. I tap my fingers on the steering wheel. Leah shifts in her seat.

Suddenly, I hear Julia in my head. *There's clearly sexual tension between you two, Alex. You need to make a move.* Her tone would be jokey, but she would be dead serious. Kevin and Zoe would laugh and agree with her. Morgan would say something inspiring about telling Leah how I feel before it's too late and Madison would shoot me a meaningful look. I can feel the tips of my ears grow hot as the reality of my situation sinks in.

It's prom night.

I'm in my car.

Alone with a girl.

"So…" Leah laughs nervously. "Why were you asking me about college earlier?"

"Oh, right." I had forgotten about my desperate need to know where Leah would be living next year, but now, once again, it feels like a crucial piece of information I'm missing. I can't make a move if there's no move available. I try not to let on how invested I am in her answer.

"Yeah. Uh, I was wondering where you were going to school next year. If you're going somewhere at all. Obviously, not going to college is a valid life decision too. But I mean…" I stammer into silence. So much for keeping it cool.

"I'm going to Middlebury," Leah says. "In Vermont."

"Oh." I keep my eyes focused on the tree outside my window. If I look at Leah, I might start crying, which would be horrifying. We only met twelve hours ago. I shouldn't be *this* devastated about losing a girl I met twelve hours ago. "Well, that makes sense."

"What makes sense?"

"You going to Middlebury." There's a lump forming at the back of my throat. I cough a few times to shoo it away. "I mean…there are a lot of parks in Vermont. Plenty of geese to evict from their natural habitats."

"Oh. My. God." Leah swats at my arm. "We were having a moment, and you had to bring up the geese. You know, for a guy who claims to have all these great values, you sure don't seem to value independent thought. You do realize people can have different beliefs than their parents—"

I cut Leah off. "We were having a moment?"

She nods. Then smiles.

This time, my entire body grows hot, not just my ears. So Leah won't be my lifelong partner. That doesn't mean we can't hang out before she leaves for Vermont. People have summer romances all the time. Especially the summer before they leave for college. That's the premise of every teen romantic comedy ever made.

"Don't look happy," Leah says.

"What?" I'm suddenly concerned I misread this entire situation. "Why shouldn't I look happy?"

"Because I leave right after we graduate."

"Why? What kind of college starts in June?" Now I'm enraged at the thought of Middlebury taking Leah away from me too soon. I'm really experiencing the full range of human emotions tonight.

"Not for school," Leah says. "My family has a home in Martha's Vineyard. We go there every summer." She sighs and rests her head on my shoulder. I'm tempted to say something snarky about how upsetting it must be to have a vacation home, but I can tell she's actually sad.

"Otherwise…" Leah pauses. "Otherwise, I would have asked you out already."

I somehow start choking on my own spit. Leah removes her head from my shoulder as I'm overcome by a coughing fit. "Alex! Are you okay?" Leah hits me a few times on the back. "What's the matter with you? Are you opposed to the girl asking out the guy or something?" She grins. I know exactly where she's going with this, but I'm hacking too much to interject. "I have to say, that's not very progressive of you. For someone who values the environment so much, I would expect a more feminist perspective."

"I have no problem with a girl asking me out," I say once the coughing has dissipated. "Just because it's never happened before doesn't mean I'm opposed." Leah laughs. "However, I am opposed to you leaving Oregon right after I met you. Believe it or not, I was actually about to ask you out myself."

"No way. You're too indecisive."

"I was! Did you not see how much I was blushing?"

"Okay, true. You were totally freaking out over there. I thought you were going to have a heart attack or something." Leah cringes. "Sorry, bad analogy."

"No, it's okay." I close my eyes. "Halmoni's going to be sad though. I'm pretty sure she thinks you're my only chance at a legitimate girlfriend." Now that I know I can't actually date Leah, I'm less concerned with the word. None of it makes a difference anymore.

"You skipped your after-prom party because you liked

me." I state this like it's a fact, which I'm pretty sure it is, but it's still not something I would have dared to say aloud six hours ago.

"Obviously." Leah smiles. "Why would I stay overnight in the hospital with some random acquaintance? Nobody's that nice."

Leah and I settle into a comfortable silence. There are so many unspoken words between us. So many missed opportunities and painful what-ifs. After a few minutes of bittersweet quiet, Leah's hand creeps over toward mine. I reciprocate by intertwining my fingers with hers.

"I killed my hamster," Leah announces.

"Um, okay?" I'm not sure why Leah decided rodent deaths were a good topic of conversation. Does she think I'll be less sad about her leaving if I know she's a cold-blooded killer?

"I went skiing over spring break with some friends. And I forgot to tell someone to feed my hamster. When I got home five days later, he was dead."

"Uh, thanks for sharing, I guess?" If anything, the rodent story makes Leah even more appealing. She was starting to seem a bit too perfect (other than the whole daughter of a nappeun nom thing). I appreciate that she's flawed enough to accidentally murder a beloved pet.

"My point is I'm not up for a distance thing," Leah says.

"Ah." Honestly, I hadn't even considered a long-distance

relationship. That level of commitment makes sense for established couples like Kevin and Julia, and their colleges are only fifteen minutes apart. Starting something long-distance with a girl I met twelve hours ago would be ludicrous. "Yeah, definitely not. I don't want to end up like your dead hamster."

"Poor Rigatoni."

"Rigatoni is the hamster's name?"

"Yeah."

A wave of sadness floods through my body. I don't have the strength to tell her my childhood guinea pig was named Macaroni. It would be too tragic. "That's a funny name," I say finally.

The sun is starting to peek over the horizon. For the first time in my life, I have officially pulled an all-nighter. I can't help but wonder if this is what every weekend with Leah would be like in a different world. One where she wasn't going first to Martha's Vineyard and then to Vermont.

Would we stay awake until sunrise, exchanging stories about our childhoods, talking about the future, and arguing about the merits of arts education? Or maybe we'd wake up at dawn and go for romantic bike rides together. I'm bad at both waking up early and riding a bike, but I would learn for Leah.

"This sucks," she says.

"So much suckiness." I squeeze Leah's hand. She

responds by stroking my wrist with her thumb.

"There is one thing…" She bites her lip and then shakes her head.

"What?"

"I know about…" Leah giggles a little. It's possibly the cutest sound I've ever heard. "I know you lied to me earlier."

"What? How did I lie?" I'm quite indignant at the accusation. If anything, I've been far too honest with Leah tonight.

"About the sex pact. You said it was a joke." My face must look guilty because Leah snaps her fingers. "Aha! I knew you were lying."

"How did you know?"

"You forget Julia and I are lab partners. That's the closest bond any two people can have."

"My lab partner and I have never said anything to each other that didn't involve beakers and chemical compounds."

"Alex, we've already established that you need to socialize more." Leah pokes me in the ribs. "Anyway, the second Julia started talking about the sex pact, I knew she was serious." Leah procures a sticky note from her purse. "Also, she gave me this when we met up for pictures." It's only when she hands me the note that I realize there's a condom taped to the back.

"I'm going to kill her," I mutter.

"Read the note," Leah instructs.

"'Dear Lele.' Oh my god. Do people call you Lele?" I look up from the Post-it.

"Absolutely not," Leah says. "I refuse to accept such a hideous nickname."

I keep reading. "'I know I had to beg you to come with us…' Wow, that's rude."

"She didn't have to beg me."

"'But should you and Alex decide to join our sacred pact…' Okay, that's offensive to every religion. 'I thought you should be prepared. Love, Julia.'"

I peel off the condom and hand it to Leah, who's staring intently at the dashboard.

"You didn't throw it away," I say, pointing out the painfully obvious.

"I was intrigued."

"By the sex pact or by me?"

"Both."

"I've never even kissed anyone. I don't know how to have sex." It's the most awkward thing anybody could say before a possible sexual encounter, but I figure it's best to be up front about my lack of experience. Besides, Leah would figure that out soon enough.

"And you think I do!?"

"I don't know how many people you've been with before," I say. "I would never judge or discriminate against someone based on their sexual history. See, I'm a feminist."

"Alex…" Leah moans.

"Sorry. Does arguing with you kill the mood?"

"No, the opposite." Leah grabs my shirt collar and presses her lips against mine. Our bodies tumble into an awkward pile in the front seat. "I mean, obviously, I'm always right," she says when we come up for air. "But, god, is your stubbornness attractive."

"Oh really?" I smile sweetly at Leah. "Should we maybe discuss how disenfranchised the elderly are in American culture? Or how the geese are only going to get angrier if your dad keeps building stuff on their homes?"

"Literally shut up and take your shirt off," Leah says, slipping the straps of her dress off her shoulders. "I mean... only if you want to do this."

My shirt is off before Leah finishes her sentence.

Madison

I can tell Morgan has entered the store by the sound of the door flying open.

"Mad!? Where are you? Madison!"

I take a bite of my Pop-Tart. I'm confident Morgan will find me without any help. I'm the only customer in the store. I'm sprawled in the middle of an aisle. And there are silver Pop-Tart wrappers scattered around my legs.

"Oh thank god." Morgan appears at the end of the aisle with a nervous Kevin hovering behind her. She runs toward me, kicks the trash out of her way, and kneels next to me. "How are you feeling? Where's the pain at?"

"A little better. Probably a six or seven now."

Morgan eyes me suspiciously. "Promise?"

"I swear it's better." I'm not saying this for Morgan's sake. Ever since Jake and I officially parted ways, my body has been feeling a tad lighter, my joints slightly less achy than before. This is still a bad lupus flare, but I think the relief of ending things with Jake has eased a bit of the stress I was feeling.

"Did Jake seriously abandon you here on the floor? What an asshole." Morgan grabs a Pop-Tart from the box I'm currently working on. I appreciate that she doesn't question my decision to eat products before I've paid for them. And that she hasn't made any nagging comments about the evils of junk food.

"I broke up with him," I say. "And then begged him to leave. He honestly did everything right. I didn't give him a choice."

"Um, of course he had a choice. He could have ignored your stupid request and insisted on staying with you. That's what I would have done."

"You're my sister."

"Genetics has nothing to do with it! No decent guy would have left you stranded at a gas station. Right, Kevin?"

"Uh…" Kevin looks up from the box of macaroni and cheese he was studying. "I don't know what I'm supposed to say here."

"You're supposed to tell Madison you would never abandon her if she was suffering," Morgan says.

"No, you're supposed to tell Morgan you would respect my wishes as a human being with personal autonomy."

Kevin looks back and forth between me and Morgan. "Yeah, there's no way I can win this one." He places the mac and cheese back on the shelf. "You know what? I'm really in the mood for some Gatorade. I'm gonna...yeah. Gonna look for some Gatorade." Kevin hurries out of the nonperishable snack aisle and toward the glass-fronted refrigerators at the side of the store.

"Kev would have stayed," Morgan says.

"You're biased. You automatically hate everything about Jake."

"Maybe so. But that doesn't mean I'm wrong."

I stretch out my fingers and evaluate the stiffness in my joints. Although the pain is better, I still feel dull aches all over. I can't possibly imagine moving from this exact spot on the mud-streaked tile floor. Morgan notices my movements. Normally, she would insist on telling our mom or starting a bath for me, but all she does tonight is place a comforting hand on my thigh.

We sit together in the relative silence of the convenience store. The sole employee is coughing intermittently at the checkout counter and I can hear Kevin pacing in front of the beverage case, but it's surprisingly peaceful under the quiet buzz of the fluorescent lights. I'm waiting for Morgan to talk. Whenever we get into arguments, she always apologizes first. I'm definitely the more stubborn twin.

Morgan doesn't disappoint. After a few more seconds of quiet, she takes a deep breath. "I'm really sorry, Mad. I feel like you ended up in this situation because I was being so controlling and worrying all night. Like, you pushed yourself too hard because you had to prove me wrong or something. I know I need to calm down and let you live your life, but I get so paranoid. I feel like I should see a therapist or something."

"You should definitely see a therapist," I say.

"What we need is couples counseling," Morgan says. "And we should bring Mom. She's the worst of all of us."

"Our poor mother. How many times did you call her tonight?"

"Twice," Morgan says.

"Hey, me too!" I break off a piece of my blueberry pastry and hand it to Morgan. She chews thoughtfully.

"So do you forgive me?"

"Yes and no."

"WHAT!?" Crumbs fly out of Morgan's mouth. "I thought that was a good apology! Hold on. I'll try again."

"No, that's not what I mean. I obviously forgive you because I always forgive you, but…"

"But what?" I can tell Morgan is panicked at the thought of this conflict not being resolved immediately. She's the "never go to bed angry" type. Though it's really more the "never move on from any scenario until everybody has forgiven everybody" type.

"But…and I don't want this to sound bad…" I choose my words carefully. "But you're kind of making it about yourself again. You don't need to apologize because I decided to climb on a roof and then go to a party at four in the morning. That was all me."

"Yeah, you were pretty dumb."

"Hey, it's a little bit your fault."

"I don't know," Morgan says. "Maybe we should start blaming you for everything. Would that make up for my years of self-centeredness?"

"No. Well, maybe. Who knows."

I'm relieved everything is semi-normal between us. I have no doubt Morgan will be attempting to micromanage my life again in no time, but I feel like she's starting to understand my side of things a little better. Morgan, however, doesn't seem like herself. Apologies are her favorite thing in the world. Usually, once our issues are resolved, she starts planning a spa day or scouring eBay for twin-sister necklaces. In my jewelry box at home, I have three charm bracelets, four pendants, and a dog collar. All twin themed. But her face is glum.

"Are you okay? You seem down."

Morgan shrugs. "Stuff with Zoe. We've been fighting all night."

"About me?"

Morgan glares at me. "Now who's making everything about herself?"

"True, sorry."

"It's just been weird," she says.

I want to press Morgan to elaborate, but I sense a figure behind us. I twist my head to see Kevin walking in small circles at the end of our aisle. He's holding no Gatorade.

"Kevin, what are you doing? Are you spying on us?"

"What? No!" Kevin wanders over. "I felt awkward because the cashier was looking at me all funny."

"Because you were loitering in the refrigerator aisle," I say. As if Kevin loitering is somehow weirder than me eating unpurchased merchandise on the floor.

Kevin doesn't bother to think of a witty retort. He continues rambling. "I thought I should walk by the front counter to not seem suspicious, you know? But then the lady asked what we were doing, and I didn't know what to say. So I was like, 'My friends are sampling Pop-Tarts,' and she said, 'That's not allowed.' So then I said I would obviously pay for the Pop-Tarts, but I didn't know how many you had eaten already, so I bought the equivalent of twenty-five boxes. So if we could maybe all chip in for those…I'm a little tight on cash at the moment."

"Twenty-five boxes! How could I even—"

"And then she said she doesn't like having random people in the store at night if we're not going to buy anything because there was a holdup here last month. A guy with a gun. She was here and everything." Kevin finally stops talking. He looks back and forth between me and Morgan as the importance of what he said registers.

"Oh my god. Julia was right." Morgan sounds justifiably astonished. Julia's habit of catastrophizing isn't normally based in reality. "We should get out of here. It's not safe. And we don't want to freak that woman out more." Morgan looks at me. "Are you okay to walk?"

"Yeah, if you can lift me a little," I say. "There's no way I'm staying here any longer."

Morgan helps me off the ground while Kevin gathers as many boxes of Pop-Tarts as he can hold. My joints are feeling better, but it's still easier to walk with someone to lean on. Morgan holds my waist with one arm and I use her shoulder as a crutch. My sister may not have the strength that comes with two-a-day baseball workouts, but she's been supporting me for so long that she's grown used to it.

"So what's going on with you and Zoe?" I ask as the three of us walk out of the store. Morgan glances at Kevin, but he's too busy balancing his armful of blue boxes to care about what we're saying.

"I can't tell you." Morgan briefly drops my arm to push open the door. The sun has started to rise, and I have to squint to see Kevin's car at the other end of the parking lot.

"You have to tell me," I say. "It's only fair because you know everything wrong with me."

"I can't." I roll my eyes at Morgan, who only holds out

for another three seconds. "Okay fine." She lowers her voice. "But you can't tell anybody until Zoe says so."

"Ooh, okay." I lean in closer. I'm a sucker for secrets, but isn't everyone?

"Zoe got off the Yale waitlist." Morgan whispers this like it's some grand conspiracy theory nobody saw coming, but I'm not particularly surprised. I was shocked when Zoe was waitlisted in the first place. As the smartest person in our grade and a legacy student, I assumed she must have been somewhere high on the list.

"Interesting," I say carefully.

"Interesting!?" Morgan's eyes are wide with excitement, and she's clutching my arm way too hard. It's not difficult to fill in the blanks. My twin sister is a genuinely good person. She doesn't get jealous or resentful when cool things happen to her friends. In fact, she's the total opposite. It's easy to imagine her excitement level shooting off the charts with little regard for Zoe's feelings. Which, I'm assuming, were some combination of angst and ambivalence.

"How in the world did you guess all of that?" Morgan asks after I've relayed this hypothesis to her. The two of us have reached the car first. Somehow, a chronic auto-immune disease is less of a handicap Kevin's mountain of Pop-Tarts.

"I don't know." I shrug. "Didn't you notice how much more excited Zoe seemed about college after she didn't get into Yale?"

"I...I really didn't." Morgan slumps over the hood of the minivan. "I assumed Yale was still her dream. How was I supposed to know she wanted me to ask her to stay? That's so un-Zoe like."

"Hey, guys? We need to go back to the store." Kevin finally catches up with us and drops some of his boxes on the hood.

"Why?"

"I was counting while I was walking, and I think I only have twenty-three boxes," Kevin says. "I want to make sure I get my money's worth. Or I suppose I can ask the lady to refund a couple of them."

"That's not happening." Morgan grabs Kevin's keys from his pocket, unlocks the car, and starts tossing Pop-Tarts into the backseat. "Madison is sick, and I have things to do at the house."

"Like telling your girlfriend you want her to stay in Oregon?" I whisper as Morgan helps me into the car.

"Like not getting caught in the middle of an armed robbery!" Morgan says loud enough for Kevin to hear. Then she turns back to me and smiles. "But also your thing."

Kevin grumbles but slides into the front seat and quickly starts the engine. I close my eyes as Morgan pulls my seat belt across my body and locks it into place. I'm fully capable of putting on my own seat belt, but for once I don't complain. Sometimes, it's nice to have help.

Julia

I don't know how we got to this point, but I'm the only one looking for Demon Cat. Me, Julia Bethany Harmond, self-avowed cat hater. The only person who would be okay if the cat turned up dead. I'm the person who's searching for the darn thing.

Zoe is still outside with me, but she's trailing behind, caressing the cat collar, and wallowing in an avalanche of self-pity.

"My life is over. The cat is dead. My life is over." Her voice cracks on the last word. I ignore her dramatics and continue my search of the shrubbery lining the driveway.

"Have you considered helping me find the freaking thing?" I ask.

"I am helping," Zoe says. "I'm holding the flashlight."

"Zo, the sun is coming up. We don't need the flashlight anymore."

"Huh." Zoe stares at the horizon as if she's noticing for the first time we're not surrounded by darkness. "That's cool."

"Right. So how about you put the phone down and get searching?"

Zoe stares at me. Then she nods and drops her phone. It lands on the gravel driveway with a muffled crunch. She could not be more dramatic about the whole ordeal if she tried.

"I've been focusing on the bushes because I swear I saw some movement. It could have been a rabbit or something, but at least it's a lead. If you want to…Zo?" I turn around to find my friend lying in the rocks next to her phone.

"Are you freaking kidding me? Do you even want to find this cat?" I storm over to Zoe and try to pull her up, but gravity is on her side. She holds up a hand to block the sun, swinging the collar from a dangling finger. The tinkling of its bell is truly pitiful.

"I appreciate you trying," Zoe says. "But we found his collar. A crow or bear or something must have eaten him and left it behind. I'm accepting the fact that Bulldog is dead and my life is officially over."

"What in the world are you talking about?" I tug on Zoe's arm again, and this time she sits up. "Cats wear collars that come off really easily, so they don't get stuck on things." Shockingly, I'm the person in this conversation with an intimate knowledge of cat safety. "It's not great the collar came off, but it doesn't mean Demon Cat is dead." *Unfortunately*, I think to myself.

"Really?" Zoe looks like she's about to cry. "I had no idea." I try to rub her forearm in a soothing way, but I'm not the best at comforting emotional people. "Thanks for not giving up on Bulldog. I know you don't like him."

"Absolutely despise him," I say, and Zoe smiles.

"I guess let's get to searching again." She stands up and wipes away the gravel stuck to her legs. "I'll have to call my uncle if we don't find him soon. Which means I'm definitely going to be stuck at Yale." Zoe groans and kicks a few pebbles into the grass.

"Wait, what are you talking about?" This time, I'm the one pulling her back. "What does this have to do with Yale? Didn't you get rejected?" I wince. That wasn't the kindest way to remind Zoe of such a colossal disappointment, but I'm thoroughly confused.

"I got off the waitlist," Zoe says glumly. "But I don't really want to go. That's what Morgan and I were fighting about."

"Oh, wow." That's a lot of information to take in at once, but I can tell from Zoe's sullen expression she's not interested in an in-depth conversation on the subject of college waitlists.

"How is Yale related to the cat?" I ask instead.

"My uncle is super Yale obsessed," Zoe says. "He'll be devastated if I choose Oregon. *And* he'll be devastated if I lose his cat."

"So you're worried that much devastation at once would kill him?"

"More like it would instigate unsolvable family drama."

"Got it." Honestly, I feel like a severed relationship with Zoe's uncle might be best for her family. I distinctly remember her mom calling him a self-obsessed sociopath, and I don't think Zoe's dad is particularly fond of his brother either. That doesn't quite feel like something I should say out loud though. "Well, then let's find this cat. So you don't have to go to Yale, I guess."

Zoe nods.

We walk side by side down the winding driveway with Zoe tiptoeing on the grass and me treading as lightly as possible on the gravel. The rising sun has woken a horde of mosquitos, and I find myself swatting away one of those bloodsucking monsters every few seconds. Between mosquitos and cats, I'm not sure which species I would eradicate first if I possessed godlike powers. Probably mosquitos, mostly because everyone hates mosquitos and I'd be a hero, but it would be a close call.

"See anything?" Zoe whispers.

"Nope. But I swear he was in a bush earlier."

With every step we take, I sense Zoe growing more and

more despondent. One look in her direction confirms my suspicions. Her shoulders are hunched, she's barely picking her feet up off the ground, and she's not even pretending to look for the cat.

I don't understand why Zoe's so bummed about getting off the waitlist. She's been talking about Yale ever since I've known her. But people change, I suppose. What really doesn't make sense is the connection between Yale and Demon Cat. The logic is faulty, especially for Zoe, the queen of rationality.

"Why do you even care what your uncle thinks?" I ask.

"I mean, I don't usually," Zoe says. "But if I lose his cat, I'm going to feel pretty shitty."

"Right, but losing Demon Cat will be your fault whether you go to Yale or not." She glares at me. "Wait, no, forget I said that."

Zoe and I keep walking. Neither of us is really looking for the cat now. I'm more concerned about making her see reason, but that's proving difficult. We haven't slept in twenty-four hours, and I don't have Zoe's logical mind. My own application to Yale was rejected outright, after all.

"My point is, this is your life," I say. "You shouldn't let your family keep you from making the best decision for you. And it's not even your whole family! It's your super obsessive uncle and maybe your dad who want you to go to Yale. I would much rather you stay here."

Zoe stops in her tracks. "You want me to stay here? You're not just saying that?"

"Well, yeah." I don't know why she's being so weird about this. "You obviously shouldn't make major life decisions based on what I want. But of course I would prefer to have you in the same state as me."

Zoe's face crumples, and she flings her arms around my neck. I'm learning Zoe is a person who definitely needs a full night's sleep. Or maybe I'm just remarkably skilled at keeping myself sane while sleep deprived. That's something for the special skills part of my résumé. I could be an ER doctor. Or some kind of scientist who studies nocturnal animals.

"I've been wanting somebody to say that," Zoe mumbles into my shoulder. "I hate how Morgan seems fine and dandy with me moving across the country."

I pat Zoe's back as she continues to gasp and hiccup and cry. Not to sound harsh, but Zoe would be a terrible nocturnal animal scientist.

"I don't understand what's wrong with me," Zoe continues. "I can usually keep my shit together, but everything tonight has been so emotional and—"

"Zoe, hush." I push my friend off my shoulder and stare into the bushes. "Did you hear that?" I hate to interrupt a touching moment, but I swear I heard something moving. And finding Demon Cat would alleviate some of Zoe's angst.

"Hear what?"

"Shh." I clap my hand over her mouth. There's definitely something moving, but I can't tell where the sound is coming from. It's not so much a rustling as a crunching. I scan the area, but I see no cat and the sound is getting louder. I'm briefly worried it's a larger, even scarier animal, but then I hear an engine and Alex's Subaru appears at the end of the driveway.

"Just Alex," Zoe says, sounding even more dejected than before.

"No, it's good," I reassure her, even though I'm feeling less than confident myself. "Now we have another person to help look. And we can use the car to search the whole area."

I wave Alex down the driveway like I'm an air traffic controller directing airplanes down the runway. (Perhaps another job requiring overnight alertness?) Alex slows to a stop next to us and rolls down his window.

Now, it wouldn't be evident to the average observer, but I can say with absolute confidence that Alex recently had sex. There's the rumpled hair, two undone buttons on his dress shirt, and the passenger seat tilted way farther back than any normal passenger would want it. Plus, there's the matter of the note I secretly gave Leah in the hopes she and Alex would hit it off.

"Hey." Alex sticks his head out the window.

"Hey yourself." I'm resisting the urge to immediately

ask him about any intimate moments with Leah. Alex is a private guy, and I was taking a risk even giving Leah that note in the first place. Any invasive questioning will have to wait until we're alone.

"You guys looking for a cat?"

"Yeah, we've been searching but…Wait."

I was so distracted by Alex partaking in romantic activities I didn't notice the grin on his face. And it's not your average I-just-had-sex grin. (Not that I have much experience with those.) No, this is a smug, I-know-something-you-don't-know grin.

"What?! Did you find him?"

"I don't know for sure. I never saw what he looked like." Alex waves us to the car. Zoe and I peer through the tinted glass into the back seat. Next to Alex's wrinkled tie (even more evidence he had sex if you ask me) is not one, but two cats. The evil pile of orange fluff commonly known as Demon Cat and a mangy Siamese with bright green eyes.

It looks like during Demon Cat's escape from the cabin, he found a friend. A friend he is now grooming contentedly in the back seat of Alex's car.

Zoe

"You're such a good kitty. Did you know that, Bulldog? You're the best kitty cat in the whole world."

I'm scratching Bulldog behind the ears. His whole body vibrates as he purrs happily, and he leans into my hand to get scratches on the other side of his head. The tumultuous hour I spent apart from Bulldog has enhanced my love for this furry guy. Maybe I'll even offer to cat-sit for Uncle Ross when he's out of town. Maybe.

"I can't believe it's morning," Julia complains. "I need to figure out what's wrong with my vagina. At exactly nine o'clock, I'm going to call my doctor. I can't wait any longer."

"It's Sunday," Alex says. Bulldog's new friend is sitting peacefully next to him on the arm of the sofa.

"Well, then I guess I'll wait a little longer. But Monday morning, I'm calling her first thing."

"We have an AP test on Monday."

"Will you stop arguing with everything I'm saying, Alex? I'm trying to make a point."

"And what is your point exactly?" I ask.

"That it's completely unfair I orchestrated this entire sex pact, and I didn't get to do it! Even stupid Demon Cat managed to find a mate."

"Yeah, I don't think their relationship is sexual."

"Why? Because they're both males?" Julia cranes her head to see the private parts of the Siamese. Alex and I laugh. We're both cuddling our respective cats while Julia paces in front of the television. "You of all people should know that cat love is cat love. Why can't you respect the wishes of—"

"Julia, please shut up." To her credit, Julia pauses her tirade against homophobia in the world of house cats. "Bulldog is neutered, so he won't be engaging in any sexual activity. His friend is probably fixed too." Bulldog's new-found companion was collarless, but Alex volunteered to get him checked for a microchip when the vet opens.

"Take that, you stupid cats." Julia points an accusing finger at Bulldog. "You won't have sex before me. How's that for karma?" I pull Bulldog closer to protect him from

Julia's wrath. Bulldog, of course, is uninterested in my affection and squirms out of my grasp.

I'm feeling calmer after talking to Julia outside. She was right, of course. There was no logical connection between losing Bulldog and going to Yale. But since we found the cat, my decision to attend the University of Oregon is even easier. Who cares what my uncle thinks? Though there is the slight matter of his busted doorknob I need to explain.

"How's your grandma?" Julia asks Alex.

"Yeah, how is she?" While I was working myself into a dramatic frenzy over college admissions all night long, Alex was dealing with actual problems.

"The surgery went really well. It took a little longer than—"

"We're ba-ack!" Morgan announces as the front door swings open.

The twins come inside first. Madison's face is pale and she's leaning on Morgan for support, but she's smiling. They walk slowly toward the couch, and both Alex and I jump up in unison to make room for Madison.

"Don't worry, guys. I've got the Pop-Tarts. It's no problem!" Kevin yells as he stumbles inside. His face is hidden behind the enormous pile of Pop-Tart in his arms. He grunts and drops a couple boxes of Blueberry and a Brown Sugar Cinnamon on the floor before he manages to deposit his stash on the kitchen table.

"Holy crap. That's so many Pop-Tarts," Julia says. She runs over to check out Kevin's haul, and Alex follows.

I wait while Morgan hands Madison pillow after pillow and drapes a fleece blanket across her legs. Only when Madison has sighed three times and pointedly glared at her does Morgan turn her attention to me. Some things will never change.

"Hey," Morgan says.

"Hey," I respond.

In the early morning sunlight, Morgan looks exhausted. My girlfriend is beautiful in any situation, but I'll admit she looks a little rough at the moment. There are bluish-purple patches under her bloodshot eyes, and her hair is frizzing out of control. I can't imagine how unattractive I must look. Crying for hours doesn't enhance anyone's natural beauty.

"I'm so glad you found the cat," Morgan says. "And a spare one too."

"And you guys managed to get an entire store's worth of Pop-Tarts."

"It's a long story," Morgan says. "Kevin's not good under pressure."

"Can you two speak up?" Madison asks from the couch. "I want to eavesdrop, but they're being loud."

"Oh my god." Morgan drags me down the hallway and into the first bedroom, the Yale-themed extravaganza I avoided all night. Even with the door closed, I can hear Alex, Kevin, and Julia shouting in the kitchen.

"Is this room okay?" Morgan asks.

"Yeah. I'm fine with it now." I glance around at the banners and posters and baseball caps. All the navy blue and white feels less threatening than it did six hours ago.

"Listen…" Morgan starts, but I shake my head.

"Let me go first." I take a deep breath. "Obviously, I've decided I don't want the waitlist spot. I decided way before I even told you if I'm being honest. And it wasn't fair of me to expect you to react a certain way. This is what's best for me, regardless of what it means for us." I think back to how emotional I got when Julia casually mentioned she wanted me to stay in Oregon. "But I really hope you're happy I'm going to be here. Otherwise…"

I stare down at my bare feet. My stomach churns at the possibility of Morgan being disappointed in my decision. But when I look up, she's smiling, and that puts me at ease. "Okay, you go."

"All I was going to say is I want you to stay," Morgan says simply.

Relief floods through my exhausted body. It was nice when Julia expressed a similar sentiment, but it was validation from Morgan I had been craving all night.

"I didn't want to be selfish," she explains. "I wanted you to make the decision that was right for you. But according to Madison, I definitely missed all the anti-Yale vibes you've been sending out."

"I mean, being straightforward from the beginning

would have been the mature way to handle things."

"But then we wouldn't have had our super fun night of sobbing and scone making."

"Oh my god, my scones!"

I don't know how long it takes for dough to go bad, but it can't be good that my unbaked scones have been sitting on the counter for hours. I rush to the door but pause to make sure Morgan is following me. When I turn around, her face is inches from mine. I give her a quick peck. Normally, I wouldn't want to stop kissing her, but Morgan's breath is not enticing at the moment.

"I love you," I whisper.

"Love you too," Morgan whispers back.

We walk hand in hand down the hallway and back into the living room. Madison gives us an obnoxious thumbs-up from the couch while Julia, Kevin, and Alex barely notice us. They're too busy organizing an elaborate Pop-Tart tasting.

"Are you guys sure you want Pop-Tarts for breakfast?" I ask. "I was making everyone scones."

"You mean the pile of mush in the kitchen with a family of ants living inside it?" Julia asks. "I'm gonna have to pass."

"Seriously?" I run to the kitchen. Julia was exaggerating—there are two or three ants, not hundreds—but even a couple ants probably mean I should give up on my dough. The scones were going to be overkneaded anyway.

When I return to the living room, Julia is ready with a handful of pastries for me to sample. She starts reading off the labels. "We've got Brown Sugar Cinnamon. We've got S'Mores. We've got Chocolate Chip. We've got Special Edition Strawberry Milkshake. We've got every variety of berry in both frosted and unfrosted form."

"I want all of the strawberry milkshake ones," Madison says, and Julia tosses three boxes onto the couch for her.

"I guess I'll take unfrosted blueberry." I curl up in an empty armchair and tuck an available blanket across my legs. "Can we pitch in for these, Kev?"

"Alex can pay for them with his lotto winnings," Julia says.

"Wait, did you actually win the lottery?" I ask.

"Kind of." Alex shrugs.

"What does 'kind of' mean?" Madison asks. She's trying to sit up, but she's struggling. The second Morgan sees her in pain, she rushes over and adjusts the pillows so Madison is in a more upright position.

"All but one of the numbers matched. So it wasn't the whole pot, which is worth millions. But my grandma won fifty thousand dollars."

"HOLY CRAP!"

"Oh my god!"

"Seriously?!"

Alex blushes at all the attention. After assuring us the money will go toward his college education and possibly reimbursing Kevin for a store's worth of Pop-Tarts, he suddenly busies himself on his phone. Julia smiles at him.

The six of us sit in our lopsided circle and exchange stories as the sun rises outside my uncle's ostentatious bay windows. I announce I will officially be attending the University of Oregon to cheers from Julia, Madison, and Morgan and a great deal of confusion from the boys who never knew there was another option. Julia provides an embellished play-by-play of our attempt to catch the cat, and I don't bother correcting her when she adds somersaults off the porch and bloody paw prints in the gravel for dramatic effect. Madison tells everyone about her and Jake's rooftop adventures and Morgan manages to laugh along. And Julia describes in uncomfortably vivid detail the pain she felt when she and Kevin tried to have sex.

"What did WebMD say?" Madison asks.

"There were a whole bunch of things," Julia says. "The top one was endometriosis, but I'm really hoping it's something less serious. I can't call my doctor until Monday though, so maybe I'll try the quiz again."

"Let's not encourage Julia's obsession with WebMD," Kevin says.

"Hey, don't criticize WebMD," Madison says. "My mom figured out I had lupus from their self-diagnosis tool."

"Yeah, and then the actual doctor diagnosed you, like, thirty minutes later," Morgan says, and everyone laughs.

I grab another Pop-Tart. Julia turns on a song by the German singer she loves. Alex and Kevin are sitting next to each other on the floor, Alex busy texting and Kevin cuddling with both cats. On the couch, Morgan is watching Madison, whose eyes are fluttering open and shut.

"Sorry we all failed at having sex," I say to Julia once the song ends. Partly because I know she's disappointed by tonight's outcome and partly because I can't stand listening to another Fynn Ludwig ballad.

"Eh." Julia shrugs. "The sex pact wasn't a total failure."

"Wait, what? Did someone have sex?"

I look around the room. It clearly wasn't Julia and Kevin as she was in massive pain whenever they got close. Me and Morgan were also a no-go. I would have given Madison and Jake decent odds at the beginning of the night, but there's no way Madison did anything physical in her condition.

Which leaves Alex. Who's texting furiously with pink-tinged cheeks.

The guy with the longest odds came through. Probability is a beautiful thing.

I look to Julia, who nods the tiniest bit and smiles. If Alex isn't going to say anything, I certainly won't share his secret. Besides, Leah is headed to Middlebury next year, so whatever happened between them must have been complicated.

"I'm obviously talking about the cats," Julia says.

"Ew, what!?" A few crumbs of Morgan's Pop-Tart fly out of her mouth. "That's why the other cat is here? That's disgusting."

"The cats are not sexually active," I repeat for the benefit of the entire room.

"It was Alex's idea," Julia says, ignoring me entirely.

"No, it wasn't!" Julia's accusation is enough to make Alex put down his phone. "I happened to find two cats together on the side of the road, and I didn't know which one was ours."

"You guys!" I pound my fist on the cushioned edge of the couch, which does little to silence my friends. "Bulldog is not biologically capable of having sex."

"You mean Demon Cat," Julia says.

"I've been calling him Spider-Cat," Madison says.

"Whatever you want to call him, this guy is not having sex."

We all stare at Bulldog, who's busy licking his tail, blissfully unaware of the heated debate about his sex life. His new friend squeaks and curls up next to him.

Under her pile of blankets, Madison starts to snore. It's only a couple minutes before Morgan is asleep next to her. Julia and I chat for a while about the potentially lucrative business of cat matchmaking, but then she dozes off as well. On the floor, Kevin slumps lower and lower into Alex's lap. Alex is unfazed and simply rests his phone on top of his friend's head.

When Alex sees I'm still awake, he puts down his phone, quietly opens a packet of frosted strawberry Pop-Tarts, and hands me one. We tap our pastries together like we're clinking champagne glasses. I take a bite, but Alex is too busy smiling and sneaking glances at his phone.

"How was it?" I whisper. Not because I want to embarrass him but because I'm genuinely curious.

"I'm that obvious?" Alex whispers back.

"Well, Julia gave you away a little bit too."

"Subtlety is not a skill she possesses."

"Never has," I say.

We chew in silence, and I don't think he's going to answer my question. But after a few more bites of his Pop-Tart, it's too much for Alex to keep to himself.

"It was unexpected. And awkward. And kind of messy," Alex says as he licks the sugar from his fingers. "But mostly, it was amazing." He smiles and turns back to his phone.

Outside, the day is getting brighter, and I know I should start cleaning. But there's no way I'm fixing this mess by myself, and my friends look too peaceful to wake. In ten minutes, I'll get everyone up. We can clean and formulate a believable excuse for the busted door. An excuse that doesn't involve his cat going missing and my friends engaging in fantasy-themed role-play ideally.

I glance back at Alex. His eyes have fallen shut as his head bobs and he slips in and out of consciousness. I gently remove the phone from his grasp and place it facedown on the carpet. With everything Kevin's been through tonight, I doubt he would appreciate being woken up by a cell phone colliding with his skull.

I settle back into my chair, tucking my feet underneath my butt and resting my head on the cushioned armrest. As I watch my friends sleep peacefully, I can feel my own breathing slow, and a familiar stillness passes through my body. There's something else too. It's not exactly happiness—can anyone truly be happy after staying awake for twenty-four hours? No, it feels more like contentment.

I don't know if I'm making the optimal college decision. Or how my uncle will react to his busted door. I don't know what will happen to me—or to any of us, really—after graduation. That kind of unpredictability usually sends me spiraling. But if tonight has taught me anything, it's that a bit of unpredictability isn't so bad after all.

Acknowledgments

You read my book! What?! That's still unbelievable to me. (Unless you skipped to the acknowledgments. In that case, you chose the most boring part. Go back to the beginning.) But seriously, thank you for picking up this book, reading it, and possibly liking it. Your existence in the universe makes me extremely happy.

Just in case it's two in the morning and you need to sleep but you still somehow care about these acknowledgments, I'll keep this brief:

Thank you to my agent, Stacey Kondla, for liking my writing. And for not getting annoyed by all my emails. You are an incredible champion of my work, and I'm so grateful to have you in my corner.

Thank you to my editor, Christina Pulles, for believing in this project. From the beginning, you completely understood my vision for this book, and collaborating with you has been everything I hoped being a real-life author would be.

Thank you to every English teacher I've ever had. I discovered my lifelong love of the five-paragraph essay in your classrooms, and I would not be here today without you. (Sorry, I still haven't finished reading *A Tale of Two Cities*. Someday.)

Thank you to the religion department at Carleton College. When people ask why I chose that major, I always say the religion department had the best writing teachers. (I also haven't finished reading the New Testament. That one seems less likely.)

Thank you to the entire Hamline University MFAC program. I rediscovered my love of writing among you awesome people, and I have the strength of this community to thank. I appreciate every student, every faculty member, every workshop leader—especially my advisors, Marsha Qualey, Swati Avasthi, and Emily Jenkins. I aspire to attain even a fraction of your brilliance.

Thank you to my wonderful writing group for being the best critique partners, cheerleaders, and friends I could wish for. This book would be much different (and much worse) without your thoughtful feedback.

Thank you to my family who never doubted my ability to do this whole writing thing. You frequently overestimate my abilities, but I am eternally grateful for your unwavering support.

And, finally, thank you to my husband, who occasionally feigned interest in my writing and even more occasionally kept our dog quiet while I was working. This book would definitely exist without you, but I appreciate you nonetheless.